The Distant L

Amazon:

A Distant Light

A Distant Miracle

A Distant Dream

Barnes & Noble:

A Distant Light

A Distant Miracle

A Distant Dream

THE INN AT NAPATREE

Lorraine Solheim

Special thanks to Jennifer Arata for her help with the financial aspects of this story and to all my friends and family who continue to support me in countless ways.

Contents

CHAPTER ONE

September

The door to Jeanne's memory bank swung open as she glanced around her late mother's sizeable country-style kitchen. Although the room had been remodeled since her mother's passing, the new stainless-steel appliances, along with a fresh coat of paint, had done little to erase the true spirit of the room. The memories were so real she could almost taste the fresh-from-the-oven macaroon cookies her mother had made famous. She smiled and raised her first-morning coffee to her lips while visions of cozy yet animated family dinners, so many years ago, served at the same pine plank table where she now sat, danced across her mind.

She glanced at the picture of her mother which stood on a nearby counter and recalled her mother's final hours and deathbed request.

"Our home has been in the Stanton family for over a hundred years. Please promise me you girls won't sell it."

Of course, they had pledged to uphold her wish. How could they not? But as a former financial analyst, Jeanne knew honoring her request would take some doing. The house boasted eight bedrooms, nine and a half baths and stood on a bluff in the posh town of Watch Hill, Rhode Island. If her calculations were correct, the taxes alone would prove more than she and her sisters could afford. So, after laying their mother to rest alongside her husband inside the wrought iron gates of the Swan Point Cemetery in Providence, she and her two sisters had put their heads together to devise a way to honor their mother's last wish. After endless hours of discussion, and when they thought they couldn't make it work, a gem of an idea took root. Before long, they had a plan to convert the sprawling Colonial into a bed and breakfast.

A familiar thud from the front porch, a sure sign the morning paper had arrived, interrupted her thoughts. "Perfect." She took in a mouthful of coffee, swallowed, and headed outside. As she thought, the Providence Journal, wrapped in plastic, lay on the porch. She cast her eyes to the sky and then back to the paper. Strange. Why cover it on a cloudless day? She picked it up, then gazed at the rolling lawn still lush from the summer rains that stretched from the house to a stone wall bordering the property from the street. A new sign installed days earlier identified the house as The Inn at Napatree. Although autumn was still weeks away, the morning temperature had already begun to change. She pulled her robe tighter against the new degree of crispness.

As she slid the paper from the bag, an envelope tumbled out and landed at her feet. Jeanne frowned and picked it up. Her name was scrawled across the front in bold, red letters. What the heck? It couldn't be an expiration notice since they hadn't been able to bring themselves to remove their mother's name. She tucked the newspaper under her arm and tore open the envelope.

The morning calm shattered like one of her mother's bone china plates. Pasted to a sheet of white paper were clipped headlines about FNB, the bank she had worked for, declaring thousands of jobs lost. Then below were three more headlines—one about a triple murder, another citing arson, and a third about three deceased family members. Then written across the bottom of the page in the same chicken scratch, *you'll pay for what you did!*

Jeanne pressed her hand to her mouth to stifle a scream. Her heart felt like it was about to leap from her chest. She instinctively glanced over her shoulder to ensure no one was lurking nearby. The ominous note fell from her shaking hands to the floor. "What does any of this have to do with me?" she whispered.

"Who on earth are you talking to?" Hannah, her younger sister stepped onto the porch with her Clumber Spaniel, Fenway, in close pursuit.

Jeanne jumped and clutched her chest. "Jeez, don't creep. You scared me half to death."

"I wasn't creeping. And it's not like you to be so jittery. What's up?"

Jeanne swallowed her fear, forced a smile, picked up the note before Hannah could question it, and waved her hand.

"Don't mind me. I was running through some last-minute things needing to be done before our grand opening. Besides, we're all a little jittery, don't you think?"

Hannah raised an eyebrow. "You're not having second thoughts about converting the house to an inn, are you? Some money thing you haven't shared with us?"

Jeanne swatted her sister's shoulder. "Of course not. Don't be silly."

<hr />

As Hannah made her way down the driveway with Fenway, Jeanne raced up the stairs to her bedroom, threw open the door, and leaned against it while she tried to calm down. She had to talk to someone about this. But who? Certainly not her sisters. They would freak out. While her thoughts collided like bumper cars at the state fair, her friend Marcus came to mind.

During her employment at FNB, she had always considered him a trusted ally. She had even nurtured a killer crush on him shortly after they'd met, but when all he did was flirt, never once indicating he might want to take things further, she had locked away her feelings.

Since one of the headlines mentioned the bank where she had worked, a former coworker could surely help her think through this. She punched in his number. "Pick up," she muttered. "Please, Marcus. Please."

"Hi, Jeanne, good to hear from you." He'd obviously seen the caller ID. "What's up?"

Jeanne flopped on her bed, filled her lungs, then let out a long breath. "Marcus, I need your help."

"Sure. What can I do?"

Although her nerves had reached a fever pitch, the sound of his voice still made her insides stir. "I need a friendly ear to help me hash something out, but I'd rather do it in person."

"Are you still in Rhode Island?"

"Yes. My mother passed shortly after I returned, and since she wanted us to keep the house, we've spent the last several months fixing it up. At the end of the week, we will open our home as The Inn at Napatree. Our first guests arrive Friday."

"Sorry for your loss."

"Thank you."

"Converting the house must have been quite an undertaking. Not to mention stressful. No wonder you want someone to talk to. Are you sure you and your sisters are up for the strain?"

"As much as we can be, I suppose. But you're right. It has been hard. Most of the work needing doing fell to us, and what we couldn't handle, like electrical upgrades and plumbing, we farmed out to professionals at a considerable cost." Jeanne lowered her voice a notch even though she knew no one could hear her through the thick plaster walls. "Although I have done my best to contain my nerves, I'm a wreck. If my sisters knew how edgy I am, they would lose their cookies."

"Opening your home to strangers and taking on the role of Miz Fix-It would make anyone anxious."

Jeanne looked at her blistered hands and wished it were all she had to worry about. "Desperate times call for desperate measures. And believe me. I have the healing blisters to prove it."

"What can I do?"

"I know it's short notice, but I'd appreciate it if you could arrange to come here in the next several days."

"Seriously?"

Jeanne squeezed her eyes shut. "Yes."

For what seemed a lifetime, Marcus didn't say a word. Jeanne was sure he had hung up when he finally spoke.

"Okay, getting away might do me good. I'll bring my laptop and work on a book I'm writing when I'm not busy helping you."

"What is the book about?" Jeanne asked, glad for the opportunity to think about something other than the note.

Marcus paused. "The collapse of the bank. I had drinks one night with a friend who works for a publishing house here in the city. He convinced me it could be a worthy investment of my time. If I'm lucky, it might sell and make me some money. Living off my nest egg won't last long. That's for sure."

"Banging out a book might be good therapy."

"For now, all I can say is it keeps me busy."

"I take it you still don't have a car."

"Not with public transportation a few steps away, not to mention the paycheck problem lately."

"Okay. The best way to get here is to hop the train at Grand Central and get off at—"

"Westerly, right?"

Despite her anxious state, Jeanne's heart fluttered. "I'm surprised you remembered."

"How could I forget your mother's Fourth of July bash?" He laughed. "If I remember correctly, you took pity on me when you heard I planned to celebrate our country's independence with a hot dog from a pushcart vendor on the streets of Manhattan."

"As I recall, you made quite a hit with my mom."

"She was a lovely woman." He paused. "Who knows, with all the fresh air you Rhode Islanders stock, maybe I'll hang out more than a few days. If it's okay?"

"You're welcome to stay as long as you like." She couldn't help smiling.

"Hold on. What's your going rate?"

"Oh, please. You won't be a paying guest. I'll even reimburse your train fare when you get here. I appreciate this, Marcus. I truly do."

"Nice of you to comp my stay, but there's no need to pay for my transportation. I'll use some of my time there to research my book by refreshing my memory on your take about what caused the failure of the bank. Consider any money I spend as my first literary tax deduction."

"Our guest suites are all booked for the weekend, so I hope you won't mind bunking on the third floor with us staff people."

"Bunk with you?" His voice was flirtatious.

"Of course not. You'll have your own room."

"Too bad."

Despite how nervous she felt, she laughed. "You haven't changed a bit, have you?"

"No. And I don't intend to." He paused. "Even though I'd love to pursue this discussion, you said your guests start arriving in a few days, right?"

"Yes. We expect the first four Friday afternoon and the last one late that night."

"Okay, I'll check the train schedule and book a seat early Friday morning. Is your younger sister still living there?"

"Both my sisters are here with me."

"I thought your older sister Phoebe was married."

"She was, but they divorced."

"Sorry to hear about the breakup, but it's good to know you're not trying to pull this endeavor off alone." His voice took on a soft sexy tone. "I can't wait to see you. And for what it's worth, I think it will be good for you and your sisters to have a man around when strangers begin their invasion."

His comment warmed Jeanne's heart. "Call and tell me what time I should expect you. I'll pick you up at the station. Mom left me her Cadillac, so I have wheels now."

"Will do. And in case you forgot what I look like, I'll be the dapper guy racing off the train to sweep you into my arms."

Jeanne shook her head. "Do you ever stop flirting?"

"How else am I going to get you to notice me?"

Jeanne's face warmed. "What would you do if I did?"

He chuckled. "Probably ask to feel your forehead. Hey, I have another call coming in. I'll see you Friday."

When Jeanne walked into the kitchen, Phoebe, surrounded by sheets of paper, was sitting at the kitchen table.

At five feet eight, thirty-nine-year-old Phoebe was three inches taller and five years older than Jeanne and held the distinction of being as prim and proper as Hannah was cute. Like Jeanne, she had brunette hair, model-like cheekbones accenting her face, and hazel eyes often taking on the color of whatever she wore. Her skin was flawless, rarely hinting at the slightest imperfection.

"What are you doing?" Jeanne asked.

Phoebe didn't look up. "Double checking my menus against my food inventory. I want to be sure I have enough. Including us, assuming no one cancels, there will be eight mouths to feed." She plucked a pencil from behind her ear and jotted a note on a piece of paper. "I should be fine with the extra I bought."

"Figure on nine. I spoke with a former colleague and invited him here for the weekend. I thought having a man around when we welcome our first guests might be a good idea," Jeanne said, mimicking what Marcus had suggested. "He'll be here Friday."

Phoebe threw the pencil down and glared at her sister. "You can't go inviting people and not tell me."

"Hey, take it easy. We just hung up. And you said you bought extra. What's the big deal?"

Phoebe shook her head and sighed. "I'm sorry. I didn't mean to snap. I simply want everything to be perfect."

"It will be. By the looks of it, you have everything under control."

Phoebe huffed. "Easy for you to say. You're not the one having to adjust my recipes for potential allergens or having to stand at the counter while I tie bread dough into dozens of little knots." She waved a hand as if shooing a fly. "Okay, okay, tell me who this guy is you've invited."

"You know him."

Phoebe arched an eyebrow. "I do?"

"My friend Marcus. Remember he came here a few years ago for one of Mom's Fourth of July extravaganzas?"

Phoebe nodded. "Ah, yes, Mr. GQ." Phoebe gave Jeanne a sly look. "Is having a man around the *only* reason you invited him?"

Heat crept up Jeanne's neck to her face. "Of course. Why else?"

"By the way you are blushing, maybe you'd like it if he were more than a friend. And this weekend offers the perfect excuse to get the ball rolling."

"Stop. It's nothing more than what I said."

Phoebe gathered the papers covering the table into a neat stack. "Since it looks like I won't get anything juicy from you, I'm off to the store."

"Store? I thought you said you bought extra."

"I did, but not a whole 'nother man's worth of extra."

Jeanne parted the shower curtain surrounding the claw foot tub in her bedroom's adjoining bathroom and stepped in. Snapshots of happy times of living in Manhattan before she tried to warn the bank executive of her fears crossed her mind. How long ago it seemed. Almost as if those days had belonged to someone else. Someone whose nerves weren't on edge, waiting for who knew what to happen next.

She rinsed off and stepped onto the fluffy white bathmat in time to hear her cell phone ring. Jeanne grabbed a towel, threw it around herself, and ran to her bedroom. She picked up her phone and checked the caller ID for spam.

Blocked.

Jeanne frowned. Should she answer it? What if Marcus is calling to say something has come up? "Hello?"

"You've ruined so many lives, Jeanne," the voice-disguised caller said. "Soon, you will know what it feels like to lose everything and everyone *you* care about."

Click.

CHAPTER TWO

Jeanne waved and quickened her steps when Marcus stepped off the train. She checked her watch and nervously smoothed her hair. "You're early."

"Pedal to the metal, I guess." His smile was the same one which always had made the butterflies in her stomach take flight.

Ten years earlier, a crush she thought to be mutual had blossomed. Then, she discovered he flirted with a host of women at the bank where they both worked, meaning he didn't consider her special. So, she let her feelings go. But now, when she recalled those times, she kicked herself for not wearing make-up or dressing in something nicer than jeans and a tee shirt.

In Jeanne's opinion, Marcus, or Mr. GQ, as Phoebe had dubbed him years earlier, not only won the prize for attractive and sexy but also garnered the award for best confidant. Unlike anyone else, he always had the uncanny ability to make her see both sides of the proverbial coin.

He hugged her. "You look like a fresh-faced college grad, Jeanne. New England life must agree with you."

Her blood pressure spiked and warmed her cheeks.

He stepped back and took her hands. "I love to see you blush."

Jeanne rolled her eyes and tried to mask her wandering thoughts. "I'm afraid it's a perpetual flush which started the day I called you."

"What the heck is going on?" he asked, shouldering his bag.

"I prefer we talk elsewhere. You know what they say about small-town ears. Are you hungry?"

"I am. I only had time to down a half glass of OJ and a four-day-old bagel before I left."

"Normally, I would take you straight to our house. Phoebe is a world-class cook. But I prefer to talk away from prying ears. There's a deli not far from here. It serves awesome breakfast sandwiches. While we eat, we can talk. My car is right over there." She pointed to her Cadillac.

After sliding into the passenger seat, he fastened his seat belt. "Since we are alone, tell me what is happening."

Jeanne put the key in the ignition and angled her body to face him. "Someone is threatening me."

"Have you called the police?"

"No. The inn opens today." She backed out of the parking spot. "I can't do anything to jeopardize it. If I call in the authorities, it could kill our hopes for success, which is why I asked you to come. Maybe you can help me think through this."

"How long has this been going on?"

Jeanne put the car in drive. "The day I called. Inside our local newspaper was an envelope with a note and several headlines."

Marcus's mouth fell open. "Wait. Are you saying someone came to your *house*?"

Jeanne nodded. "Uh-huh. I thought it odd because the paper came rolled inside a plastic bag. The delivery person usually only does so during inclement weather."

"What were the headlines about?"

"The fall of FNB, one about a triple murder, and other horrible things."

"What did the note say?"

"I will pay for what I've done."

"Did they say what they think you did?"

"It's my fault lives have been ruined."

After a long moment, he said, "Since one was about FNB, do you think someone from there could be responsible?"

Jeanne pulled into the deli's lot and parked. "I don't know *what* to think."

"Jeez, Jeanne, I never expected anything like this when you said you needed help. I thought you wanted an extra pair of hands because you opened the house to guests."

"I wish that were true. You know me, Marcus, I don't scare easily, but this terrifies me."

They walked into the restaurant, ordered at the counter, and sat at a back table away from the other patrons.

Jeanne rubbed her cold, clammy hands on her jeans, glad to have ordered tea to wrap her hands around the cup for warmth while she tried to calm her nerves.

Marcus leaned across the table and patted her arm. "Don't worry, Jeanne. I'm here now. We'll sort this out."

Jeanne inhaled and blew her breath out slowly. "I hoped it would stop with the newspaper."

"There's more?"

"Yes. A voice-disguised call." She couldn't stop rushing her words. "The caller knew my name and had my cell number, so I can only assume this is no mistake. Besides telling my sisters, what else should I do to get to the bottom of this?"

"Forty-six!" the cook shouted.

Marcus sprang to his feet. "I'll get it."

He returned with the sandwiches and put the tray on the table. "Here." He took her tea and sandwich off the tray and slid them to her. "First of all, I suggest you not tell your sisters. At least not yet."

"Why?" Jeanne added a teaspoon of sugar to her tea. "They deserve to know. They could be in danger."

Marcus picked up his egg and Canadian bacon sandwich. "They will likely freak out. I suspect the grand opening is probably causing enough stress. Until we have time to think this through, why pile on more?"

Jeanne brought her cup to her lips and blew gently. "Maybe you're right."

"Do they know I'm here?"

"Yes, I told them it would be good to have a man around when we welcome guests for the first time."

"Perfect." Marcus shook his head. "This is bizarre. I can't think of anyone at FNB who would want to scare you or harm you."

Jeanne shook her head. "Me, either. Which is why I called you. I thought you might have heard something after I left."

"Ken Marshall reacted strongly when he learned you'd escalated your concerns about the bank's financial condition. Not surprising though since he was the Chief Financial Officer."

Jeanne grimaced. "What a mistake I made going up the chain of command. Talk about a pompous ass. The CEO treated me like I didn't have a brain in my . . ." Jeanne made air quotes. 'Pretty little head.' Made me want to spit nails."

Marcus took a bite of his sandwich then put it down. "Hey. Something occurred to me. Maybe this is connected to what churned through the rumor mill after you left."

"What was that?"

"Remember Dan, Ken Marshall's nephew, who worked in the fixed-income department?"

"I never thought much of the slime bucket."

Marcus nodded and smiled. "I'm pretty sure the feeling was mutual. He spread some major stuff around about you being in cahoots with the SEC."

Jeanne chewed quickly and swallowed around the lump in her throat. "Marcus. That must be it. Someone heard the rumor and blamed me for the failure."

"Maybe. But hearing rumors and turning them into threats are two different granola bars. This is way crazy."

"And unfair." Jeanne leaned back, rubbed the back of her neck, and pushed her plate away. "But it's the only thing which makes even a scintilla of sense."

Marcus glanced at Jeanne's sandwich. "Are you finished?"

Jeanne slid the plate in front of him. "Be my guest. I've lost my appetite."

"Thanks."

"Do you think Ken or Dan could be behind this?"

"Before we play name the suspect, is there any other reason you might be on someone's radar? Perhaps a jilted lover? Or maybe a local who is upset you and your sisters have turned a residential property into a B and B?"

Jeanne took a sip of tea and shook her head. "No ditched Romeo or letters to the editor. There is a hotel right down the street from us, so that doesn't fit either."

Marcus snapped his fingers. "Not so fast. Maybe the owners don't want the competition."

"No way. Their property is ten times the size of ours, and they don't appear to be hurting for business. And besides, how would they know where I worked since one of the headlines mentioned FNB?"

Marcus wiped his mouth. "Did you keep the stuff you received? Maybe I'll see something you didn't."

"You might recognize the handwriting, but unfortunately, the caller ID won't help."

"Why?"

"The number came up blocked."

"Not surprising. A lot of people use it, even me."

⸎

Jeanne pulled into the circular driveway fronting her house. "Here we are."

Marcus's eyes grew wide. "This place never ceases to amaze me. I can see why you decided to stay after your mom passed."

As lovely as it was to inherit the house, in Jeanne's opinion, the best part of the legacy was holding onto the memories their family home cradled within its walls.

"Come on, let's get you checked in."

A few minutes later, Jeanne grabbed a key from the pegboard behind the registration desk. "I'll show you to your room."

When Jeanne crossed the second-floor hallway on her way to the next flight of stairs, Marcus pointed to one of the closed doors. "I think I stayed here last time." He followed her to the third floor.

"You did, but we've converted this floor to guest rooms. My sisters and I have relocated up here. Which is where our spare room is." Jeanne unlocked the door to the room next to hers and handed him the key. "I hope this is okay."

Marcus scanned the room. "Considering the threats, I'd rather be close to you and your sisters with strangers in the house."

Jeanne grabbed the door frame to steady herself when his comment brought to mind unbearable images of what could happen. She grimaced when she envisioned her sisters carried out on stretchers. Or a kitchen explosion maiming Phoebe.

Marcus reached for her. "Hey, are you okay?"

"The thought of what could happen scares the life out of me. I know what you said, but maybe I should tell my sisters and postpone the opening."

Marcus wrapped his arms around her and gently rubbed her back. "I promise you. Nothing will happen on my watch. If this *is* someone from FNB, they wouldn't be foolish enough to show their face here. And if you postpone the opening, your guests will blast this place on the internet. And make it hard for you to attract future business. I'd hate to see that happen. You've come too far to blow it now."

Jeanne's eyes glistened, and her lips trembled. "I've never felt this scared."

"I know, Jeanne. I know."

CHAPTER THREE

Phoebe sighed and eyed the mess on the table. "I can't believe we made it through the first night's meal.

Jeanne picked up the four-by-six-inch, scallop-edged, tented menus at each place setting on the dining room table and read them over.

A warm beginning:
New England clam chowder—succulent clams,
finely chopped celery, and potatoes swimming
in a thick sea of cream
From the garden:
Greens and heirloom tomato wedges dressed
with raspberry vinaigrette and bleu cheese crumbles
From the sea:
Atlantic Flounder with a delicate lobster stuffing
From afar:
Peruvian asparagus drizzled with Hollandaise Sauce
A happy ending:
Warm apple crisp with homemade vanilla bean ice cream

"Your dinner was a home run," Jeanne said, helping Phoebe load one of two commercial-grade dishwashers.

"Thanks. I had such fun coming up with what food combinations would appeal and how best to present them."

"Well, it showed." Jeanne lowered her voice. "Did you hear Doug, the guest in room three, tell his wife they wouldn't need a marriage counselor if she could cook like you?"

"What a jerk. I'd be willing to bet it's not her cooking putting their marriage on the rocks," Phoebe shook her head. "If you ask me, he has quite the roving eye. He practically cornered Hannah when she came in from the clinic."

"And I thought I caught him sizing up the divorcee in room five."

Marcus ended their discussion when he walked in wearing a smile guaranteed to make most women swoon. "Ladies, how can I help? I figure it's the least I can do if my first meal here is any indication of what's to come." He glanced at Jeanne. "If I keep eating like I did tonight, you will have to wheel me out to the car." He patted his stomach. "Haven't felt this stuffed in a long time."

Phoebe's cheeks pinked. "I'm glad you enjoyed it."

"Oh, it was far more than *enjoyable*. It was downright fabulous."

Phoebe pushed the start button and closed the first dishwasher. "Since it's only seven-thirty, do you two have plans for tonight?"

Jeanne glanced at Marcus. "Most everything is open downtown on Friday nights, so we thought we'd take a walk."

Marcus ran a hand down Jeanne's arm. "It will help me walk off some of the calories I wolfed down."

"Thanks for covering for me when Phoebe asked about our plans for tonight," Jeanne said, as they headed down Larkin Road on their way downtown.

"No problem."

"Have you come up with anything?"

"Not yet. But it's not from lack of trying. I can honestly say it's practically all I've thought about." He motioned to a bench along a grassy area skirting the waterfront, and they sat. The few remaining boats not yet in dry dock for the upcoming winter bobbed in the water.

"I can't believe someone would do this to me. I thought . . ." Jeanne's eyes welled, and she turned toward the water so Marcus wouldn't see her tears. She wasn't usually this emotional. But since the newspaper surfaced, followed by the hair-raising call, her emotions were raw. Like the skin beneath a scab picked at and removed too soon. "I considered my co-workers at FNB friends. Well, most of them, anyway. Certainly not enemies."

He took her hand. "I can't think of *anyone* who'd want to hurt you."

She returned her gaze to him. "But the only plausible explanation is the one you came up with about me alerting the SEC. It's the only thing making any sense."

"How anyone could think FNB disintegrated because you may have gone to the authorities is beyond strange. If anything, you'd think it would *save* the bank, not destroy it."

"Not if you had a hand in what caused the bank to fail."

Marcus rested his forearms on his knees and looked at her. "I guess I can see how it could be true."

"The irony is even though I told you I planned to go to the SEC the day I resigned, once I got home and learned about my mother's cancer diagnosis, she became priority one, and my concerns about FNB slipped to the back of the line. But you said the rumor mill was ripe about what I had said, and maybe someone remembered."

CHAPTER
FOUR

Jeanne and Marcus joined her sisters on the front porch while they awaited the arrival of a guest.

I'm so glad we decided to hang those flowers," Phoebe pointed to the plump baskets suspended from the ceiling overflowing with an assortment of lavender and deep purple pansies.

"And those pots we filled with mums along the walkway's edge make the stone pop," Hannah added.

Moments later, a car pulled into the driveway, and a seventies-ish woman approached with a wide smile. "Which of you pretty ladies is Jeanne?"

Jeanne walked down the porch steps and extended her hand. "I'm Jeanne."

The woman took her hand. "Nice to put a face with a name. I'm Josephine Reasoner. We spoke the other day. No relation to Harry." She chuckled. "Although you girls are too young to remember...." She rolled her eyes. "Don't mind me. I tend to ramble these days."

"Nice to meet you, Mrs. Reasoner." Jeanne gestured toward her sisters. "These are my sisters, Phoebe and

Hannah. Phoebe is our chef, and Hannah is a veterinarian. And this is our friend Marcus."

"Welcome to our home," the two sisters said, almost in unison.

"Why thank you," the woman said. "Please call me Jo. Although I was married for fifty-two years, whenever someone calls me *Mrs. Reasoner,* I still think they are referring to my late mother-in-law."

The women laughed.

Marcus picked up her bags. "I'll take your luggage inside."

"This is lovely," Jo said after entering the front door. "It's exactly as I envisioned it. And what a beautiful location. It must be nice having the Atlantic for a neighbor." Her eyes moistened. "My late husband would so approve."

"We hope you enjoy your stay," Phoebe said.

"I'm certain I will." She glanced at the polished mahogany staircase, then shifted her attention to the waist-high, turn-of-the-century, captain's desk inside the front door. "Is this where I register?"

Jeanne went behind the desk. "It is."

"How utterly charming."

After returning the woman's credit card, Jeanne grabbed a room key from the peg board behind her.

"Marcus, would you mind taking Jo's suitcase upstairs?"

He grabbed it. "I'm ready when you are."

"Right this way," Jeanne swept her hand toward the stairs.

Jo followed Jeanne and Marcus into the second-floor room.

He set Jo's bag on an upholstered bench at the foot of the bed while Jeanne pointed out some of the room's features.

"What an inviting space. I love your choice of paint color. Pale blue and yellow bring the ocean and sunshine right inside, don't you think?"

"I'm glad you like it." Jeanne went to a group of windows along a padded sitting area, pulled back the curtains, and gestured. "Your room features a water view."

"How wonderful." Jo leaned in for a better look. "I take it these windows open."

"They do."

"Then I'll do so tonight and let the sound of the waves lull me to sleep."

Jeanne led the way to the bathroom. "And this is your ensuite."

"Mercy me. I haven't seen a claw-foot tub in oh so many years. What a charming way to soak away one's consternations."

Jeanne handed her the room key. "There are additional towels next to the sink, another blanket in the bottom drawer of the bureau in case you get chilly, and two more pillows in the closet. If you need anything else, please let one of us know."

A little after eight the following morning, while rinsing dishes to put in the dishwasher, Jeanne gazed out the window. Sandy-haired Aaron Downing was stretching his hamstrings on the back porch.

He had arrived late the previous night and told her he'd chosen their B and B because of its location on the water.

"Well, we're not quite *on* it," Jeanne remembered saying.

"Close enough. Being born and raised in Orient Point, Long Island, when I'm away from the water, it's like being in a foreign country," he'd said.

She watched him straighten and bound down the porch steps. He hadn't gone more than a dozen feet when the door to the porch flung open, and Hannah yelled, "Fenway, stop!"

Aaron pulled up, turned around, and squatted, arms wide, as the friendly canine barreled toward him.

Jeanne dried her hands on a dishtowel, tossed it on the marble-like, quartz countertop, and went outside.

At thirty, Hannah could best be described as a pixie. Her face and petite form had always favored their mother. At five-foot-two, she considered it a catastrophe if her weight ever exceeded one hundred and five pounds. And unlike her sisters, who had learned at an early age to think twice and speak once, Hannah never fully grasped the concept and often spoke her mind without regard to the consequences.

"I'm so sorry," Hannah shouted, sprinting down the porch stairs.

The dog's tail wagged madly as he licked Aaron's face.

Laughing, he took the exuberant pup's head in his hands. The light breeze carried Aaron's voice to the porch. "What's your name, boy? You're a fine one, aren't you? Yes, you are."

"His name is Fenway. I'm Hannah Stanton." Hannah extended her hand and then snapped a leash to the dog's collar. "I'm sorry if he bothered you."

"No problem. I'm Aaron Downing. Nice to meet you." He swept his arm toward the ocean. "It would take more than a few sloppy kisses to ruin such a beautiful day. This is one heck of a location you have here."

"Thank you, but the credit belongs to our ancestors. Our home has been in the family for over a hundred years. But I agree, they did make an awesome choice."

"Your website said my stay includes a history lesson. Are you the resident professor?"

Hannah smiled. "My sisters and I share the distinction."

"Well then, I'll be sure to look for one of you after I check out the beach and get some breakfast. Then maybe I'll take a walk and check out your downtown."

"It's very quaint." Hannah smiled. "If this were summer, the carousel would be running. It's always a treat to watch."

"Maybe I'll take a look, anyway."

"You won't see much. The panels go up right after Labor Day. It's amazing how our town transforms for each season. As beautiful as the summer months are, it's my least favorite time of year because of the truckloads of tourists it ushers in." She looked at her watch. "I better get going. I have to get to work."

"You work on Saturdays?"

"Only until noon. I'm a veterinarian." She pointed to the carriage house behind her and to the left of the house. "My practice is right over there."

"Convenient."

"Can't imagine it any other way." She tugged on Fenway's leash. "Come on, we have patients to see. But first, we have to go for a walk."

CHAPTER FIVE

Jeanne had gone to bed at her usual time but couldn't sleep. Scenes reminiscent of a B-level thriller movie played and repeated in her mind. After tossing and turning most of the night, she rolled over and glanced at the clock for the umpteenth time. Four-fifty-eight. She pulled the covers over her head in a last-ditch attempt to try to get some sleep. After realizing it was hopeless, she threw off the blanket, put on her slippers, and padded to the bathroom. She washed her face, brushed her teeth, and slipped on a pair of jeans and a cream-colored long-sleeved shirt.

Since the headline-stuffed edition of the paper had arrived days earlier, Jeanne made it a point to be the first to intercept it so she could check it before anyone else could. She flipped on the light at the foot of the stairs. Was there someone crouching on the porch? Jeanne gasped, clutched her chest, and flipped on the porch light. She peeked out the curtained-glass side light of the front door. The only thing on the top step was the paper.

"Only the paperboy, I guess." She eased open the door, hurried toward the rolled paper, and prayed for nothing more ominous than world updates. She scanned the surrounding area, picked up the newspaper, unrolled it, and let out a long stream of air. "Thank goodness."

A hand grasped her shoulder. She jumped and let out a squeal.

"Are you okay?" Marcus asked.

She gulped. "You scared me. I thought you were still sleeping."

"Has something happened?"

"When I came downstairs, I thought I saw someone on the porch, turns out it must have been the paperboy."

"Why are you down here so early?"

"I couldn't sleep and wanted to examine this." She held up the paper. "Before anyone else had a chance to."

Marcus pointed to an envelope protruding from the mailbox next to the door. "Yesterday's mail?"

Jeanne's heart started to race. "I brought it in. Maybe I *did* see someone other than the paperboy."

Marcus took the envelope. "I'll open it."

"Why?"

"In case . . ."

"In case what?" Jeanne's hand went to her mouth while her mind traveled to past news accounts of ricin reportedly being sent through the mail. "You don't think this person would send *poison,* do you?" Jeanne spun on her heel. "We should call the police. If there's powder in there, it could be deadly."

"Wait. Turn on the outside light."

"Marcus, don't open it."

"Please turn on the light."

Marcus tapped the envelope on the porch rail and held it to the light. "No mounds of powder or indication of a postmark." Before Jeanne could stop him, he tore it open and pulled out a piece of paper the size of an index card. "It's clean. Only a note."

Jeanne watched his eyes go wide. "What does it say?"

"Your sisters should enjoy life while they can. Time's wasting. Tic-Toc. Tic-Toc."

Jeanne conjured every ounce of control she possessed not to run upstairs and spill her guts to her sisters, then bang on all the guest room doors to tell them to run for their lives. "I have to tell Hannah and Phoebe. This is out of control."

Marcus gently held her shoulders. "Calm down. We agreed it's not a good idea to tell them yet. Besides, you have your guests to consider. You can't throw them out."

Jeanne flexed her back muscles and stretched her neck to relax the knot forming at the base of her skull. "I've never lied to them."

"You're not. You've only decided to withhold information for a more appropriate time. There's a difference."

At mid-morning, Jeanne walked into the dining room to find Phoebe, who had set up tea, coffee, and an assortment of cookies on the antique sideboard. "Is there anything I can do to help?"

"I'm all set. I thought I would swing by the sitting room to see if anything needs doing."

"I'll join you."

Jo was seated by a front window, munching on a shortbread cookie topped with a dollop of raspberry jam in its center.

"Mind if we join you?" Jeanne asked.

"Please do. And forgive me for dunking," Jo said, a cup of tea in one hand and her cookie poised in the other.

"Cookies are made for that." Phoebe took a seat beside Jeanne on the sofa. "I hope you enjoyed your breakfast."

Jo eyed the cookie with what looked like a trace of embarrassment. "How could I not? I'm usually not a big eater, but I have gobbled down two of your glorious cheese crepes, and now I can't stop inhaling these cookies. Where on earth did you learn to be such a superb cook?"

Phoebe was unlikely to promote herself, so it was Jeanne's job to do so. "Phoebe attended Johnson and Wales Culinary Institute here in Rhode Island."

Jo nodded and dipped her cookie. "In my younger days, I dreamed of donning a chef's hat. But I suppose, as with other things, it wasn't meant to be. Once my daughter came along, all my focus went to her upbringing."

"We have something in common then," Phoebe said. "I left JW a semester short of my degree to give birth to my son Rob. Since he's now a freshman at Penn State, our idea to turn our home into a B and B gave me a chance to return to my passion."

Jo raised her cup to her lips. "What made you decide to open your home to guests?"

Phoebe smiled. "If we didn't, we had little hope of keeping it after our mom passed away. She made it clear she wanted the house to remain with us, but large as it is, the expense would have been more than any of us could afford. So, we created The Inn at Napatree to honor her wishes."

"How lovely of you girls to respect your mother so."

Jeanne studied the woman seated in one of the three wing chairs across from her. Slight in build, her nearly wrinkle-free face framed by short silver hair, showed a hint of blush on her cheeks while her lips bore a light shade of rose lipstick. *You sure do remind me of Mom.*

"Do you have any plans for the day?" Phoebe asked.

"Not really. Other than maybe to poke around your beautiful property and breathe in the salt air. It's so different here from the spit of land I own on Staten Island. It would be nice if I could bottle this wonderful sea air and bring it home."

"Have you lived there long?" Jeanne asked.

"All my life. Frank and I are natives, a scarce thing these days." Jo looked away before returning her attention to the sisters. "Funny how I still think of him in the present tense. What I should have said is he *was* a native." She shook her head. "Forgive me. I find it hard not to drift into yesterdays." She offered a soft smile. "I guess it's a sign of my advancing age." She pushed her lips together. "Now, what was I saying?"

Phoebe gave her a soft smile. "You were telling us about Staten Island."

"Of course. I live in a town called Willowbrook. When I was a child, the area where my current home stands was vast farmland. Now the only thing growing is its population. I'm afraid tract housing replaced green fields long ago." She sighed. "It's all I've ever known."

"I'm sure it's lovely." Jeanne stood. "Well, I should get going. And don't forget. You can always come back to refill the bottle you mentioned."

CHAPTER SIX

Jeanne and Marcus sat huddled over cups of hot cocoa at the kitchen table after all the guests and her sisters had retired for the night.

Marcus licked his lips. "Hands down, this is the best hot chocolate ever."

"It should be," Jeanne said. "Phoebe creates the mix from scratch with chocolate she special orders. Last night I bet we chopped and ground blocks of it for over an hour." Jeanne held her mug with both hands while she surveyed the architecture of Marcus's face. Phoebe had pegged him right when she called him Mr. GQ. His eyes were so dark they seemed almost black and matched his wavy, gel-infused, hair. Yes, Phoebe was right.

A dab of whipped cream clung to the tip of her nose when she lowered her cup.

"How cute are you?" Before she could wipe it away, Marcus reached across the table. "Don't move." He gently wiped the cream off with his finger, brought the same finger to his mouth, and with a flick of his tongue, the cream disappeared.

She fought to maintain control as hormonal high jinks washed over her.

"Let's talk about this morning," Marcus said as if his tongue action hadn't been the least bit sexy.

"The recent note took direct aim at my sisters. If something happens to them . . ."

"Trust me, nothing will. We'll figure this out. And in the meantime, I'll do everything I can to protect all of you."

"How much longer can you stay?"

"Until we have a handle on this, if that's what you want."

Jeanne stared into her lap. "I've already monopolized too much of your time. I'm sure you have a million things to do at home. Like finish your book and find a job."

"My resume's on my laptop. I can search and send from anywhere. Besides, being here helps me with my book."

"How so?"

"It gives me a chance to ask you some questions. But, enough about me, let's review what we know so far."

Jeanne nodded. "Okay. As far as the note is concerned, the printing looked like a first grader. Which doesn't give us much in the way of clues."

"Was the envelope sealed?"

"No. Which eliminates checking for DNA." Jeanne glanced over her shoulder to ensure no one was within hearing distance. "I don't feel right leaving my sisters in the dark. Do you still think we should hold off?"

"Absolutely. Let's wait until after your guests leave. Then you can tell them."

Doubt and fear strong-armed Jeanne. "O-k-a-y."

"I've been thinking about this, and if it turns out the way I think it might, you may not need to tell them."

"What do you mean?"

"Since you didn't shut down the inn when you received the threats, this weirdo may realize you aren't easily frazzled and grow tired of his or her attempts to scare you."

"Or step things up."

The next day

Jeanne knocked on Hannah's bedroom door and stuck her head in. "You decent?"

Hannah coughed out a laugh. "Of course. It's two-thirty in the afternoon, and I'm fresh in from the clinic. What makes you think I wouldn't be?"

Jeanne walked in and sat on the edge of the bed where Hannah sat crossed-legged, balancing a Sudoku puzzle book in her lap. Jeanne shrugged. "Oh, I don't know. I thought you might be changing into something prettier than scrubs."

"Why?"

"Aaron Downing. You two seemed to hit it off yesterday morning."

Hannah tossed the book onto the bed. "*Puh-lease.* I was only being friendly to one of our guests. I wouldn't have bumped into him if it weren't for Fenway." She looked down at her sleeping dog, head on his paws on the braided rug beside the bed.

His ears pricked at the sound of his name, and he raised his head. But when no one seemed to need him, he resumed his nap.

"Sure, blame Fen. You can't deny Aaron is cute."

Hannah laughed. "You're right. He is cute."

Jeanne faked a swoon. "And those heart-stopping eyes."

"I know. They remind me of faded denim. Almost makes you think you can see into his soul."

"Lots of sun-kissed hair, too. Might make *some* women want to run their fingers through it."

"Hadn't given it any thought."

Jeanne laughed. "Yeah, right. Who are you kidding?"

Hannah giggled.

"If you ask me, I'd say he has potential."

"Speaking of which, where is Ernest Hemingway this afternoon? Working on his book?"

"I guess."

"Do you think he has a prayer of getting it published?"

Jeanne shrugged. "According to him, he does, which surprises me because, from what I understand, publishers aren't anxious to take chances on unproven authors nowadays. Although." She paused. "His book is non-fiction, and since it revolves around a current event, it might make a difference." Jeanne slid off the bed and walked to the door. "I'll let you get back to your puzzle. As for me, I'm off to see if the next great author wants to take a ride and get some ice cream."

Jeanne was thrilled when Marcus agreed to go for a ride. Maybe being away would let her focus on something other than the threats.

"It feels good not to be alone with my thoughts," Jeanne said when they sat on a bench outside Wicked Good Scoops in Misquamicut. "I can't ever remember feeling this jumpy. While I was out for a run this morning a car backfired, and I had to control the urge to hit the ground." She shook her head. "It doesn't take much to spook me these days."

"It's only natural considering what you're going through."

Jeanne choked back the lump growing in her throat.

"It's okay to be scared, you know." Marcus' voice was smooth as the ice cream dripping down what was left of his cone.

She finished her ice cream, covered her face with her hands, and released her pent-up tears.

He gently pulled her to him. "Go on. Let it out."

She fumbled in her pocket for a tissue, then dabbed at her eyes. "Maybe if I tell my sisters, it will take some pressure off. I've never lied to them, and their not knowing what's going on is eating at me. Besides, they have a right to know."

"If it makes you feel better, and since we haven't come up with anything, I'll support your decision."

"I'd like you to be there when I tell them." Jeanne took a cleansing breath and wiped her tears.

"Of course." Having finished his cone, he wiped his hands on a napkin, took her chin in his hand, raised it, and looked at her. "I'm here for you, Jeanne. Whatever you need."

CHAPTER
SEVEN

On Sunday afternoon, the sisters assembled on the front porch to say goodbye to the last of their weekend guests.

"Walk me to my car, Doc?" Aaron asked.

Hannah blushed. "Sure."

Phoebe opened the door to go inside. "Coming?" she asked Jeanne.

"In a minute." Jeanne claimed one of the rockers and watched Hannah and Aaron chatting. *It looks to me like you're smitten, little sister. And who can blame you? He's good-looking and too nice to know it. Yep, I'd say the guy has potential.*

Hannah returned to the porch a few minutes after Aaron left.

"I guess, like yesterday, you were only being friendly to one of our guests."

"Okay. If you must know, I like him."

Jeanne smiled. "I think it's mutual."

"I wouldn't read too much into it. The last year has been rough on him."

"Sounds like you two have been talking." Jeanne smirked.

"It's not like you to miss a trick. I'm surprised you didn't notice us sitting outside by the fire pit last night."

Normally she *would* have noticed, but after the last few days, she found it hard to do anything except dwell on her circumstances.

"I think it did him good to talk to someone about it."

Jeanne knew exactly how he must have felt. "Did he lose his job during the pandemic?"

"No. He inherited his late father's pharmacy, much like I inherited the clinic from Dad."

"Is he a pharmacist?"

"Yes."

"Since it's not job-related, what did he talk about?"

'I'll tell you if you promise not to say anything to him, assuming he decides to return."

"My lips are sealed."

Hannah pulled over one of the rockers and sat next to Jeanne. "He is a widower."

Jeanne touched her sister's forearm. "He's awfully young. How old is he?"

"Thirty-two."

"Was his wife sick?"

"No. A driver ran a red light and broadsided her vehicle. To make matters worse, not only did he lose his wife, but she was seven and a half months pregnant with their son."

Jeanne winced. "How sad."

"It's easy to see how lost he is without her. By the sounds of it, she meant the world to him."

"Was he in the car?"

"No. Gillian taught at the local elementary school. The accident happened on her way home from a parent-teacher conference one night. He said the only comforting thing was he learned she died instantly. He said he couldn't handle it if he had any inclination she had suffered."

"Did he say what brought him here?"

"He needed to get away. He first tried the New Hampshire mountains, but the isolation proved too much. He said all he did was think, which made a bad situation worse. He checked out the following day." She shrugged. "I guess this time he decided to try something where he wouldn't be so alone."

"Well, since he stayed the whole weekend, I guess it worked out for him."

Hannah gave her sister a sly smile. "He met me, didn't he?"

Jeanne nodded. "He did."

"If you ask me, he would be better off if he sold his house and moved elsewhere. The memories must be overwhelming. And apparently his route to work takes him past the school where she taught and the intersection, where she died. According to him, whenever he approaches that stretch of road, he imagines the tires squealing and the bang of metal hitting metal."

Hannah leaned back against her chair and sighed. "He's so nice, Jeanne. It breaks my heart when I think of what he has gone through." She glanced at her sister. "I like him. A lot. But who knows if I will ever hear from him again." She leaned forward in her seat. "Do you think a year is long enough to move on after losing your wife?"

"Everyone has checked out." Jeanne joined her sisters at the kitchen table. "I reviewed our upcoming reservations, and our next guests, a couple named Estes, won't arrive for a few more days."

Phoebe glanced at the calendar held in place by a chef's hat magnet on the refrigerator door. "Doesn't give us much time. It's only three days away. And we have the open house the day before."

"You said everyone left." Hannah looked at Jeanne. "But Marcus is still here, isn't he?"

Jeanne nodded. "I don't consider him a guest. He plans to stay for at least a few more days. As a matter of fact, I want to talk to both of you when he comes downstairs."

Phoebe lifted an eyebrow. "About?"

"I'd rather wait for him to be here."

"What's up with that?" Hannah asked. "Since when do you need him here to talk to us?"

An awkward silence filled the room.

"Jo and Aaron are great, aren't they?" Jeanne said, trying to fill the void.

Hannah grinned. "Aaron is better than great. He's an answer to a woman's prayers."

Phoebe frowned. "Did I miss something?"

Jeanne laughed. "Sounds like big sister has had her head under a cabbage leaf for the last two days."

Phoebe glanced from Hannah to Jeanne. "What are you talking about?"

Jeanne grinned. "Our baby sister is crushin'."

"Really?" Phoebe looked at Hannah. "Is that true?"

Hannah shrugged.

"I guess I was so caught up with cooking I didn't notice."

"And you loved every minute of it, didn't you?" Jeanne laughed.

Phoebe flashed a wide smile. "Absolutely. But I want to hear about what I missed."

"I'm going to pour myself a coffee." Jeanne rose. "Anyone care to join me?"

"Me." Hannah held out her cup.

Phoebe waved her hand. "No thanks. I've had my fill. I'll be bouncing off the walls if I have any more."

Jeanne poured herself and Hannah a cup then placed the carafe on the table. "Jo Reasoner is a real sweetie, isn't she?"

"She is," Hannah said. "She makes you feel like you've known her forever."

"I know what you mean." Phoebe toyed with a napkin. "It broke my heart to see how sad she became whenever she mentioned her late husband. It made me think of Mom after Dad died."

Jeanne gave a knowing nod. "I don't know about you two, but she reminds me a little of Mom."

Hannah knit her brow. "Since you mention it, I see what you mean."

Marcus strolled into the kitchen and raised his chin in acknowledgment. "Good afternoon, ladies." He tilted his head toward the refrigerator. "Okay, if I grab a water?"

"Of course. I'm glad you're here," Jeanne said. "I told Phoebe and Hannah I want to talk to them but preferred to wait for you."

Phoebe directed her attention to Marcus. "No offense, but we don't understand why she needs you here to speak to us."

Marcus pulled a water bottle from the fridge and sat beside Jeanne. "No offense taken. I'll let Jeanne explain."

"I don't like the sound of this." Hannah narrowed her eyes at Jeanne. Then switched her attention to Marcus. "I hope you haven't convinced Jeanne to return to Manhattan."

"Not even close." Jeanne swallowed.

Phoebe's eyes moved from Jeanne to Marcus and back again. "Will one of you please tell us what's going on?"

"Someone is threatening me." Jeanne whooshed out her words.

Phoebe's eyes went wide. "Threaten. By whom? And more importantly, why?"

"Yeah, why would anyone want to threaten *you*?" Hannah asked.

"The only thing I can come up with is someone must believe I'm a whistleblower and caused the bank where I worked to collapse."

Phoebe refilled her cup. "Why on earth would they think that?"

"Because I said I would turn them into the SEC the day I quit."

"When you say threatened, what *exactly* do you mean?" Hannah rested her elbows on the table.

"A few days before we opened, an envelope arrived inside the Providence Journal. There was a note inside the envelope."

Hannah pointed at Jeanne. "Even though you denied it, I knew something wasn't right that morning."

"Are you saying this person came to our *house*?" Phoebe's voice traveled up a few octaves. She shook her head. "Oh, Jeanne, you should've told us before now."

"Blame me." Marcus put the cap on his bottle of water. "When I found out, I suggested she wait. I felt certain you both were stressed about the upcoming opening, so why make it worse? And I thought maybe given time, Jeanne and I could figure this out, and you wouldn't need to worry unnecessarily. But as it turns out, we haven't."

Phoebe looked at Jeanne. "What did the note say?"

"I will pay for what I did, and attached to it was a newspaper headline about the fall of FNB." Jeanne opting not to disclose the other headlines about murder and mayhem.

Phoebe lowered her voice to a whisper. "Jeanne, this is frightening. I shudder to think what could happen if this lunatic comes here posing as a guest."

"I doubt whoever is behind this would be bold enough to risk being identified if it turns out to be someone from the bank," Marcus said. "And in my humble opinion, if they wanted to hurt her, they could have by now. I think they only want to scare her."

"Have there been any other incidents?" Hannah asked.

Jeanne nodded, trying to decide how much more to tell them. Should she also mention the note she thought might have contained ricin? No. They were already freaked out over someone coming to the house. "The next day, I got a call. I thought it was Marcus saying he changed his mind about coming, but—

"What did the person say?" Phoebe pushed, clearly anxious. "Did you recognize the voice?"

"No, it sounded like one of those voice synthesizers. And as far as what they said, they told me I will know what it feels like to lose everything and everyone I care about."

Phoebe gasped.

"What about caller ID?" Hannah asked.

"Blocked."

"Which, of course, doesn't narrow the field since many people use it," Marcus added. "Even me."

Hannah ignored him. "Phoebe's right, Jeanne. You should have told us."

Phoebe looked at Marcus. "Now I understand why you came."

Marcus nodded. "Jeanne called the morning the newspaper clipping arrived and asked me to come as soon as possible, so I caught the early train the next morning."

"I assume you've spoken to the police, right?" Phoebe said.

"Not yet."

Phoebe slapped the table. "For goodness' sake, what are you waiting for?"

"The note and call could easily be nothing more than mischief," Marcus said. "Until we have a better handle on this, I've advised Jeanne to hold off. Getting the police involved could hurt your business. In the meantime, I'll keep watch until we find out who is behind this." He smiled at Jeanne. "Or until you decide you don't want me around anymore."

Hannah huffed, pushed back her chair, and paced. "I assume you told this person you didn't do anything. Right?"

"I didn't have a chance. They hung up too fast."

"I suppose because of the voice disguise, we can't even narrow down gender," Hannah said.

Jeanne shook her head. "Nope."

"Great. Just great." Hannah stopped pacing. "We don't know anything about this wacko, and our doors are open to the public."

"Do either of you have any idea who it could be?" Phoebe asked.

"Even though everything points to the contrary, it's hard to believe it's anyone we know." Marcus tossed his empty bottle in the recycle bin. "But the bank employed more than a thousand people at our location, so we can't know for sure."

"I'm afraid to ask if anything *else* has happened since the call?" Phoebe asked.

Jeanne bit her bottom lip. "Not so far."

"Well, at least we have that going for us." Phoebe sighed. "What do you suggest we do now? This person has already come here once that we know of. We can't sit around until he tries to do more than leave a note or make a call."

"I agree." Hannah looked at Jeanne. "Not only are you in potential danger, but we all are, including our guests."

Phoebe faced Marcus. "We appreciate your offer to stay, but unless you have a squad of Delta Force Ranger Seal Marines in your suitcase, I vote we call the police."

"I agree," Hannah said with a definitive nod.

Marcus shook his head. "Police will swarm all over this place. Is that what you want?"

Hannah's shoulders slumped. "He's right. Once the cops are involved, it will be a matter of time before the media finds out and latches onto the story. The publicity it generates will torpedo our hopes of the inn being successful, not to mention the effect it could have on my practice. Who in their right mind would want to stay here or bring their animals to me when they know one of the owners is being stalked?"

Marcus rested his elbows on the table. "I have a plan."

"Let's hear it," Hannah said.

"I'll keep watch overnight. I think it's a fair assumption the note was probably planted while everyone was asleep. I'll keep my cell and a can of mace Jeanne carried in Manhattan with me. If I see anything suspicious, I'll call the police. Not only will we catch the jerk, but we'll also minimize an investigation which could leak to the press."

"That's very gallant of you." Phoebe glared at him. "But too dangerous." She looked at Jeanne. "I'm surprised you'd even consider it. You're not thinking straight."

Marcus gave a half-hearted laugh. "Trust me. I'm no hero. I won't be stupid enough to put myself in harm's way."

"Thank you for your offer," Phoebe said. "But I have a better idea."

Jeanne side-eyed Marcus and thought a flicker of anger crossed his face. "What?"

"We could hire a private investigator. Then we can find out what's going on without the police, and we won't risk having the inn plastered all over the news. The person making these threats could decide to turn words into action if we wait too long."

"Not a bad idea." Jeanne tipped her head to the side. "But how do we find someone reputable?"

Phoebe traced her finger through a spot of coffee on the table. "I can give you someone to contact."

Jeanne raised an eyebrow. "*You* know someone?"

"Yes. I've hired him in the past."

"Why?"

"I had to confirm my suspicions about my ex's philandering weren't the result of an overactive imagination."

"I'm sorry, Phoebe," Jeanne said.

Phoebe shrugged. "I knew I was right. But I needed proof to propel the divorce forward. So, I waited for Rob to leave for college, then called a friend who had a similar problem, and she suggested I call Ray Grossi. His office is in Providence. He did exactly as he said he would. Got me the proof I needed and at a reasonable price."

Jeanne eyed Marcus. "I think Phoebe may be on to something. A private detective sounds like a good place to start."

"In the meantime, I think I should still plan on hanging around if it's okay with the three of you."

"Fine." Phoebe stood.

Hannah grinned. "Second."

"Give me his number." Jeanne sighed and held out her hand to Phoebe. "I'll give him a call."

CHAPTER
EIGHT

"His office is over there," Jeanne said, pointing at a structure in downtown Providence as they left the parking garage. "It's called The Turks Head building."

Marcus stared at the stone building. "Weird name. Where did it come from?"

"Legend has it that back in the mid-seventeen hundreds, the house which once stood on the property had a carving of a Turk's head on the front porch. So, the architect who designed this, kept that in mind and fashioned the head at the top of the building." They turned the corner. "Look up."

"Cool."

They entered the building and took the elevator to the sixth floor.

Well-marked, heavy, wooden doors lined the hallway, making it easy to locate suite six-two-seven without any trouble.

Jeanne turned the knob and pushed open the door. A balding man of medium build sat at the reception desk talking on the phone. He waved her in and wrote something on a yellow pad. "Sounds good. I'll wait for your call." He hung up, stood, and extended his hand. "Jeanne

Stanton, I presume. I'm Ray Grossi." He looked at Marcus. "And you are?"

"Marcus Reynolds."

"I made fresh coffee. Beans are from a local coffee shop. Better than any other, in my opinion. Interested?"

"Yes, thank you," Jeanne said.

Marcus nodded. "Make it two if you don't mind."

Ray gestured toward an open office. "Go in and have a seat while I rustle up the java."

Jeanne glanced around the office. Phoebe said to expect a mess, and she was right. The desk and two metal filing cabinets were piled high with file folders. And the windowsills looked like they hadn't seen a duster in months.

Ray returned carrying a tray with four mugs. Three filled with coffee, and the fourth holding an assortment of creamers, sugar packets, and stirrers. He walked around the desk and put the tray on the only small amount of available real estate. "Pardon my office. Best intentions don't always translate into a done deed."

"No worries. Your housekeeping skills are the least of my concerns. My sister spoke highly of you, and she's not easy to please."

"Your sister is a nice woman." He shook his head. "I never get guys who drive a woman like her to need my services." He pulled a fresh yellow pad from his left-hand desk drawer and picked up a pen. "Let's talk about you."

Jeanne took a sip of her coffee. "I've received three threats and think they may be connected to my former employer, a highly respected Manhattan based bank named FNB. At least until they *weren't* respected."

"If my memory serves me, they closed about two months ago, am I right?"

"Yes. Three months after I left."

Ray made a note on his pad. "How long were you employed there?"

"Ten years."

Another note.

"Long story short, I thought a good portion of the bank's investments took a risky turn when interest rates rose. Instead of liquidating when the current values started to tank, they doubled down. And as I predicted, those values continued to drop, which lost the bank its ability to borrow. When the news leaked out, there was a run on the bank. And the rest, as they say, is history."

"Did you share your concerns with anyone?"

"Yes, my boss, and when he wouldn't listen, I raised them to the president."

"How did it go?" He didn't look up from taking notes.

Jeanne huffed. "Talk about a colossal waste of time. The president was condescending and pelted me with sexist comments. It made me so angry, I resigned a few hours after leaving his office."

Ray flipped the page and wrote something else. "Did you have any enemies there?"

"I didn't think so at the time. Although I never had much use for one guy who, in my estimation, played a significant role in the problem and only kept his job because of his connections."

"Did he know what you thought about him?"

Marcus threw his head back and laughed. "Oh, he knew all right. Jeanne's not one to hide what she thinks."

Ray made another note and sat back. "When did the authorities get involved?"

"After I left."

"Would your boss or the president have reason to believe you might have reported your suspicions?"

"Possibly. The rumor mill at the bank was quite active."

"Did you tell either of them you intended to turn them in?"

"No, only Marcus."

Ray jotted a note, pursed his lips, put his forearms on the desk, and leaned forward. "Could you have been overheard?"

Jeanne shrugged. "I suppose."

"The question is, *did* you report them?"

"I never had the chance. When I arrived home, I discovered my mother had been diagnosed with pancreatic cancer. Within a few days, I left Manhattan and came to Rhode Island to be with her."

Ray's face softened. "Hard to hear." He leaned back in his chair. "How long did she live?"

"Thirty-nine days." Jeanne bowed her head. "It was pretty fast."

"I'm sorry for your loss," Ray said.

Jeanne raised her head and looked over Ray's shoulder at the semi-closed vertical blinds covering the window so he wouldn't see the tears building in her eyes.

"I take it the SEC got relegated to low priority and caring for your mom shot to the top."

She returned her gaze to him. "Honestly, I never had any intention of going to the authorities. I said what I did in a fit of anger. I had to find another job, and I knew prospective employers would shy away from hiring me if they learned I walked out. So why make a bad situation worse by going to the feds?"

Ray took a sip of his coffee. "Have you since found employment?"

"No. Mom requested my sisters and I keep the house where we were born. And to do so, we devised a plan to turn it into a B and B." She knocked on the wooden desk. "If all goes well, we'll be able to keep our promise and maintain a roof over our heads."

Ray leaned back in his chair. "A bed and breakfast up this way is quite a change from the bright lights of Manhattan."

Jeanne nodded. "Indeed."

"Considering your current situation, I'm sure you realize having your home open to the public threatens your safety."

"No one I worked with has expressed a desire to stay at the inn." She tilted her head toward Marcus. "Not even Marcus until I invited him."

Ray tapped his pen on his chin, made a note, and looked at Marcus. "Where do you fit in?"

"Jeanne and I have been friends for ten years. She called after receiving the note and asked me to stay at the house the weekend they opened."

Ray pointed his pen at Jeanne. "Let's talk more about the threats."

Twenty minutes later, Ray put his pen down. "Okay, we can help you. I'll handle the investigation myself and ask my associate Woody to do the fieldwork."

Jeanne raised an eyebrow. "Fieldwork?"

"Yes. And if you're willing, Mr. Reynolds, I'd like to enlist your help as well."

"Of course."

"Do you think you could arrange a meeting with some of your former colleagues?"

Marcus hesitated. "I suppose. But for what purpose?"

"If you talk about the closing, maybe even mention Jeanne's name, someone might shine a light on themselves."

He turned to Jeanne. "If I do this, it means leaving you and your sisters alone. Are you okay with that?"

"I want this nightmare to end. If it means catching this guy faster, I'm all in."

"Good. I'll want Woody to join you." Ray pointed his pen at Marcus.

"People are bound to ask what he's doing there." Marcus frowned. "So, what do I say?"

"Introduce him as a friend who is staying with you for a few days. I don't think it will present a problem. And maybe with some careful coaxing and a few drinks, loose tongues will prevail, and we might learn something." Ray redirected his attention to Jeanne. "In the meantime. I'll ask a friend of mine on the local police force to do me a favor and send a few patrols past your house on their graveyard shift."

"We prefer not to get them involved," Jeanne said.

"If you're worried, he might ask questions, don't be. He's known me long enough to know better than to ask."

CHAPTER
NINE

As much as Marcus wasn't a fan of returning to Manhattan to set up the meeting Ray had requested, he knew it would be in his best interests to appear cooperative. So, he had given the impression he would do whatever was necessary to help flush out the perp regardless of the trouble it could bring him. But before he had time to come up with how best to present his request, out of the blue, Ken Marshall, the former FNB CFO, phoned and suggested they get together.

Although he had worked his charms over the years to convince Ken, he considered him a friend, the truth was, Marcus considered him nothing more than an acquaintance. An acquaintance who, as it turned out, had provided invaluable insights into the bank's financial condition he would not have otherwise had. Getting together with Ken was not what Ray had suggested, but it might help to grease the skids for a larger meeting. But he couldn't help wondering if Ken had somehow gotten wind of his visit to Jeanne and intended to grill him about it. It would take some doing not to get himself in hot water with his former colleague. But what choice did he have?

What came as more of a shock than the call was the meeting place Ken had suggested. Nick's Steak House was considered one of the most upscale restaurants in midtown. But then again, why was he surprised? Hadn't Ken always been known for playing the part of big man in town?

⁓⊙⊗⊙⌇⁓

Marcus had been so deep in thought about how to respond to any questions Ken might raise, he walked past the restaurant and had to double back.

"I'm meeting a friend, but it doesn't look like he is here yet," he told the maître d after scanning the restaurant's interior.

"Do you have a reservation?"

"It's probably under Marshall."

The man scanned his IPAD. "Yes. Here it is. A table for two. Would you like to be seated, or do you prefer to wait until the other party arrives?"

"I'll be seated, thank you."

The man led Marcus to a booth at the rear of the restaurant. "The reservation requested privacy, sir. Will this do?"

"Yes. Thank you." *Why had Ken requested this particular seating?* He glanced around at the nearly empty space and slid onto the leather bench seat facing the door to keep an eye out for Ken.

A few minutes later, a waiter stopped by. "May I get you something from the bar while you wait, sir?"

"Yes. Scotch with a splash if you don't mind."

Ken hadn't arrived by the time Marcus had almost finished his drink. He checked his watch. Strange. Ken had always prided himself on his punctuality and was known for not tolerating anything less from others. As Marcus reached for his phone, his former colleague rushed through the door, out of breath.

When Ken approached the podium, the maître d gave a discreet nod in Marcus's direction.

"Sorry I'm late." Ken took a seat. "My life these days is one hot mess."

The waiter appeared. "May I start you off with something to drink, sir?"

Ken glanced at Marcus's glass. "Scotch?"

"Yes."

"I'll have the same."

"Very good, sir."

"So, how goes it?" Marcus asked, anxious to get to the bottom of why Ken asked to meet.

Ken shook his head. "Not good. Not good at all. I guess you haven't heard about my son."

"Is he sick?"

Ken sighed. "If only. He passed away three weeks ago."

Marcus put his glass down. "Oh, man. I'm *so* sorry. What happened?"

Ken's eyes glistened. "As you may recall, he had a history of seizures, which isn't at all uncommon for kids on the Autism spectrum. Unfortunately, this time it happened when he was taking a bath. According to the autopsy results, he sustained a blow to his head which rendered him unconscious, and as a result, he drowned. My wife blames herself. She had only left him alone for a few minutes." He looked down at the table and shook his head. "I still can't believe my boy is gone."

"What a tragedy. I don't know what to say."

"There isn't anything you *can* say. What makes the whole thing worse is this didn't have to happen."

Was he blaming his wife?

"If FNB didn't go under, I wouldn't have had to replace his trained nannies with less qualified help. The guilt of his death will follow me the rest of my life."

"Is there anything I can do?"

Ken huffed a breath and ran his hand down his neck. "Nothing can bring him back. And no one can fix the mess I'm in."

"I thought the reason you called was to tell me you found a job and maybe offer me a position."

"Things aren't good on that front either. I've networked all my contacts and clogged the Internet with resumes. All my efforts have produced have been interviews, one the day my son died. I thought they all went well, but I never heard back."

The waiter returned with Ken's drink. "Are you gentlemen ready to order?"

Marcus looked up. "We need a few."

"Of course, sir. I'll check back."

Ken raised his glass, and Marcus followed suit. "To good friends and better days." They tapped their glasses together. "How about you? Have you landed anything?"

"I haven't started looking," Marcus said. "Wait, that's not exactly true. I did some searching right after we found ourselves on the street. But then, one night over drinks, a friend who works for a local publisher suggested I put my search on a brief hold and dedicate my time to writing a book about the collapse." Marcus shrugged. "He made it sound like it could be a worthy investment of my time. I figured, why not. Stopped schlepping resumes and took up writing."

"Seriously?" Ken took a pull on his drink.

Marcus nodded. "Yeah, but I will resume the job search after the first of the year. By then, the book will be in the hands of the publisher. And I will be running low on cash."

"I wish I could afford to do the same, but because of my insider status I was forced to hold onto my stock options." Ken grimaced. "The only thing those things are good for these days is a substitute for toilet paper." He lowered his glass. "Come to think of it. Some of the conversations we had put you in the same boat." He gave a half-hearted chuckle. "I guess you were better than me at salting money away."

The last thing Marcus wanted to get into was a discussion about his stock options. "I'm sure it's only a matter of time before things start to turn. Considering your reputation, I bet your phone starts ringing with head spinning offers before too long."

"Well, before too long, it will be October first, and the rent will be due. Unless something pops up fast, it will be too late."

"Too late for what?"

"Holding on to our condo. We've begun searching out of the city for something smaller, but no matter where you go, everything is so damned expensive when you don't have a paycheck."

"Why not go to your place in the Hamptons for now?"

"No can do. It's for sale. And if I don't get an offer and close soon, I'm looking at foreclosure." He shook his head. "No matter where I turn, all I see are brick walls. I guess my in-laws were right when they tried to talk Eileen out of marrying me."

"Why would they do such a thing?"

"They always thought she could do better. And I guess, based on my current situation, they were right. They even issued her an ultimatum when they suspected I might be on the verge of proposing." His face brightened. "Thank goodness, she saw something in me they didn't. She's the best thing to happen to me."

"But surely, after all this time, they've come around."

He sighed. "Eileen and her parents haven't spoken for years. I thought my success at FNB might finally make a difference. Then the feds swoop in and shutter the company. Imagine how I felt when I had to go to them with my hand out to pay for my son's caretakers."

"I'm sure you had no choice. His care and education must carry a steep price tag."

"You don't know the half of it. We had recently hired a new nanny and except for the price tag, things were going great. He seemed to like her, and unlike the others, who wanted to stay at the condo all day and encourage him to watch television, she took him everywhere. We were starting to see a difference before everything blew up."

"I take it the loan didn't materialize."

"Not even close. My father-in-law demanded to know what caused the failure, implying I must have had a hand in it since I was the CFO." Nothing I said made a difference. He didn't want to understand. All he was interested in was proving they were right about me. I tried to tell them I wasn't asking for a gift and would pay them back as soon as I found a job. But did it make a difference? No. It did not." He ran his fingers through his hair. "As it turns out, it was all for nothing because my son died soon after. And since then, the grief over my son's death and the prospect of vacating our home has taken a toll on my marriage. I wouldn't be surprised if a divorce is the next landmine I have to maneuver." He paused. "Thank you for agreeing to meet. As you can see, I need someone to talk to. Someone I could trust. I don't mind telling you things can get dark when I'm alone with my thoughts."

This guy was getting attacked from all angles. And as much as Marcus wasn't a fan of Ken, his heart still went out to him. "I know nothing can bring back your son, but as far as your other troubles, I'm sure things will turn around. Before long you'll be back on your feet again."

"I'm not holding my breath."

"It seems times are tough for a lot of people. You're not my only friend to need a kind ear."

Ken took a long pull on his drink and swallowed. "Someone from the bank?"

Marcus nodded. "You remember Jeanne Stanton, don't you?"

"Yeah. What's her problem?" Anger filled his words.

"She and her sisters inherited their family home, but to keep it, they had to convert it to a B and B."

Ken narrowed his eyes. "Doesn't sound bad to me. If I remember correctly, she came from Watch Hill, Rhode Island, before taking the job with us. I suspect the house must be worth a bundle. Why didn't they sell it and pocket the money?"

"They promised their mother they would keep it in the family."

"She inherits what is sure to be a multi-million-dollar property and will likely rake in more than enough income to float the place, so I repeat, what's her problem?"

Marcus didn't intend to share why Jeanne had contacted him, especially since it was apparent she wasn't on Ken's good side. "There probably won't be one. But still, it is a huge undertaking."

"I wouldn't worry about her if I were you. Her kind always comes out smelling like French perfume. What surprises me is you obviously consider her a friend."

Marcus twirled the half-inch of scotch left in his glass. "Why?"

"Because she's the reason we're out pounding the pavement."

Marcus coughed out a nervous laugh. "What makes you say that?"

"She made it clear she intended to go to the SEC after being denied a promotion she thought she deserved. Those in the know believe she got her revenge. Which doesn't surprise me since Jeanne always struck me as a spoiled little rich girl accustomed to getting her way."

Marcus was torn. On one hand, he wanted to defend Jeanne, but on the other, if he weren't careful, he could blow everything. "I don't think you have your facts straight."

Ken leaned back. "Really? Did she tell you when Rick hauled her into his office, she said she had proof of corporate fraud and would go to the SEC if he fired her?"

"I understand *she* is the one who prompted that meeting, not the other way around. As far as I know, no one fired her. She quit."

Ken laughed. "And you believed her?"

"Why would she lie?"

"Ego."

"Did you ever stop to think maybe she suspected some of what you shared with me? Maybe she realized we were sitting on a powder keg and only wanted to save the company."

"Unless you told her." Ken glared at Marcus. "There is no way she could have known what took place."

Marcus held up his hands. "She didn't hear it from me."

Ken wiped his sweaty forehead. "Good to hear. You had me wondering there for a minute. For what it's worth, I'm the one who deserves the thanks for keeping us going for as long as we did after the values of our investments tanked. Not her."

To ensure Ken wouldn't harbor the sense he may have tipped Jeanne off, he said, "Although I remember you talking to me, I honestly can't recall the details."

"I got the idea how we could pump up asset values to facilitate our loan requests when we needed cash infusions to keep the doors open after the market was in free fall."

Marcus snapped his fingers. "Oh, right. Now I remember."

"If I must say so myself, it was nothing short of a stroke of genius. The sad thing is it worked until your *friend* pulled the rug out from under us. The beginning of the end came when the feds started sniffing around."

The waiter came to the table. "Have you gentlemen had time to peruse the menu?"

"Why don't we share an appetizer?" Marcus said, after glancing at the prices.

"Sounds good." Ken looked at the waiter. "Do you still serve the seafood sampler?"

"Of course, sir, it is one of our specialties."

"Sounds good." Ken held up his near-empty glass. "And please bring us each a refill."

"Very good, sir."

Marcus choked back his words. Hadn't Ken spent the better part of their time together complaining about his financial straits? Only to order the most expensive item on the menu. Unbelievable. *I sure hope he plans to pick up the tab.*

"You remember Dan, right?" Ken said, interrupting Marcus' thoughts.

"Sure, your nephew. The guy who headed up the fixed income department."

"If you want to give anyone credit, it should be Dan. He was the brains behind the research which led us to the stellar returns we enjoyed for several years."

"But when inflation hit, and the interest rates started rising, wasn't it his portfolios losing value?"

"True. Which is where my asset-pumping scheme came in. All we had to do was secure loans until we got past inflation. And we would have been home free."

"Why not dump the investments?"

"The loss would have been too much to bear. As they say on the street, all we had at the time were paper losses. If we sold, the losses would have become real. So, the plan was to ride out inflation and use leverage to keep us going until things turned around."

"Since you said Jeanne didn't have a clue as to what was going on, how can you think she had a hand in the company's failure?"

Ken pointed a finger at Marcus. "I don't *think*. I *know*." He lowered his voice. "Regardless of what she may or may not have known, I have it from a reliable source the Feds got to someone on the inside, and she fits the bill. We think she raised enough red flags to prompt the authorities to get involved." He curled his lip. "Miss know-it-all. Miss I-crap-chocolate-ice-cream."

Marcus sat back. "I know Dan is your nephew, but I hope he's not your reliable source."

"Listen, I know neither you nor Jeanne ever thought much of him, but as I said, he did a lot for the bank. Like me, he was willing to put his neck on the line to try and pull us out." Ken paused. "It's true, he may have been the first to give me a reason to suspect her, but he certainly wasn't the only one."

The waiter returned with fresh drinks. "Your seafood platter will be out momentarily.

Ken downed the last of his first drink and pushed his glass aside.

Marcus's mind was spinning. The tone of Ken's voice had been so harsh it could peel paint off the walls. He had to redirect the conversation before he dug himself any further into a hole he couldn't get out of. "Hey, I've been thinking of getting together with a few of our former colleagues. I thought it would do us good to forget our troubles and talk about old times. What do you think?"

Ken's expression softened. "Sounds good. But whatever you do, don't invite Stanton."

Marcus held up his hand. "Are you kidding me? Based on what you've said, it would be like leading a pig to slaughter."

"You got that right."

"Why don't you call a few and I'll do the same."

"I'll take care of letting Dan know." Ken stared into his glass.

"Sounds like a plan. Who knows, maybe some have found jobs and can give us a few leads."

Ken leaned forward and lowered his voice. "Who's going to hire me with all the rumors flying around?"

"What rumors?"

"From what I have heard, The Federal Banking Committee is about to issue subpoenas, and some expect to be called to Washington to testify. As the former CFO, I'm sure I'll be on the shortlist. You might want to go. Then you'll see what I've said about Stanton is true. You shouldn't have to be there too long because as I hear it, the rat will be up first before the Feds have a go at us. I promise you this, if I don't get called, I still intend to be there even if it means I sleep on the street."

"Why?"

"So, I can have the satisfaction of giving miss goody-two-shoes an earful, so she knows in no uncertain terms what her holier-than-thou attitude has caused."

CHAPTER
TEN

"*Rats*? We don't have rats!" Jeanne answered the door to the Rhode Island Health Department Inspector.

The man dressed in gray slacks and a white shirt clasped an attaché in one hand. "I'm here to conduct an inspection, but before I do, state law requires I speak with the licensed food service manager."

"That would be my sister Phoebe." After checking his credentials, Jeanne opened the door and motioned him inside. "She's in the kitchen. Follow me."

"Phoebe, this man is from the health department. He thinks we have…" Jeanne lowered her voice. "Rats."

Phoebe gasped. "What? You must be mistaken. You can eat off my floors. And the rest of the kitchen is no different."

Jeanne placed a reassuring hand on her sister's shoulder.

"No mistake." The inspector took in the pristine room. "We received an anonymous complaint regarding unsanitary conditions. I took the call myself."

Jeanne felt the hair on her arms stand at attention. "Complaint? Who would say such a thing? Our guests have given us nothing but glowing reviews."

Phoebe was right. The floor didn't feature so much as a crumb, the stainless-steel appliances exhibited not a hint of fingerprints. Even the row of four small pots of herbs lining the windowsill above the sink didn't show evidence of a single dead leaf.

The inspector opened his attaché, removed several plastic bags and cloths, and looked at Phoebe. "When did you last have guests?"

"Two days ago."

"Did anyone report being sick?"

Phoebe looked at her sister and then the inspector. "Not exactly."

"Not exactly? As in, yes?"

"We did have to call paramedics for a guest. But it had *nothing* to do with anything he ate here."

"My investigation might reveal differently."

Jeanne watched Phoebe fume with indignation as the inspector marched across the kitchen, meticulously wiping the countertops with test cloths, moving on to the refrigerator and at every stop he ceremoniously dropped the wipes into his little specimen bags.

"On the surface, everything appears in order, but we will have to wait until we get the results back from the lab." He placed the bags into his case. "Is this your only refrigeration?" he asked, gesturing at the subzero stainless-steel unit.

"We have a smaller one in the garage for overflow."

"Okay, I'll check there on my way out."

Phoebe crossed her arms over her chest. "I know of nothing anyone could find fault with, and we certainly don't have any *vermin*."

"My sister is a stickler when it comes to cleanliness. I'm shocked anyone could think differently."

The inspector eyed the kitchen, all but ignoring Jeanne's comment. "Looks like all I have left to check is the pantry."

Back straight, head high, Phoebe walked across the room, opened the door to the large walk-in storage area, turned on the light, and stepped aside. "Be my guest."

Cereals, dried fruits, breadcrumbs, an array of spices all in alphabetical order, along with an assortment of gluten and gluten-free flours, and five different brands of sweeteners lined the lower shelves.

The inspector examined two-thirds of the pantry without incident, turned his head, and eyed a three-step ladder on the side wall. "May I?"

"Of course." Phoebe opened it for him. "The top shelf is for excess."

He climbed to the second step and turned on his flashlight.

Jeanne corner-eyed Phoebe.

Three-quarters of the way along the third shelf, he reached behind a canister, pushed it aside, removed his phone from his pocket, and snapped a picture. "What do we have here?" He lifted a box of rat poison.

Phoebe's hand flew to her mouth. "Where did that come from? *I* know better than to put it there."

The inspector stepped off the ladder and looked inside the box. Then reached in with a gloved hand and lifted a dead rodent by its tail from the container.

Phoebe shrieked, "We have *never* had rodents." She looked at Jeanne. "Mom would have mentioned something, and she never did. And I certainly have never seen any. I swear that box wasn't on the shelf when I cleaned and rearranged everything before we opened our doors."

"Usually there's…" He bent over and shined his flashlight around the area. "Huh, no droppings. Must not have been in here too long." He took another picture.

"There are *no droppings* because we *don't* have rodents." Phoebe was nearly screaming.

He straightened. "Then how do you explain the finding?"

"I can't because I have no idea how the box or the…" Phoebe shuddered. "Rat got there."

The inspector took a pen from his pocket and made a note. "I will need the name and contact information of the guest who became ill."

"Why?" Phoebe said, her voice shaking.

"Until I speak with him, I can't finalize my report. In the meantime, your facility is closed until further notice."

Phoebe looked at Jeanne, her eyes wide, hand covering her mouth.

Jeanne choked back thoughts of defeat. The mere idea they might have to break their promise to their mother made her knees buckle. How could this be? Hours earlier, she and her sisters had rummaged through a stack of unpaid bills joyfully knowing they could now be paid thanks to the success of their opening weekend. Jeanne took a deep breath to maintain her control. "I'm afraid contacting Mr. Estes is out of the question."

"Why?" the inspector asked.

Jeanne swallowed. "He died on the way to the hospital."

CHAPTER ELEVEN

"When will we hear back from the health department?" Hannah asked as she and her sisters rocked on the porch two days after the inspection.

"He led me to believe finishing his report would take a few days once he contacted Mrs. Estes," Phoebe said. "Which I know happened because she called to tell me."

Jeanne peered around Hannah to Phoebe. "Did she say how it went?"

"She gave us high marks and confirmed her husband died of an aneurysm. I apologized for having to involve her at such a difficult time. Thankfully, she was very understanding."

Hannah shook her head. "What a shame. It's not bad enough she lost her husband, but then she had to rehash the event because of some bogus claim." Hannah sighed. "When we lost Mom, I don't know if we would have been as gracious."

"We should come up with a way to thank her," Jeanne said.

"How about a gift certificate for a couple of nights when she feels up to it?" Hannah suggested.

Phoebe nodded. "Great idea. Once we get the all-clear, I'll send it out."

⸺⟆⟢⟣⟤⸻

Jeanne was on the last quarter mile of her morning jog when her cell phone rang. Panting, she pulled up, slid the phone from her waistband holder, and looked at the screen. Blocked. She debated on whether to answer. *But maybe it was Marcus.* "Hello?"

"Sooner or later, rats end up dead. Like the one in your pantry."

Click.

With shaking hands, Jeanne slid the phone back into the holder and, at full speed, took off for home.

"Phoebe, Hannah!" She flung the front door open and sprinted through the hall. "Where are you?" she yelled.

"In the kitchen," Phoebe called out.

When Jeanne entered the kitchen, her older sister was standing at the long counter making tiny cones out of wonton wrappers.

Phoebe stopped what she was doing and looked at her sister. "What's wrong?"

"I got another call," Jeanne said breathlessly. "Where's Hannah? You both need to hear this."

"She left for the clinic." Phoebe went to the fridge, pulled out a water bottle, and handed it to her sister. "Sit down." She pulled out a chair and sat. "Tell me about the call."

"He knew about the rat." She heaved a breath. "And said sooner or later, rats end up dead. Like the one in your pantry."

Phoebe's hand flew to her chest. "The only way he could know about the rat episode is if he planted it or has an inside source at the health department."

"Or paid someone to attend the open house, to plant it because the mastermind feared being recognized."

"Did you call Ray?"

"Not yet. I wanted to make sure you and Hannah were okay." A thick knot formed in her throat. "Oh, Phoebe, what are we going to do?"

"You call Ray, and I'll go to the clinic to ensure everything's okay there and to let Hannah know the latest development."

"Okay." Jeanne picked up the phone in the kitchen and dialed the private investigator.

"You've contacted the office of Ray Grossi. I'm either on the phone or with another client. Please leave the reason for your call and your phone number, and I'll call you back as soon as possible."

Jeanne left a message, hung up, and punched in Marcus's number.

"There has been another call," she said before he could say hello. "This one scared me even more than the others. Not only did the caller mention something only my sisters and I know about, but it took things to a whole new level when he alluded to murder."

"Slow down. Take a deep breath and tell me what you're talking about."

Jeanne blew out a stream of air. "A few days after our last guest left, a Rhode Island Health Department inspector paid us a visit."

"Why?"

"He said he received a complaint about unsanitary conditions complete with rodents."

"What? That's crazy."

"What's crazier is he found a box of rat poison in the pantry with a dead rodent inside."

"How is that possible?"

"We have no idea. Phoebe was shocked. She knows better than to have poison near food. And we have never seen rodents anywhere in the house. The question is, who put it there, and when?"

"Have you come up with anything?"

"I think a guest must have planted it or someone came to the open house and carried out orders from whoever is behind this. But Phoebe stayed in the kitchen to keep an eye on things during the open house and didn't see anything suspicious, so we don't know what to think."

"You should have told me about the inspector. I would have come back."

"My sisters and I agreed not to tell anyone. It's not exactly something proprietors of a new B and B want to broadcast. Not even to friends. Besides, I didn't want to disrupt your attempts to set up the meeting."

"It's in the works. Coincidentally Ken Marshall called after I returned and asked to meet for drinks. I used the time to suggest the get-together."

"How did it go?"

"Okay. Until I mentioned I had spoken to you."

"Why would you bring me up?"

"When I asked him why he wanted to meet, he said he needed someone to talk to, and I said he wasn't the only one who had recently needed a friendly ear."

"You didn't tell him about the threats, did you?'

"Of course not."

"Did he indicate he could be behind this madness?"

"Although he isn't a fan of yours, I can't imagine he has any part in this."

"How can you be so sure?"

"He has too much going on to have time to plant notes or make calls."

"Why? Is he working?"

"No. He's juggling a bunch of financial issues, and then there is the passing of his son to deal with."

"Was his son sick?"

"No. The kid was autistic and had a history of seizures. Unfortunately, this time he seized while in the tub, hit his head, and drowned."

"How awful. When did this happen?"

"About three weeks ago."

Jeanne's thoughts raced like an Indy car taking laps at Daytona. "That coincides with what's been happening here. For all we know his son's death could have sent him over the edge."

"Ken may be many things, but threatening people is not one of them. Have you called Ray?"

"I did, but I had to leave a message."

"Okay, let's think about this for a minute."

"What's to think about?" She cringed at the near hysteria in her voice. "For all I know, whomever is doing this could be lurking across the street."

"I know you're upset. But don't let your imagination get the best of you. If we're going to figure this out, you have to stay clear-headed."

"Easier said than done." Jeanne huffed a breath. "Answer me this. Does Ken think I'm a whistleblower?"

Marcus didn't answer.

"Does he?" Her voice climbed to new heights.

"Yes. But he had his facts all screwed up."

Jeanne sank into a chair. "Did you set him straight?"

"What do you think?" The irritation in Marcus' voice was loud and clear.

"What do you mean, he didn't have his facts straight?"

"He swears you were fired. Which prompted you to go to the authorities with bogus claims to seek revenge."

"That's not true. I resigned."

"I think Dan Bradbury may have started the rumor and helped stir the innuendo pot."

"Slime ball. I would not put it past *him* to go to the authorities to save his skin since he was probably knee-deep in the shenanigans there."

"Hey, I know you never liked him, and I suspect the feeling was mutual, but I doubt he would have any reason to go to the authorities. I think all he might be guilty of is filling Ken with propaganda to puff himself up and maybe redirect attention away from what a mess the portfolio he was responsible for turned into."

Jeanne's shoulders sagged, and she let her head drop. "I'm so frightened. My sisters could be in danger. I don't know what I'll do if—"

"Maybe it's time to alert the police."

"I should talk to Hannah and Phoebe again before I do. This affects all of us. It's not only the success of the inn at stake, but Hannah's clinic as well."

"Would you feel better if I come back?"

"Yes." She sighed. "It will at least give me some peace of mind knowing we aren't here alone."

"On second thought, I can't. I'm still waiting to hear back from Ken about the get-together I'm supposed to set up."

Her voice caught, and tears dropped into her lap. "Marcus, I—"

"Forget the meeting. I'll call Ken and tell him something came up. Keeping you and your sisters safe is far more important than a meeting which, in my opinion, isn't likely to produce anything worthwhile anyway. I'll make my reservation for the train and text you with the time."

She had to maintain some level of composure, or everything she and her sisters had worked so hard for would crumble around them. The phone rang. Jeanne checked the screen. Ray Grossi. She answered on the first ring.

"Ray here. What's going on? You sounded frantic when you left your message."

"I've had another call." Panic rose within her as she revisited the call. "This time, he knew about a visit we had from the health department."

"Health department? When did this happen?"

"Shortly after our last guest checked out. The inspector came to investigate a complaint someone lodged against us claiming unsanitary conditions."

"Did he find anything?"

"A box of rat poison in the pantry containing a dead rodent. Phoebe swears—"

"Trust me, the rat was not in the pantry when it was breathing."

Ray's deep voice was reassuring, but was he right? "How can you be so sure?"

"When rodents ingest poison, they search for water, usually outside. Which is where they die. You can rest assured the rat *did not* die in the box."

Although she had believed Phoebe when she said she had no idea how the box got there, hearing Ray confirm it sent relief over her. "What do you suggest we do?"

"Step things up. I'll arrange for a couple of my guys to keep watch at your house twenty-four seven. How's Marcus doing with setting up the meeting we discussed?"

"I asked him to return, so we put it on hold."

"It's far more important for him to stay put and follow our plan."

Jeanne's back stiffened. Easy for him to say it wasn't necessary for Marcus to be there. He wasn't the one living in constant fear every day. And although twenty-four-hour protection sounded good, it would no doubt cost a boatload of money. Maybe Ray needed to be reminded she and her sisters may be living in a beautiful Colonial in the heart of Watch Hill, but their financial status had nothing to do with it.

"Sounds expensive."

"I'll call in a favor and arrange to have the local police increase their drive-byes. Which will minimize the hours my staff and I spend there. I'll do what I have to get to the bottom of this so you and your sisters can have the peace of mind you deserve."

Jeanne's throat tightened, and she fought back the tears. "I appreciate that, but I still need a sense of how much you think this will cost."

Ray gave her a ballpark estimate.

Although the amount would make a severe dent in the savings she had left, she had to do whatever was necessary to protect her sisters. If it meant wiping out her nest egg, then so be it. Besides, what choice did she have without getting the police officially involved? Marcus certainly couldn't be expected to stay until all this was hashed out. And what if the situation turned dangerous, and he became an unintended victim? How would she live with herself if something were to happen? "I'm on board with your suggestion, and will mention it to my sisters. I can't imagine they will have an issue, but I want to keep them informed."

"Of course. In the meantime, I'll speak with the police chief and see how far he can go without an active investigation. Then once I know what exactly he can do, I'll be in a better position to know if I can further decrease my estimate. But you have my word. It will not be any higher than what I have already told you. You and your sister's safety are my main concern, so rest assured I will do my best to keep my expenses down."

Jeanne let out a sigh of relief. "Thank you."

"I will keep watch tonight myself. I only ask for Phoebe to keep me fed in exchange for not charging for my time. With no wife and a severe lack of culinary skills, anything she creates will more than make up for me doing my part gratis. Then I'll arrange for Woody to start in the morning. Okay?"

"Sounds like a plan. And Phoebe will take great joy in making sure you are well fed. And I'll call Marcus to tell him to stay put."

"By the way, how did the inspection turn out?"

"Phoebe had to agree there wouldn't be any poison stored anywhere near the kitchen, which of course, she already knew. Then once she signed a statement to that effect, they gave us the go-ahead to reopen."

"No big surprise there. The problem is since the caller's efforts failed to put you out of business, I predict whoever complained will try something else."

CHAPTER
TWELVE

Aaron took a deep breath, cracked open the door to the nursery, and stuck his head inside. He hadn't entered the room since the night his wife and unborn son had died. He took another deep breath, let it out, and pushed open the door. A pine crib hugged one wall. A floating shelf behind it held a collection of stuffed animals. Small, plastic, rainbow-colored zoo critters hung from a mobile. He recalled the day he had painted the walls a light blue after learning they would welcome a son. In some ways, happy times seemed like yesterday. In others, it was like an ocean away.

A faint musty smell hung in the air as he glanced around the room. A changing table and a chest of drawers filled the remaining wall space while a rocker sat in one corner. Aaron went to the crib and turned on the mobile. The sweet music filled his ears. Vibrating with grief and anger, he tried to push aside the dark thoughts still plaguing him despite his best efforts. His eyes blurred. He headed for the rocker, sat down, and opened a manila folder he was holding. Newspaper accounts of the FNB failure stared back at him.

Day passed to night as he rocked and recounted the worst days of his life. On top of their deaths, the recent collapse of the bank had put an end to fulfilling his late wife's last wishes. Oh, if he could only turn back time. Why had he parked her entire inheritance at the bank based on her late father's confidence without the proper research? He stared out the window at the starlit sky and closed his eyes. *I'll do what's necessary to honor your wishes, Gillian. No matter what. You have my promise.*

He laid his head against the back of the rocker, recalling countless dreams of his late wife. Each dream was pretty much the same. She would call his name from across the room. When he tried to respond, his lips seemed sealed. What he wouldn't give to be able to reach out to her, tell her how much he loved and missed her, and how sorry he was for losing her money. Instead, he would awaken awash in perspiration, his heart pounding, always trying to make sense of the dream. Were they intended to be a reminder of what he had done? A call to action? When he opened his eyes, the only illumination came from a streetlight across the road. His eyes grew heavy, and before long, he drifted off.

Gillian revisited, but when she opened her arms to him this time, he stepped into her embrace. He reveled in the closeness. Told her he loved her. And how he had only existed in a stumbling state of numbness since her death.

She stroked his face.

Aaron leaned in for a kiss, but instead of feeling her lips on his, he woke and glanced at a small digital clock on the nearby side table. Nine fourteen. He rubbed his eyes and shook off the sleepy cobwebs. *Was he dreaming?* Nine fourteen was the exact time the clock on Gillian's dashboard had frozen for eternity, the same time the red-light-running driver had taken the lives of his loved ones.

CHAPTER THIRTEEN

Hannah sailed into the kitchen and snatched a banana from a bowl of fresh fruit on the counter. "Aaron called." Her voice was like a teenager in the throes of her first love. "He's at a pharmaceutical conference at The Waldorf."

"Nice place to have a meeting." Phoebe filled a kettle for tea.

"Since the conference ends on Friday afternoon, he asked if we had any availability this weekend."

"I take it you jumped at the chance to see him."

"Of course. We plan to go to Mystic Village right after I close the clinic on Saturday afternoon."

"Sounds like fun." Phoebe tapped her chin. "I can't remember the last time I went there. But I do remember loving the eclectic mix of quaint shops."

"I doubt we will have time to do the shops since I want to go to the aquarium." Hannah peeled back the banana skin. "I haven't been there since they renovated it. The last time Mrs. Murphy brought Rambo in for his shots, she said it was worth the trip."

Phoebe chuckled. "Rambo? Sounds like a hundred-fifty-pound Rottweiler."

"Not even close." Hannah chuckled. "More like a six-pound Yorkie."

"Jo, how nice to hear from you," Jeanne said after answering the phone at the front desk.

"I thought I'd call to see how you girls are doing."

"How sweet of you. We're fine and are discussing how best to decorate the house for the holidays."

"Whatever you decide, I'm sure it will be beautiful. Your house is lovely as it is, but with lights, festive decorations, and maybe a Christmas snowfall, it is easy to envision it looking like a postcard scene."

"Thank you." *Jo was right. Their home was indeed beautiful. But more importantly, it cradled warm memories in every nook and cranny.* "Should we look forward to seeing you sometime soon?"

"You read my mind, dear. That is the other reason for my call. I'd love to come up next week and stay for three nights, Tuesday, Wednesday, and Thursday. And I would appreciate it if I could have the suite I had last time. It was such a comfy space."

Jeanne clicked on the inn's online calendar. "The eighteenth, nineteenth, and twentieth, correct?"

"Yes, dear. Please say you can have me."

"You're in luck. A guest canceled two days ago. So, the room is yours." Was she hearing things, or had Jo muttered, *yes?*

Jo cleared her throat. "I guess it was meant to be."

Phoebe put her broom aside and stopped sweeping the front steps when Aaron pulled into the circular driveway. He grabbed his bag from the trunk and walked toward her, wearing a broad smile which could quickly melt a woman's heart.

"Phoebe, how nice to see you again."

"Welcome back. The last time I checked, Hannah was still at the clinic, but only one car was parked in front, so she should be here soon."

He looked at his watch. "I'm a little early. The conference I attended wrapped up sooner than expected. I was anxious to get here, so I took advantage of an early start to avoid the traffic."

"I'm glad you made it safe and sound. I hope the same holds true for our other returning guests."

"Returnees must mean you're doing a great job. Do I know this other guest?" Then he squeezed his eyes shut as if blocking out a memory. "Not the divorcee, I hope."

Phoebe chuckled. "No, thank goodness. Although I spent much of my time in the kitchen, I heard about her antics. And yes, you've met the woman who is coming back. It's Jo Reasoner."

"Ah, yes. I liked her."

"So did we." She motioned him inside. "Come on in, and I'll get you registered, so you will be all set when Hannah gets here."

"Is it okay if I leave my car out front until we finish? Or would you prefer I move it around to the side?"

"Leave it where it is. Rumor has it you and my sister are headed to Mystic Village this afternoon, so why go to the trouble of moving it?"

Aaron picked up his bag. "Did she tell you we plan to go to the aquarium and then grab some dinner?"

"She did. Sounds like fun." After checking him in, Phoebe handed him the key to his room. "The room is on the second floor, first door on the left. Do you need me to show you the way?"

"Thanks, I got it." He grasped the handle of his bag, headed for the stairs, then looked over his shoulder at Phoebe. "Uh, what's for dessert tonight?"

Phoebe laughed. "I thought you were eating out."

He grinned. "We are, but I can always save room for one of your delightful treats."

CHAPTER FOURTEEN

Much like the alcohol, the conversation flowed in rounds at the get-together Marcus and Ken had arranged.

First round, office stories.

"Remember the guy who fat-fingered a transaction and entered a million instead of ten thousand?" Marcus said.

"Yeah, I thought he would lose his lunch," another added. "How 'bout the redhead who drank herself sick at the picnic two years ago and had to be sent home in a cab by the head of human resources?"

Round two. The collapse of FNB.

A man seated near the middle of the table glanced around and asked, "Anyone find a job yet?"

When no one raised a hand, Marcus said, "I guess we're all in the same boat."

Another former colleague, decades older than Marcus, shook his head. "Who would have thought we would find ourselves beating a path to church every Sunday to pray for a paycheck?"

"I assure you," Ken said. "Not me."

Marcus lifted his drink while his mind raced around. *How could he bring Jeanne's name into the conversation without making it seem odd*? But he knew he had to come up with something quickly because for the last ten minutes, Woody, Ray's associate, had been giving him a look saying, come on, let's get this ball rolling.

"Looks like I'll be heading to DC." Ken poked the ice in his drink with his finger.

"Job offer?" Woody asked, earning him an icy glare from Ken.

"My wife and I wouldn't be moving out of our Fifth Avenue apartment into some dump while I watch my Hampton place go into foreclosure if that were the case."

"What's with DC?" a woman seated across from Ken asked.

"I received a subpoena to testify before the Federal Banking Committee. They have reason to think something needs explaining, and the politicians are hungry to hang someone."

"What's to explain?" Woody asked.

Ken ignored the question. "If I only could get my hands on—"

"Does anyone need a refill?" A server interrupted their discussion.

"I'm good." After the waiter left, Woody returned his attention to Ken. "Are you the only one being called on to testify?"

Ken raised an eyebrow and, for a moment, glared at Woody as if to say, what's it to you? "No. Four of us. The

CEO, COO, me, and…." He leaned his shoulder against his nephew. "Danny boy here."

A woman Marcus remembered as a middle-of-the-totem-pole employee raised an eyebrow. "Why did they call *you*? You were only…."

Dan leaned forward, clearly annoyed. "Only what? A nothing? Someone not qualified to shine your, could-feed-a-family of four for-a-month-on-what-they-cost, shoes?"

The woman reddened. "I only meant—"

Dan put a hand up like a policeman directing traffic. "I know what you meant, and I'm not surprised. You and Jeanne were tight. She did a great job of spreading unsupported allegations about me." He drained his glass and rotated his shoulders. "You think what you want, but at least *I'm* not a rat like your friend."

Marcus almost sighed in relief someone else had brought Jeanne's name into the conversation.

"Who's Jeanne?" Woody asked, expertly playing the role of an unsuspecting friend. "One of the executives?"

"Hardly," Dan scoffed. "More like a financial analyst. And not a very good one, if you ask me."

Woody gave Marcus a look that said, here's your chance to jump in and defend your friend.

Not wanting to be seen supporting someone most people seated at the table probably considered a traitor, Marcus bit his tongue.

"Thanks to her, we are all pounding the pavement." Dan huffed. "She always thought she was smarter than the rest of us."

Woody picked at the label on his bottle of beer. "How could someone in the position you described do anything to crater a company? Unless, of course, she had proof of wrongdoing."

"Regardless of what you think, anyone can go to the SEC," Ken spit out. "And she was bold enough to try. I can tell you this." Ken was beginning to slur his words. "I will be hard-pressed not to give her a piece of my mind when I see her."

"What makes you think she will be at the hearing?" another former colleague asked.

"Rumor has it there's a whistle-blower, and my money, if I had any, would be on her."

<hr />

After saying goodbye to Aaron on Sunday afternoon, Hannah sulked as she walked into the house and found Jeanne in the hallway.

"Something wrong?" Jeanne asked.

Phoebe rounded the corner before Hannah had a chance to answer. "What are you two up to?

"I was asking Hannah if something is wrong. She looks like one of her patients died."

"What's wrong is Aaron left."

"You like him a lot, don't you, baby sister?"

Hannah nodded. "I think he could be the *one*." She headed for the sitting room. "Let's have a seat."

"For goodness' sake, you've only been with him twice." Phoebe shook her head and took a chair. "Don't you think it's quick to jump to that conclusion?"

Hannah shrugged. "When you know. You know."

"Have you two made plans to see one another again?" Jeanne sat on the love seat.

Hannah grinned and joined Jeanne. "I'm going to his house next week."

"Big step," Jeanne said. "Are you sure that's a good idea?"

Phoebe knit her eyebrows. "I don't like the idea you will be staying with a man you hardly know."

"Don't get your apron in a knot." Hannah frowned at Phoebe. "It's not like he's a serial killer. And if it makes you feel any better, I'll be staying in his guest room."

Phoebe's laugh bordered on sarcastic. "Hah! You expect us to believe that?"

"Believe what you want. I'm a grown woman and can make my own decisions. Thank you very much."

CHAPTER FIFTEEN

After collecting them from her garden, Phoebe dumped an armful of plump yellow, purple, white, and deep tangerine-colored mums into the sink. She then took a porcelain vase from an overhead cupboard, filled it with water, cut each stem on a diagonal, arranged the blooms, and carried it to the dining room table.

Hannah came up behind her. "How pretty."

Phoebe tightened her grip on the vase and spun around. "You scared me half to death and almost made me drop this. I agree with Jeanne. You do have a knack for sneaking up on people."

"I wasn't sneaking. Maybe you and Jeanne should get your hearing checked."

Phoebe put the vase in the center of the table. "If you ask me, as quiet as you can be, you'd make a great cat burglar."

The comment earned Phoebe an eye roll. "I came to find out if you are ready to take me to the Cross Sound Ferry. It leaves at four." She glanced at her watch. "I thought my last patient would never stop asking questions."

"Hmmm, a talking canine." Phoebe winked.

"Ha, ha, ha. Very funny. You know what I mean."

"Don't stress. New London is only thirty-five minutes away." Phoebe resituated the vase until she deemed it perfect. "We have plenty of time. It will take me a few minutes to pack the sandwiches I made for us to eat while we wait for the ferry. Do me a favor and get the cooler from the basement."

"No problem."

"Aaron knows to pick you up once you arrive, right?

"Of course." She blew out a stream of air. "I wish you and Beans would stop treating me like a child."

Phoebe smiled. She hadn't heard Jeanne referred to by her nickname in ages. "I don't want you to be hurt."

"No worries." Hannah leaned over the table to smell the mums. "Nice. They remind me of college football games."

~⊙⌒⊙⌒~

"I'm glad you're getting a break from all this craziness," Phoebe said on the way to New London.

Hannah stared out the car window. Make sure to call me if anything else happens. Especially if we get another visit from the state. One more, and we are as good as done."

Phoebe nodded. "The inspector made it quite clear if they receive another complaint, the next investigation will be far more extensive."

"How much more extensive could it be? He even called one of our guests."

Phoebe shuddered. "Please, let's not talk about it. It drives me crazy. I know I've done everything possible to prevent another visit. I even put a lock on the pantry door."

"What happened isn't your fault. If you ask me, I think this nut job is someone Jeanne knows."

"Like who?"

"Marcus. There is something about the guy that rubs my fur the wrong way."

"Really?"

Hannah reached for the cooler behind the driver's seat. "I'm hungry. You ready for your sandwich?"

"Not now. I'll wait until we get there."

"What are we having?" Hannah spread a napkin on her lap.

"Curried chicken salad."

Hannah removed a water bottle from the cooler and stuck it in the cup holder. "Take a minute and think about what I'm about to say when it comes to Marcus." She shifted in her seat. "First, Jeanne told him she was going to the SEC the day she quit, am I right?"

"Well, yes, but—"

"And second, his caller ID comes up as blocked, the same as the calls she has received." Hannah paused to take a bite of her sandwich. "And I have a feeling Ray thinks the same."

Phoebe blushed at Ray's name, which drove her crazy. The man was simply not her type, but . . . "Why?"

"Because he told Jeanne to tell Marcus to stay home after the most recent call."

"Interesting theory, Columbo. But Ray is only against him coming because of the meeting he wants Marcus to set up in Manhattan."

Hannah huffed. "Take your blinders off. He's out of work like the rest, and didn't the headline say thousands out of work?" She took another bite of her sandwich. "Mmmm, good, Pheeb-Meister."

"A lot of people block their number. Jeanne said so herself."

"If you ask me, he's too damn sure of himself. Always right there with an answer for everything." Hannah pointed out the window. "There's the sign for the Cross Sound Ferry."

"Got it."

Phoebe took the next exit ramp and followed the signs directing her to the graveled entrance. She pulled in and parked. "I'll take my sandwich now."

⁓◦⦿◦⁓

Jeanne sat on the cushioned window seat in the sitting room, pulled her knees to her chest, and sighed. *This has got to stop. I have never dreaded being alone. And now all I do is worry about what this maniac will try next.*

She pushed back the sheer curtains and glanced outside. "Glad Phoebe and Hannah aren't here to see me acting like a scared rabbit." She swung her socked feet off the cushion and padded toward the kitchen. *What I need is another brownie. That will be what? Three? I won't only be a scared rabbit but a fat one.*

The landline in the butler's pantry rang. She went to the old push-button phone sans caller ID and hesitated before picking up the receiver. On the fourth ring, she answered. "Hello." Jeanne immediately recognized her older sister's voice.

"Everything okay there?"

Jeanne let out a pent-up breath. "Yes."

"Good. Hannah is on the ferry, and I'm on my way home. I'll be there within the hour."

"Glad to hear it. I need someone with willpower, so I stop inhaling your brownies. I've already made a serious dent in them, and I'm on the verge of doing even more damage to my waistline."

"That's what they're—"

"Phoebe? Hello?" Jeanne heard a dial tone. *She probably forgot to charge her phone before she left.* She shrugged, hung up the phone, went to the kitchen, and stared at the platter of plastic covered brownies. *Should I? Tea will do, and it has fewer calories.* She plugged in the electric tea kettle.

The phone rang again.

Jeanne dashed to grab it. "You didn't have to call back. Your brownies are safe. I'm having tea."

But it wasn't Phoebe calling back.

"Mind if I join you?"

Jeanne dropped the receiver, letting it bounce off the side of the lower cabinet, while the caller's words drifted upward in a muffled fashion.

"What's the matter, Jeanne? Not up for company?"

Jeanne picked up the receiver and brought it to her ear. "Listen to me. I don't know why you're harassing me. But you're mistaken if you think I had anything to do with the fall of FNB. I'm warning you. Leave us alone, or you'll find yourself in jail."

She slammed the phone back into its cradle and stared at it momentarily while her hands and legs shook.

The doorbell rang.

Jeanne froze, took a deep breath to steady herself, tiptoed to the front door, and looked out the peephole.

The mailman stood on the porch.

She let out a long breath. With shaking hands, she opened it.

"A little too much for the mailbox, considering what is already in there." The carrier pulled a manila envelope from the box and put it on top of the pile he held in his hand. "I didn't want to leave it on the porch." He looked around. "The wind is picking up."

"Thank you." Jeanne took the mail and closed the door.

Her attention went directly to the manila envelope. It bore the same bold printing as the last one. She ripped it open and pulled out the contents revealing a photo of Phoebe walking toward the garage. An attached note read,

"Next time, it won't be a picture I'm shooting. Bang. Bang. Who's dead?"

Jeanne dropped the envelope and picture, ran to the phone, and called Ray's cell. He answered "Grossi" on the second ring.

"It's Jeanne Stanton," she said, breathing hard. "I received another envelope. This time he's threatening to kill Phoebe!"

⸙

Phoebe was headed to the front door when Ray pulled in and parked behind her. She tried to quell the blush creeping up her face. "Hi Ray, what're you doing here?"

"I called him," Jeanne stood in the doorway.

Phoebe blanched. "Oh no, this doesn't sound good. What's happened now?"

"There was another call, and moments later, the mailman delivered this." Jeanne thrust out the envelope.

They went inside, and Jeanne started to remove the contents.

"Don't." Ray warned. "Fingerprints."

"Too late, I've already touched it. There weren't any on the first one. What makes you think this will be different?"

"Might not be, but sometimes people get sloppy." He pulled out a pair of latex gloves and slid the picture and note from the envelope.

Phoebe looked over his shoulder taking in the musky scent of his aftershave. Her hand flew to her mouth as she stared at the picture. "What does the note say?"

Jeanne told her.

"It's time to call the police," Ray said. "Our surveillance attempts aren't enough. The next time, it could be an explosive device delivered to the house."

For a second the room spun. Phoebe staggered at the stars spinning behind her eyes.

"Phoebe? Do you need to sit down?" Jeanne asked.

"I'm okay. Give me a minute." Phoebe looked at the picture again and re-read the note. "As we've said, police presence could seriously impact our inn business, not to mention the effect it might have on Hannah's clients. We can't risk losing her income. It's the only steady source we have. I think this is nothing more than a scare tactic. If he had the time to take the picture, he certainly could have harmed me if he wanted to."

Ray shook his head and patted Phoebe's shoulder. "It's not good to second guess a psycho, Phoebe."

Jeanne looked at her sister with worried eyes. "I can't chance anything happening to you." She turned her attention to Ray. "Instead of the police, can someone move in here until this is over?"

Ray tugged on his ear. "I might be able to arrange something. But remember all my inside guy can do is offer a sense of security. The man I have in mind left PPD not long ago and is as good as you'll get. And although he still carries, he no longer has law enforcement authority."

Phoebe closed her eyes for a moment and groaned. "Trust me, I'm no martyr, but if this business fails, it'll play right into this maniac's hands. We can't let that happen. I vote for the bodyguard. He will provide more protection than we could expect from the police anyway."

"Your call, Jeanne." Ray shrugged.

"I've already made a sizeable dent in my savings with the surveillance." She shook her head. "I don't have a choice. I can't put you and Hannah in further danger. We need to discuss a few things, but when can he move in?"

"Probably not for a couple of days. Are you expecting any guests?"

She checked her phone. "Not until next week."

"Good. Until he gets here, don't book anyone else. And once he's here, as far as anyone is concerned, he's a guest. No exceptions. Got it?"

"Even Marcus and Aaron?" Phoebe said.

"*Everyone*. At this point, you cannot trust anyone except each other. Even I'm suspect."

Phoebe tilted her head and wrinkled her brow. "You?"

"I'm merely making a point."

"But Marcus is my friend." Jeanne's voice was filled with frustration.

"No one." Ray's stern words left no room for interpretation.

CHAPTER
SIXTEEN

Phoebe raised her arms, waved, and shouted her sister's name when Hannah walked down the ramp from the ferry. "Over here, Hannah! Over here!"

Rolling her suitcase behind her, Hannah smiled and picked up her pace.

Phoebe gestured with her head. "I'm parked over there. Did you have a nice time?"

"Before we go there, how's everything at home?"

Phoebe pursed her lips and frowned. "We've had another incident."

Hannah stopped. "You said you'd call if anything happened."

"Why ruin your weekend?"

"What now?"

Phoebe urged Hannah forward. "There was another call, followed by a picture and a note in the mail."

"What was the picture of?"

"Me."

"You?"

"Yes. Someone was close enough to capture me walking to the garage."

Eyes wide, Hannah pressed a hand to her throat. "What did the note say?"

Phoebe tried to calm the angst building inside her at the mention of the note. "Next time, it won't be a picture he's shooting."

Hannah gasped. "This is out of control. We have to do something."

"We're doing it. A former detective from the Providence Police Force will be moving in."

"Moving in? As in staying at our *house?*"

Phoebe nodded. "Yes, and Ray made it clear that only you, me, and Jeanne can know he's not a guest."

"What about Marcus?"

"No one."

Hannah grabbed Phoebe's sleeve and stopped walking. "I *knew* it. Ray thinks Marcus is involved, doesn't he?"

"He didn't say that."

"Then why can't he know?"

Phoebe shrugged. "The fewer people, the better, I suppose."

"Marcus is no dummy. We can't say the man is a guest if he continues to stay at the house."

"If anyone asks, including Aaron, he's a boarder. We can say we need the money."

"Why Aaron? Surely, he's not a suspect?"

"At this point, it's fair to say everyone is a suspect. It doesn't mean Marcus or Aaron can't continue to visit. But we can't tell them why the man is here."

"Are you okay with what we're doing?" Jeanne asked Hannah as the sisters walked the beach behind their house with Woody trailing behind them. "Or do you think we should get the police involved?"

"Once Phoebe explained the reasoning, I have to agree it's the only viable option."

Jeanne looked off into the distance. "My biggest worry is whoever is doing this might decide threats are insufficient. I couldn't live with myself if anything happened to either of you."

Phoebe stopped walking and spread her arms. "I think we need a group hug."

The women formed a tight circle then proceeded on.

"Can we please change the subject and discuss something more pleasant?" Phoebe asked.

Jeanne turned her attention to Hannah. "Tell us about your weekend. Is Aaron's house nice?"

Hannah tucked her hair behind her ears. "Very nice. From what he told me, it's a Craftsman built from one of those kits Sears sold years ago. I can tell you his house isn't short on character."

Jeanne picked up a small shell then dropped it back to the sand. "I've never visited Orient Point. Is it as exotic as it sounds?"

"Not at all. It's more like here. Lots of nearby farms, but the smell of the ocean is everywhere."

"When was his house built?" Phoebe hooked arms with Hannah.

"In the early nineteen hundreds by his grandfather. Like us, he has all the original paperwork and designs his ancestors handed down."

"How interesting," Phoebe said.

"The house is nice but seeing the nursery frozen in time threw me for a loop."

Jeanne kicked at a piece of driftwood. "I find it odd he hasn't dismantled it by now."

"I don't think he has set foot in the room since his wife and son died."

"What makes you think so?" Phoebe asked.

"He didn't offer to show it to me until I asked him about it, and for another, I detected a musty smell when he opened the door."

Phoebe shook her head. "How sad. His loss must still weigh heavily on him. It reminds me of how hard it was for Mom to remove Dad's clothes from their closet after he passed away."

"Makes me wonder if he is as ready to move on as I had hoped."

"Did you talk about it?" Phoebe asked.

"Not really. I feared I would open a hornet's nest if I broached the subject." Hannah shrugged. "Besides, I know how I feel, and if he wants more than a once-in-awhile girlfriend, I guess time will tell."

Jeanne linked her arm through Hannah's, putting her younger sister between her and Phoebe. "What if it's all he wants?"

"Not much I can do about it, is there?" Hannah offered up a small smile. "But I'm taking it as a good sign he asked me to return next weekend."

"*Next* weekend? But you just got back." Phoebe was always the mama bear. "Why doesn't he come here if he wants to see you?"

"He's uncomfortable leaving his business in someone else's hands too often. And you said Ray doesn't want anyone staying here until the new guy moves in."

"What about *your* business?" Jeanne asked. "Don't you think you should consider that?"

"It's easier for me. I don't have to leave until after I close on Saturday, and since I don't work Mondays, it isn't much of a problem. I will still be on call for my patients and, if need be, could refer them to Dr. Jackson in an emergency."

Phoebe bit her bottom lip. "Aren't you concerned you might be coming across as too eager?"

Hannah stopped walking, wiggled from her sisters' arms, and pushed her hands against her hips. "Not in the least. I'm not the one who asked me to come back. I even thought about calling in a temporary vet so I could stay a few extra days."

"Oh, Hannie," Jeanne said. "I know how impulsive you can be, but I don't think pushing things is a good idea."

Hannah wrinkled her brow. "I thought you liked Aaron."

"My comments have nothing to do with whether I like him. You might be coming on a bit strong after what he has been through, which could scare him away."

Hannah blew out a breath. "Do you think I would jeopardize our only source of income right now? Please, give me a little more credit. But don't think for a minute if he continues to invite me, I won't go." Hannah faced her sisters. "I only have one concern."

"What?" Phoebe asked.

"You both have to promise whenever I'm away, you will call or text me the minute something happens."

Jeanne and Phoebe exchanged glances before Jeanne spoke. "It's not like there is anything you can do from far away. Why bother you?"

"Because I said so."

"You sound just like Mom used to."

Phoebe threw up her hands. "All right."

"So, let's move on from talking about Aaron. When is the retired detective moving in?"

Jeanne urged her sisters onward. "I don't know if he's retired. All Ray said was he left the force. And regarding a move-in date, when he called yesterday, I invited him to come by tomorrow for a meet and greet. We can ask then."

"What if we don't like him?" Hannah asked.

"I guess we could ask Ray to suggest someone else." Jeanne shrugged.

"Assuming he passes muster," Hannah muttered under her breath. "What do we do until he moves in?"

"Woody will watch outside until ten at night, then come inside and stay until morning. Once the new guy starts, Woody will resume his former overnight exterior surveillance." Phoebe snapped her fingers. "Which reminds me, where should we have the new guy stay?"

"I suggest he take one of the spare rooms on our floor. I prefer we keep our guestrooms available for guests." With her arms hooked with her sisters again, Jeanne headed back to the house. "If we put him on the third floor it will keep him closer to us in case of an emergency and won't cut back on guest income."

CHAPTER
SEVENTEEN

Jeanne answered the knock at the front door to find a decidedly handsome man standing on the front porch.

"Hello. I think you're expecting me. I'm Neal Jansing."

Jeanne couldn't help but stare. The man before her did not match the mental image she had conjured up. "Um, oh. Yes. Uh, hi." She stepped back and mumbled, "Magnum PI."

He chuckled. "I get that a lot. People think I'm Tom Selleck's twin brother, except it's impossible since I'm at least thirty years younger. I even tried shaving off my mustache to lessen the comparison, but my mirror didn't know who I was, so I grew it back."

"Oh, good. I mean. Okay. I mean..." Jeanne looked down at her feet and coughed out a laugh. "I'm sorry." She raised her head. "You probably get this reaction a lot, but it isn't every day a girl opens the door to find Magnum standing on her porch."

The soon-to-be bodyguard gave her a smile accentuating his dimples, making Jeanne's insides stir. "And you are?"

"Jeanne Stanton."

"Ah, yes. Pleased to meet you. I should mention I don't wiggle my eyebrows like Tom was known for. So, there's that."

Jeanne motioned him inside. "Please come in. My sister Phoebe is in the kitchen making coffee."

Neal smiled. "Does it taste as good as it smells?"

"Better."

He waggled his eyebrows.

"I thought you said..."

He gave Jeanne a smile which almost made her swoon. "There are exceptions to every rule, or so I've heard."

Jeanne led Neal to the kitchen on legs as shaky as leaves in a storm. Once there, they found Hannah seated at the table while Phoebe, with her back to Jeanne and Neal, poured her sister a cup of the steaming brew.

"Ladies. Meet Neal Jansing."

Phoebe poured the remaining coffee into a carafe and cocked her head. "Have we met before?"

Neal shook his head. "I don't think so. I'm sure I would remember if we had."

Phoebe's face took on a rosy hue, and Jeanne smiled to herself at how flustered her older sister looked.

"Maybe not, then. It's just you look like...." She put out her hand. "Please pardon my lack of manners. I'm Phoebe. Nice to meet you."

Neal flashed the same smile which moments earlier had made Jeanne melt. "Good to put a face with a name. Ray has told me all about the three of you. And like I told your sister, it's not the first time someone has mistaken me for someone else."

Hannah cleared her throat. "Hi, Neal. I'm Hannah."

"Nice to meet all of you."

Phoebe moved a plate of butter cookies next to the carafe, and they joined Hannah at the table.

"Ray said you are a former Providence Police detective." Jeanne broke the silence.

He reached for the carafe. "Twenty years, a detective the last ten. Left four months ago."

Jeanne took a full cup from him and passed it to Phoebe. "And you've been working for Ray ever since?"

"Not exactly. I took time to be alone with my thoughts and give myself time to unwind. But boredom moved in after six weeks. Since I knew Ray from my time on the force, I called, we talked, and before I could overthink it, I accepted his offer to join his staff."

"You seem too young to have retired, so I take it you left on your own?" Phoebe put cream in her coffee and added a spoonful of sugar.

"True," Neal said without elaborating.

Jeanne frowned. *Had there been a problem, and he had been forced to quit?* Ray wouldn't have recommended him if he didn't think Neal was up for the job, so she let it go.

"I can't imagine what it must be like to put your life on the line every day," Phoebe said.

"Most days, I tried my best not to think about it. But as you might suspect, it can be hard to digest the stress a police officer has to deal with."

Hannah removed a cookie from the plate. "Were you ever shot?"

He nodded while he swallowed a mouthful of coffee. "Five years after I joined the force. A bad guy took exception to me, I guess. Then again, a year ago, during a drug bust turned ugly, I hovered for several days on death's doorstep."

"Well, thank goodness you survived." Phoebe put a hand to her chest. "Sometimes it takes an event of that magnitude to make us realize what's truly important." She gestured at her sisters. "Although we've always been close, our mother's passing and recent events have reminded us how much we mean to one another."

"I know what you mean. I love my daughters beyond measure. Once I recovered, I decided I had to take the necessary steps to be around to walk them down the aisle someday."

"You're married?" Hannah asked the obvious. "How does your wife feel about you living with three women?"

Jeanne's heated spirits dampened.

"Doesn't matter. We're divorced."

Jeanne caught herself before smiling.

"Two weeks after I gave my notice, I learned she was having an affair with a neighbor I considered a friend. A detective's hours can be wonky, and we'd been drifting apart for the last several years anyway. The irony is this detective couldn't see what was happening right under his nose."

Phoebe glanced out a window into the distance. "We often don't see what is right before our eyes."

Neal took the last mouthful of coffee and put his cup down. "Mind if I have another? It has been a while since I've had coffee anywhere near this good."

Phoebe nodded. "A pinch of salt makes a big difference."

Neal helped himself. "Okay, now you've heard my story. Tell me what's been going on here." He turned his soft brown eyes to Jeanne. "Let's start with you."

Jeanne reached for a cookie while she gathered her thoughts. "Before moving back here, I worked for a bank in Manhattan which failed this past summer. A few months later, I received the first threat. The only logical explanation is whoever is behind this thinks I'm a whistle-blower."

For the next few minutes, Neal listened intently, asking questions when necessary.

One-by-one he looked at them. Then redirected his attention to Jeanne. "I'm sure once you heard about your mother's situation, any thoughts of the SEC and your former employer went right out the window."

Jeanne's throat tightened at the memory, and she fought back the tears threatening to streak down her cheeks. She drifted back to the fateful call, remembering how sick she had felt at hearing the shocking news.

"Jeanne?"

The sound of Neal's voice pulled her back from her thoughts. "I'm sorry. The memory is still pretty fresh."

Neal's face softened. "No need to apologize. Take whatever time you need."

Even though she wasn't, she had to say she was all right.

"I'd like to know who you told about going to the SEC?"

"A former colleague. But it isn't him."

Hannah frowned. "You can't be certain."

Neal tapped his pen on the notepad. "Are you referring to Marcus Reynolds?"

"Yes."

"Why do you think he shouldn't be in our circle of suspects?"

"Maybe she doesn't." Hannah swiped another cookie. "But I'm not as sure as Jeanne."

"Why?" Neal asked.

Jeanne sat back and folded her arms across her chest. "Because he's the only person she knows who worked with me. That's why."

Hannah ignored her. "There's something about him that doesn't sit right with me."

"Like what?" Neal leaned his elbows on the table.

Jeanne kept her arms crossed. "Yeah, Hannah, like what? That he's been a good friend to me for over ten years? Or the fact he rushed to be here for us when we needed him? What *exactly* doesn't feel right? Tell me. Because I sure as heck would like to know."

"For starters, you said he's the only one you mentioned the SEC to. And then there is the matter of him being unemployed with no apparent prospects for a new job plus he uses the same caller ID as the person who called you."

If only Hannah would keep her opinions to herself. The last thing Jeanne needed was to encourage Neal to bark up the wrong tree and waste her money. She huffed a breath. "I've told you he's not looking for a job because he's writing a book."

"Hah! For all you know, he could be out looking and not finding anything and is using the book-writing thing as a cover."

Jeanne slapped the table making everyone jump. "Oh, please. How late did you have to stay awake last night to come up with such a brilliant thought?"

"I don't know why my thoughts seem so farfetched to you," Hannah said.

"Because I *know* him. It's not in his DNA to go sneaking around planting threats and making voice-disguised phone calls."

"I hope you're right, Jeanne." Neal rolled his coffee cup between his hands. "I know first-hand how difficult it is to find out a friend isn't all you think they are."

"When are you moving in?" Phoebe broke through the growing tension in the room.

"November first. There are some things I have to take care of first. But don't worry. Ray has arranged to cover for me until I can get things sorted. He told you Woody will resume his overnight watch outside once I move in, correct?"

All Jeanne could think of was how much this would cost her. Although her sisters had volunteered to pitch in, it was only fair she foot the bill since she was the reason they needed protection in the first place.

"If anyone asks, we plan to say you're a long-term guest," Phoebe said. "Okay?"

"Not only is it okay, but it's also not far from the truth. My wife got the house, so this job will give me a place to stay until I find an apartment."

***

Halloween

On a side table near the registration desk was a wicker basket filled with several dozen orange, cellophane-wrapped bundles of candy held together with black curling ribbons Phoebe had put together. "These are perfect." Jeanne said, picking up one of the small bundles. "What kind of candy did you use, Phoebe?"

"Mini chocolate bars and candy corn." Phoebe grinned. "I also found some holiday-themed chocolates with Trick printed on one side and Treat on the other, so I threw in some of those too. Come look at the decorations on the porch."

Jeanne stepped outside. A two-foot-high, glowing jack-o'-lantern and an array of stuffed witches reclined on the rockers while ghosts made from sheets hung from the porch's ceiling. "This must have taken you forever." On her way inside, she stepped on the Halloween-themed doormat. It cackled like a witch. She giggled, stepped on it again, and followed Phoebe inside.

"Halloween is such fun. I love answering the door to the little ones dressed up in imaginative costumes." Phoebe toyed with a piece of candy. "I never tire of telling them how scary or cute they look."

Jeanne hugged her sister. "You're such a mama bear."

Phoebe shrugged. "Nothing wrong with that."

"Not in the least. Tell me, how will our first Halloween together in more than a decade play out? Who will hand out the candy? Who will answer the door?"

Phoebe laughed. "Why don't we play it by ear? A little spontaneity will do you good. Instead of worrying about who does what, I say we cross our fingers and hope we have enough candy. We can always find out from Hannah how she and Mom worked things."

As if on cue, Hannah walked in, with Fenway in full trot leading the way. The dog sported an orange and black striped bandana and an orange t-shirt which said something Jeanne couldn't quite decipher. "Ask me what?"

"How many kids did you and Mom usually have on Halloween?" Phoebe asked.

"Maybe a couple of dozen," Hannah pointed at the candy tray. "How many did you make?"

"Thirty."

"We'll probably have a few left over. The number of kids each year has been dwindling."

Phoebe crouched down and took Fenway's head in her hands. "How cute are you?" She raised her eyes to Hannah. "Where did you get his tee shirt?"

"Mom bought it for him last year."

Jeanne grinned. "Leave it to her." She bent over to get a closer look at his shirt. "Ah, I see now what it says, tricks for you and treats for me." She patted the dog. "Now tell me, how did you two work it as far as giving out the candy?"

Phoebe shot Jeanne a look. "What happened to spontaneity?"

Jeanne rolled her eyes. "Humor me."

"We had a great system. And once Fenway came on the scene, we put him to work too." She leaned down and scratched her dog's head. "Didn't we, Fens?" She straightened. "It all started with watching a scary movie while we waited for the kids. Mom handled the popcorn, and I put her *Frankenstein* tape with Boris Karloff, the only good *Frankenstein* ever made, in my opinion, into the old VCR."

"What did Fenway do besides try and steal the candy?" Jeanne asked.

"He kept watch at the window and warned us by barking when kids were approaching before they could ring the bell. Which gave me time to pause the tape while

Mom and I went to the door." Tears pooled in Hannah's eyes. "Gosh, I miss her."

Phoebe went to Hannah and pulled her into a hug. "We all do."

Hannah sighed. "She had so many traditions."

"Well, I say we keep this one going." Phoebe dropped her arm. "I'll pop the corn."

Hannah's face brightened. "I'll get the tape."

"C'mon boy." Jeanne patted Fenway's head again. "Looks like you are on duty."

The sisters were seven minutes into *Frankenstein* when Fenway lumbered to the front-facing window, put his front paws on the sill, wagged his tail, and let out a short bark.

"Sounds like our signal." Hannah pushed the pause button on the remote.

Fenway pawed at the glass.

Hannah stood. "What're you doing, boy?"

The doormat cackled.

A shadow darkened the front door's glass panel.

The hair on Jeanne's neck stood at attention.

Phoebe put her popcorn aside and started for the door.

Jeanne grabbed Phoebe's wrist, "Wait," she whispered. "Let them ring the bell."

"Why?"

"Because." Jeanne went to a window overlooking the porch. She pushed back the edge of the sheer lace curtain no more than an inch in time to see someone dressed as a witch walking briskly down the driveway.

Phoebe stood behind her. "Do you see anyone?"

Jeanne put a finger to her lips. "Yes. Probably a teenager."

"Why didn't they ring the bell?" Hannah moved in front of Jeanne and opened the curtain wider. "Why come here and leave with no candy?"

"Do you see a car?" Phoebe said.

"No." The skin on Jeanne's arms prickled.

"Could be down the street." Hannah grabbed her jacket from the coat tree. "I'm going after the witch. This is going to stop here and now!"

Jeanne grabbed a handful of Hannah's haunted house design sweatshirt. "Are you crazy? Don't you think it's odd a kid wouldn't ring the bell?" She glanced over Hannah's shoulder. "Phoebe, call Woody's cell. Maybe he can tell who it is."

Phoebe's face drained of color. "I can't..."

Jeanne let go of Hannah's shirt. "For heaven's sake, why not?"

"I talked him into taking a few hours off to take his little boy trick or treating. I thought with all the kids. No one would be stupid enough..."

Jeanne shook her head. "That was a mistake. A big one. Now we're here alone. What if the person has a gun and comes back?"

"I'm sorry. I didn't think—"

"While you two decide what to do." With shaking hands, Hannah pulled on her jacket. "I'm going to catch up with the witch."

Jeanne knew better than to try to talk her sister out of something she had set her mind to. She grabbed her coat off the tree and took a candy package. "Phoebe, call Ray," she said over her shoulder. "I'm going with Hannah."

The two sisters sprinted down the lawn to the sidewalk.

Hannah pointed. "There! Hey, witch!"

The person dressed in black increased his pace.

"You there in the witch's costume!" Jeanne shouted. "You forgot your treat."

The figure stopped and faced the sisters. A mask covered the face.

Hannah ran toward the witch.

"What's the matter?" the witch asked, removing her hat and raising her mask.

"Caroline!" Jeanne sighed with relief. "Did you come by our house?"

"Yes. Mom told me to drop off an envelope delivered to us by mistake today."

Jeanne smiled at the fifteen-year-old girl who lived next door. "Thank you. We saw it," Jeanne lied holding out the candy pouch. "We wanted to give you something for your trouble."

Caroline took the bundle of candy. "Thank you."

"Why didn't you ring the bell?" Hannah asked.

"I'm in a hurry. My friends and I plan to build a bonfire on the beach behind my house and then try to guess who everybody is. Mom insisted I deliver the envelope before I went there. I'm late."

"Well, we won't hold you." Jeanne flapped her hands at Caroline. "Have a good time."

"Thanks." Caroline pulled her mask down, put on her hat, hiked her skirt, and jogged down the street.

"Happy Halloween!" Hannah called after her.

Without slowing her pace, the girl raised her arm in the air.

Hannah giggled as they walked back to their house. "She probably thinks we're crazy."

"Why wouldn't she? Two grown-ups running after a teenager in the dark. We're lucky she didn't scream."

Hannah grinned. "Good thing you had the candy. What made you think to take it?"

"Don't know."

"I do. You always have a plan, even when you don't realize it."

The sisters climbed the porch steps to find Phoebe sliding the key into the lock.

"Where are you going?" Jeanne asked.

"Nowhere now. I was worried when you didn't come right back. Did you find out who it was?"

"Yes. Caroline from next door. She said an envelope was delivered to their house by mistake." Hannah pointed down at the envelope peeking from under the mat. "Her mother insisted she bring it here before she went off with her friends."

Jeanne pulled the envelope out sending the Halloween mat cackling. With her thumb and forefinger, she grasped it by one corner. "This isn't good. The writing is the same as the others."

"Ray will be here in about forty minutes," Phoebe said. "He wasn't happy about Woody and said he would deal with him later. I tried to tell him it wasn't his fault. But it didn't seem to matter. He said until he gets here, he wants us to turn off the outside lights and not open the door to anyone but him."

⸺⧼⧽⸺

Jeanne went behind their desk, pulled a letter opener from the top middle drawer, and handed it to Ray.

He pulled on a pair of latex gloves, slit open the envelope, and extracted a sheet of paper.

"What does it say?" Jeanne's heart pounded in her ears.

Ray glanced at the sisters and then read aloud. "Shame on you. Pity the poor children who eat candy from your pantry."

"Throw the packages out!" Phoebe shrieked. "All of them. Now!" She exhaled a long stream of air. "Thank goodness we didn't hand any out."

Jeanne looked at Hannah. "Caroline."

"Who's Caroline?" Ray asked.

Jeanne explained.

"Were the candies in their original packaging when you made these?" Ray asked Phoebe.

"Yes."

"Check each one and make sure they don't appear to have been tampered with. If they seem okay, the chances the girl got the one tainted package are slim. Whoever is behind this wouldn't damage one." Ray held the envelope up to the light and raised a brow. "There's something else in here." He tilted the envelope into his palm.

A small, foil covered candy slid out, the word Trick facing up.

Phoebe gasped. "I used those in my bundles. How the heck?"

"Enough!" Hannah slashed her hand in the air. "We can't take any chances. I'm going to the beach to see if I can find Caroline and get the candy back. If she hasn't eaten it yet, I'll tell her it's stale. If she has, I'm afraid I'll have to tell her mother Caroline should see a doctor if she experiences any strange symptoms."

"I'll feel better knowing she isn't in danger." Phoebe grabbed her coat. "But you can't go alone."

"I'll go with you," Ray looked at Jeanne and Phoebe. "You two stay put and keep the doors locked."

"I don't know how much more we can take." A lump in her throat made it difficult for Jeanne to speak.

"We need tea," Phoebe said. "I'll put the kettle on."

"Forget what I said about my guy staying here." Ray pulled out his cell phone from his inside coat pocket. "It's time to call the police."

Jeanne stared at him. "I've told you we can't afford the fallout it will cause if the police are involved. Everything we have worked so hard for will go up in a puff of smoke. Think about it. Who in their right mind would want to come here if they think we are the victims of a stalker? And let's not forget about Hannah's practice. Without her income, we will be forced to close our doors and put the house on the market."

"Losing your business is better than losing your—"

"Neal will be here tomorrow night," Jeanne countered.

Ray shook his head. "Not enough."

"Maybe the envelope will show traces of DNA," Hannah said.

"Too slow." Ray put his phone back in his pocket.

Jeanne rubbed the back of her neck to relieve the tightness. "There must be something you can do other than us calling the police."

Ray let out a deep breath. "It's against my better judgment, but maybe there is."

"What?"

"Don't ask. Leave it to me. It's not exactly legal. Come on, Hannah, let's find the girl."

―――∽⊙৪৫⊙∽―――

Neal and the sisters gathered in the kitchen for lunch after he moved in the following day.

"Ray is having all the candy, including the one you retrieved, analyzed," Neal said to the sisters. "From now on, do not open anything delivered here without having me check it first. And another thing, the location of my room presents a problem."

"Why?" Jeanne asked.

"Because I can't see the garage or the right side of the backyard from my windows. Are those places visible from any of your other rooms?"

"Only Hannah's and one guest room," Jeanne lifted her sandwich.

"Then it's best if I take one of them."

"I don't want Hannah to have to move, and we'd rather not give up a premier guest room," Jeanne bit her bottom lip. "Besides, we feel better having you on the same floor as us."

He looked from one woman to the other as they nodded. "Okay, let's see how it goes. If I'm right, I may have to pull rank and insist on moving. And so you know, I'll conduct exterior inspections four to five times daily. And before I turn in, I will check the outside doors and downstairs windows to guarantee they're secure. I assume you lock the doors to your rooms, right?"

Phoebe nodded.

"Good. I'll double-check those, too, to be sure."

"By the way, the lock to the side door of the garage hasn't worked in years," Jeanne said.

"Not acceptable. I'll hire a locksmith to replace the lock and make five keys. Each of us will have one. We'll put one in a kitchen drawer, so you don't have to carry your key around in case you have to go to the garage."

"Good." Phoebe stood. "I'll put it in the drawer next to the one for the pantry."

"We'll need bottled water brought in each time someone goes out there," Hannah said.

Jeanne nodded. "I'll take care of—"

"Uh, ladies? May I continue?"

The sisters quieted.

"I will be conducting background checks on your guests. So, you must feed me their information when they make a reservation."

Jeanne frowned. "I check them out online."

"My process will be more accurate than anything you can do since I will have access to a system Ray uses."

"Oh, that's good." Phoebe looked at Jeanne. "Isn't it, Jeanne?"

"Yes, as long as the police don't get involved."

"At least not for now they won't. There is one more thing. Assuming these threats continue, the next time anything is delivered here, or something happens, get me right away. And if I'm not here for whatever reason, remember to handle letters or packages the way Ray showed you and bring the evidence to my room. Are we clear, ladies?"

Phoebe and Hannah gave a solemn nod.

Jeanne visibly bristled. "Let *me* make something clear since I'm the one paying you. Our guests cannot get the impression something isn't right. Which is why you're here and not the police."

"I will do my best to respect your request, but may I remind *you* my job is to keep you all safe while we track down the perpetrator. Trust me, if you follow my instructions, no one will suspect a thing."

For fourteen months after ending her relationship with her former boyfriend, Jeanne had vowed not to open her heart to another man before she was sure he would not break it. So when Ray insisted he didn't want them to entertain guests, including Marcus, until after Neal moved in, she had considered it a blessing and a curse. Initially, she had leaned on Ray's insistence and found relief. But as time passed, she couldn't shake the fact she missed him. By the time Neal moved in, she missed Marcus so much she called him and suggested he come to Watch Hill.

"Tell me about this Neal guy. How long will he be here?" Marcus asked Jeanne after dinner the day he returned to the inn.

She did her best to sound nonchalant as she took a clean plate he had taken from the dishwasher and put it in the cupboard. "He's freshly divorced and needs a place to stay until he decides what's next."

"What do you know about him?"

Jeanne shrugged. "No more than we know about any other guest, except Ray did a background check on him and it came up clean. She needed to be careful not to make it sound like Ray knew him. "He will start doing the same for anyone who stays here until we discover who is behind this madness."

"Are you saying he checked me out too?"

"Of course not, silly," she lied, knowing Ray had said he was suspicious of everyone. "You're a friend, not a guest." She smiled at him. "I can tell you're not a fan of having Neal here, but you can't be around twenty-four-seven. My sisters and I will have peace of mind knowing a man is here. The money we will collect for his stay will also be useful." Lying was becoming a bad habit.

Marcus took Jeanne's hand. "I can be here as much as you want."

Jeanne couldn't help but smile. "I can't keep imposing on you."

"You're not. I like being here for you." He touched the side of her face. "You're important to me, Jeanne. Always have been."

Where did that come from? And why hadn't he said anything like this before? She cocked a brow and tried to calm her racing heart. "Really?"

Hannah walked in with more dishes. "Uh, sorry."

"For what?" Jeanne felt like a child caught red-handed being naughty.

"Looks like I'm interrupting."

Although Jeanne would have preferred to keep the prior conversation with Marcus going, it was what it was. "Not in the least. While we were cleaning up the kitchen, we were talking about what to do for the rest of the night."

⸙

The following day

With the wind at her back Jeanne walked with Neal along the bluff at the back of the property before breakfast and had to bite her tongue so she wouldn't say something she might regret.

"You should've told me Marcus will be here for a few more days."

Jeanne pulled her sweatshirt hood over her head and stuck her hands in her pockets. "Why?"

"If I'm going to be effective, you have to tell me these things."

Jeanne huffed a breath. No matter how hard she tried to tell herself Neal's presence was a necessary evil, it made her uncomfortable having him under foot watching every move she and her sisters made. Not to mention being told what to do. Her resolve not to bark at him shattered. "He'll stay as long as I want him to."

Neal shook his head. "It'd be better if you stop inviting him."

"For whom?"

Neal rolled his eyes. "As Ray and I have told you, everyone is suspect until they aren't. Which includes Marcus."

"How many times do I have to tell you he is not involved in this craziness?"

"Regardless of what you think, we are still in the process of sorting through myth versus reality." Neal hunched his head into his shoulders. "Speaking of Marcus, is he a nervous type?"

Jeanne coughed out a laugh. "Marcus? Are you kidding me? He's about as cool minded as they come."

"Have you ever noticed how he jiggles the coins in his pockets a lot?"

"Of course, I have. I've always considered it an annoying habit, much like biting your nails."

Neal shook his head. "Conversely, it's usually a signal of uneasiness."

"Marcus, uneasy? You are totally off base. Marcus has always struck me as in control."

"So was Ted Bundy. Just ask the families of his murder victims."

Jeanne rounded on him and glared. "Give me a break. Now you're comparing Marcus to Ted Bundy? Instead of focusing on my friend, I suggest you and Ray put your efforts into finding the real culprit." She started to walk away, then stopped and looked over her shoulder at him. "Please stop wasting my money on micro-analyzing Marcus."

After her walk with Neal, Jeanne sat at the table to have breakfast with Marcus.

"How about we head to Foxwoods for a few hours," Marcus suggested.

"I've never been to a casino." Jeanne buttered a slice of toast. "I wouldn't know what to do."

"I'll show you everything you need to know. It's a lot of fun, and Foxwoods isn't far. Getting away from here for a few hours will do you good. We'll play a little, have something to eat, and head home." He winked. "Or if the machines like us, maybe we'll stay until they don't."

Jeanne's eyes widened, and she grinned when they entered the casino floor. The maze of slot machines, sounds, vibrant colors, and throngs of people surprised her. It was a lot to take in. She pointed at one of the machines whose rich colors caught her attention. "Let's try that one."

Marcus leaned over her shoulder after she settled into the leather seat and said, "The smallest bill it will take is a five."

She shrugged. "Nothing ventured." She pulled a five from her wallet and slid it into the slot. "Kind of like a soda machine, except more expensive," she laughed and lifted her eyes to him. "What now?"

"Select the amount you want to bet, and pull the lever or push the button, whichever you prefer."

She pushed the button and when the reels stopped spinning, three bonus icons lined up like wooden soldiers across the screen.

Jeanne clapped her hands together. "Does that mean I won?"

"Not yet. But you have yourself a string of free spins."

A man at the next machine tipped his head at them. "I played there for the last hour, and it got me next to nothing. Must be your lucky day."

Marcus chuckled. "Who knows maybe you will walk out of here with a jackpot."

The screen vibrated after each winning spin, and when her free bonus plays were over, Jeanne was two hundred and fifty-five dollars richer.

"Better return on my five dollars than at a bank. I guess I'm buying dinner." She hit the cash-out button and slipped her winning ticket into her purse.

"Maybe if you keep playing, you'll win enough not to need your long-term guest."

"Fat chance. Anyway, Neal's a nice guy."

"How *nice?*" Marcus asked while they walked to the redemption machine so Jeanne could collect her cash. "Please tell me. I'd like to know."

"Nice is nice. Why?"

"I don't like him around you all the time."

Jeanne stopped and arched a brow at him. "If I didn't know better, I'd swear you are jealous."

Marcus took her hand and gave her a sly smile. "Would that be so bad?"

They wound their way through the casino to the food court. *Had his feelings for her suddenly changed because he felt threatened by Neal? Could he be jealous because he cared for her in ways she never expected? Or had his ego been trampled when he realized he might not be the only man to vie for her attention?*

"I'm up for something light," Marcus said. "You?"

Her stomach growled. "Pizza?"

"Great. You still like veggie style?"

"Some things never change."

Marcus tugged his wallet from his back pocket. "Find us a table. I'll get this."

"I thought I was buying."

"Maybe dinner. This is a snack."

Jeanne scanned the crowded food court and found an empty two-seater on the far side next to the windows. After settling into her seat, she gazed at the forest of ancient pine trees stretching before her. She gestured to the window when Marcus got to the table. "A table with a view. How pretty."

Marcus put the tray on the table. "It is."

Jeanne stuck her straw into her soda cup, picked up her slice of pizza, and folded it in half. Something she had learned to do after moving to Manhattan. "Tell me, what do you have against Neal?"

Marcus's face colored slightly. "I only want what's best for you."

"And what does that have to do with Neal?"

"I don't like him living with you."

Jeanne put her pizza slice down. "Marcus Reynolds, he is not *living* with me. Like I said before, if I didn't know better, I'd swear you're jealous."

He shrugged. "Maybe *you* think of us as friends, but I want more."

She raised an eyebrow. "You can't be serious."

"Why is it so hard to believe?"

"How long have you felt this way?"

Marcus took a sip of his soda. "Almost from the moment we met. I never pushed it based on the company's policy about employee dating, because it would've meant a career killer for both of us."

"Maybe I would've felt differently."

"That's just it. I didn't want you to take such a chance. Of the two of us, you always had the potential to rise in the ranks. Me, not so much. I never would've asked you to consider giving up everything you had worked so hard to achieve. I would have been the one to go, and as much as I hate to admit it, the thought of the Brinks delivery truck not showing up on payday would have been more than I could bear. It was the best money I ever made."

Jeanne swallowed hard as her heart galloped at the words she had waited so long to hear. Other than the occasional flirty comments he handed out like candy to nearly every female at FNB, he had never given Jeanne any indication he wanted anything but an abiding friendship with her. Should she let the feelings she had long suppressed rise to the surface? She placed her hand over his while she collected her thoughts. "I never thought I'd tell you this, but for the longest time I harbored a big crush on you." She took her hand back. "But you always gave me the sense I was no more than your lunch buddy, so I let my feelings go. Now, after all this time, you're saying I should've kept them?"

Marcus nodded.

"Well, Mr. Reynolds, that's quite a revelation."

"The question is, what do we do about it?"

Jeanne paused. "To be honest, I'm not sure. I don't want to jeopardize our friendship for what might turn into a momentary fling."

Marcus gave her a soft smile. "Me either. Let's take things slow and see where it takes us. Now as for Neal—"

Jeanne put a finger to his lips. "Who?"

Marcus eyed the cavernous room. "I think this is one of the largest casinos in the country."

"I can see why. There must be thousands of slot machines here, not to mention table games," Jeanne said as they walked around the sprawling complex after having lunch.

"Do you want to play something?" Jeanne asked.

"As a matter of fact, I do." He took her hand. "Follow me." He led her into another section of the casino lit by enormous chandeliers. Marcus made his way to a baccarat table and gestured. "James Bond's game." He sat down at the table and threw down two twenty-dollar bills.

Jeanne stood behind him and watched as he worked the chips the dealer had pushed across the table to him. "I didn't know you liked to gamble," she whispered in his ear. "Have you played this before?"

"A time or two. A time or two."

CHAPTER EIGHTEEN

The smell of fresh apple pie greeted Jeanne and Marcus as they walked into the kitchen. Phoebe, clad in a red apron, clapped her hands together, sending a cloud of white flour into the air. "Did you win?" she asked.

Jeanne grinned. "I'm two hundred and fifty-five dollars richer."

Although the winnings were excellent, her windfall paled in comparison to Marcus admitting he had feelings for her. But now was not the time to divulge that. Besides, for all she knew, it might only be Marcus' flirty personality speaking. After all, hadn't she given him a chance to kiss her when they stepped into the elevator, yet he hadn't taken the bait?

"I guess there's something to beginners' luck." Phoebe redirected her attention to Marcus. "What about you?"

Marcus tilted his head in Jeanne's direction. "She did all the winning."

Jeanne retrieved a bottle of water from the refrigerator, passing by one of the kitchen chairs wedged under the doorknob of the side entry door. Her eyes widened. "Did something happen? I took it as a good sign when you didn't call."

Phoebe put the chair back in its place at the kitchen table. "No worries. I got a little jumpy this afternoon, is all." Phoebe sighed. "The only new development is Rob called and said he won't make it home for Thanksgiving. It seems he's failing one of his courses and found a tutor who'll help him over the holiday. I guess he takes after me when it comes to numbers. I told him if he came home, you could help him. But he said he's already committed." She shrugged. "His schooling's more important than one holiday, so I let it go."

"At least he has a good excuse." Jeanne couldn't help but wonder if her sister was telling the truth about why her son would not make it home for the holiday. Had she suggested he not come because she worried for his safety? Sure, the caller had everyone's nerves on edge, but if her sister were afraid to let her son come home, Jeanne would never forgive herself. And it would be like Phoebe not to let on how frightened she was.

Phoebe looked away. "I'm very disappointed." She returned her gaze to her sister. "On a brighter note. I saved you some leftover pie filling."

Thoughts of leftover pie filling brought Jeanne back to when her mother let her finish the remnants left in the bowl. She smiled, poked her finger in the filling, and brought it to her mouth. "Mmmm. Delicious. Phoebe, this is as good as Mom's. Marcus, you should try this."

He opened his mouth and leaned in.

Did he expect her to dip her finger into the mixture for him? And if so, how would her sister interpret that? Jeanne's cheeks grew warm as she eyed the mix, then dipped a different finger in the sweet, sticky filling and lifted it quickly to Marcus's mouth so neither he nor Phoebe would see how flustered she was. As he closed his mouth around her finger, he sucked the treat from the tip, never once losing eye contact with her, as if Phoebe weren't an arm's length away. She extracted her finger, wiped her hands on a nearby paper towel then smoothed her sweater to fight off the urge to smile like a schoolgirl.

"You're right. Delicious." Marcus gave her a sly smile.

"Aaron still here?" Jeanne asked, changing the subject to ease her racing heart. The question was merely a distraction since she had seen his car parked out front when they returned.

"He's staying until tomorrow."

Jeanne took a chair at the table. "I'm surprised he came at all after what Hannah said about his concerns with leaving his business in the hands of others."

"I'm glad he did. I prefer him here instead of her there." Phoebe checked the stove's timer.

Marcus pulled up a chair next to Jeanne. "What were they up to while we were gone?"

"They went to Galilee and had lunch at George's. They returned about a half hour ago."

"Ooh, I love George's." Jeanne licked her lips and hummed. "Great seafood."

"We'll have to go." Marcus nudged Jeanne's shoulder.

Since their discussion at the food court, Jeanne had looked at Marcus with fresh eyes. *Boy you're gorgeous.* She gave him a coy smile. "Sounds good."

Phoebe rinsed out her dishes. "Oh, and before I forget, Jo called. She'll be here in a few days."

"I guess she must like it here," Marcus said. "What's this, her third visit?"

"She's fast becoming more of a friend than a guest." Jeanne looked out the kitchen window. The row of red maples lining the property had turned a fiery fall orange, while two cardinals shared a meal at a nearby birdfeeder. "She's probably lonely since her husband passed away."

"I think you're right." Phoebe wiped off the counter and hung the wet dishrag over the faucet. "And I must say I am quite proud I was able to complete the booking on the computer without help from either you or Hannah. I followed the instructions you left at the desk and took it slow." She snapped her fingers. "Easy, peasey."

Jeanne put an arm around her sister's shoulder and squeezed gently. "My sister, the techno-wizard."

Phoebe chuckled. "If I were you, I'd check it out to ensure I didn't screw it up."

Jeanne yawned then glanced at her watch. "I know it's only nine-thirty, but I'm beat." She headed for the stairs.

"It's been a long day." Marcus followed her. "Goodnight, Phoebe."

Marcus stopped when he and Jeanne reached the third floor. "Want to watch some more TV?"

TV? Hadn't she said she was tired? "I think I'll pass."

"We can watch it in your room until you fall asleep."

Jeanne was sure Marcus had more on his mind than a television program. As much as the thought of having him in her room was enticing, she wasn't sure she wanted to further their relationship. "Maybe another time."

Marcus put his arm around her waist and pulled her close. He gazed into her eyes until she thought her knees would abandon her, then lowered his lips to hers in a soft lingering kiss.

A moment later, he stepped back, took her hand, and led her to her door.

When they reached her room, he pressed her against it, and kissed her again.

The doorknob lodged in the small of her back. When their lips separated, she reached behind her and pushed it open. What the heck. She led him to a chaise lounge fronting a trio of windows.

Neither one attempted to brighten the moonlit space or turn on the television.

"Marcus, we need to take this slow," Jeanne said, while he kissed her neck sending shivers down her spine.

"We have all night."

"I meant...."

He lifted her chin and looked into her eyes. "All night, Jeanne," he whispered, then kissed her again.

Jeanne awoke with a wide smile. Making love to Marcus had been as natural as rain on a hot summer night. Slow, gentle, passionate, igniting feelings she hadn't felt in so long.

"Good morning," he whispered in her ear, his voice heavy with sleep and his arm stretched across her waist.

She rolled over to face him and wrapped her arms around his neck. "Morning," she whispered back. "We should be quiet. I don't want anyone to hear us."

"I'd say it's a little late for that."

Despite the plaster walls, Jeanne couldn't help wondering if Phoebe had heard her and Marcus the night before, since her room was right next to hers. After Marcus slipped from her room, she couldn't help but grin. But she'd have to ditch the smile before she went downstairs. The last thing she wanted to engage in was a third-degree from her sister about why she was in such a good mood before she had a chance to down her morning coffee. As it turned out, her concern was on target when she walked into the kitchen.

"Bet you slept *good* last night," Phoebe said, her face buried in the newspaper.

Jeanne's cheeks warmed. "No different from most."

"Really? I thought you would have slept like a rock."

Jeanne poured herself coffee. "Why?"

Phoebe put the paper down and looked over her reading glasses at her sister. "Jeanne Eliza Stanton, I may be naïve about some things, but I'm not deaf!"

Jeanne sat across from her sister. "I—"

Phoebe's eyes twinkled. "Why are you embarrassed? You're certainly old enough. Besides, I've suspected for some time there's more to your relationship with Marcus than you let on."

"I'm glad someone did because I never thought so. Although I had the hots for him years ago, I never knew it was mutual until yesterday."

Phoebe leaned her elbows on the table. "Why, what happened?"

Jeanne held her coffee cup in both hands and took a sip to hide the smile failing to disappear. "He surprised me when he said he never pushed anything with me because of the FNB policy prohibiting employees from being romantically involved. My first reaction was too late buddy. That was then. This is now. Then I remembered what drove me crazy about him back then and—"

Phoebe gently slapped the table. "I could tell something had changed between the time you left here yesterday and when you got home." She gave Jeanne a wink. "So, how was it?"

Jeanne reached for the cream. "Good."

"Only *good*? Not mind-boggling?"

"Well, yeah. Better than good. Oh, I don't know." She ran a finger around the rim of her mug and stared at the coffee as if she might find an answer swimming in her cup.

"Go on."

Jeanne looked up. "There's nothing more."

Phoebe smirked. "Uh-huh."

"Why do you want me to analyze this?"

"You seem to be doing fine on your own."

Jeanne sighed. "Okay, if you must know. I *like* him. Maybe even love him the way you do a friend you've known for ten years. In the early days, my knees went rubbery every time I saw him." She chuckled. "But I convinced myself he didn't feel any differently about me than any other female at FNB."

"I can see why he would have that effect on you. He sure is handsome. The first time I saw him. I thought he could be a model!"

A moment passed. Jeanne drank some coffee and put her mug down.

Phoebe folded the paper and set it aside. "I sense a *but* coming."

"Yesterday, when he confessed his feelings, the part of me that didn't tell him it was too late flew back to a time when I would have given a week's pay to hear those words. Hearing him say what I had long given up on was flattering. Besides, he made me feel pretty, and took my mind off the trouble I've caused."

"Hannah may be cute, but you have always been the pretty one." Phoebe chuckled. "Mom always called me her porcelain doll, which honestly, I never understood what she meant, but *you* have a fresh-faced beauty women spend hundreds on products to achieve. You shouldn't need Marcus, or any other man to feel good about yourself. And stop thinking what's been happening is somehow your fault."

Jeanne reached across the table and gently squeezed her sister's hand. "Thanks, Pheeb."

"Why do you seem to be questioning your feelings for Marcus?"

Jeanne shrugged. "I guess I'm gun-shy."

"Why?"

"Because I never saw the end of my previous relationship coming. And I don't want to feel the same degree of hurt again."

Phoebe nodded knowingly. "Don't be too hard on yourself. Like I told Neal, we often don't see what we don't want to. My advice is not to let your past color your future."

Marcus replayed the previous night with Jeanne while he stuffed his clothes into his bag for his return trip to Manhattan. He'd felt the time was right to launch himself at her after seeing how flustered she became when he sucked the apple pie filling from her finger. And he had been right. Thank goodness he had listened to the voice telling him to go for it. After all, it further cemented their relationship, and Jeanne was the catch of a lifetime. She was different than other women he had been intimate with. Primarily because not only was she hot, but she also had the smarts to go with it, and that alone would aid him in ways she would never suspect.

The phone rang, interrupting his thoughts. He shoved his shaving kit into his duffel bag and answered what had become a familiar ringtone.

"What's up?" Marcus said.

"Where are you?"

"Stanton's."

"Mission accomplished?"

Marcus smiled. "What do you think?"

It had surprised Jeanne when Marcus seduced her, and it shocked her even more when she gave in to his advances. She told herself time and time again her resolve had weakened based on the high level of stress she was under.

Her phone rang, dismissing her thoughts. She picked it up from her nightstand and glanced at the screen.

Blocked caller.

She hadn't received a threatening call in more than a week, so more than likely, it was Marcus calling to say how much he missed her. She answered with a cheerful, "Hi there."

"Shame on you for blowing money away at a casino when former employees of FNB can't afford to put food on the table," the caller said.

A chill ran down her spine. How could he know about the casino? Her curiosity morphed into anger. "How many times must I tell you I'm innocent of whatever it is you think I'm guilty of before it sinks in?"

The caller gave a hearty laugh making Jeanne's skin crawl.

"Don't play dumb with me. If you haven't gotten it by now, trust me, before long, you will."

Click.

Jeanne had to relieve the tension brought on by the call. Whenever she needed to redirect her thoughts, a long jog helped. She laced up her running shoes and headed downstairs. But first, she had to let Neal know about the latest incident.

"Where're you going?" he asked when Jeanne reached the bottom of the stairs.

"I need to run off some stress. I had another call."

"You should have come to find me while you were on the phone."

"There is never enough time. The call ends before I can get a chance to alert anyone."

"What did they say this time?"

She filled him in.

"Maybe going for a run isn't such a good idea."

"I have to do something, or I will explode."

"It's not safe for you to go alone. Since you're determined, wait here. I'll be right back. I need a minute to change."

Jeanne rolled her eyes. Her emotions were a mix of frustration at needing a bodyguard and relief she wouldn't be on the streets by herself. "Okay, but remember, I'm accustomed to keeping a certain pace."

Neal laughed. "Oh, I get it. You think I'm too old to keep up with you."

Jeanne's face warmed. "I didn't mean—"

"Yeah, right." Neal took the stairs two at a time. "Stay right where you are. I'll be back down in a few minutes."

When she was sure he was out of earshot, she muttered, "Nice going. Insult the bodyguard."

A few minutes later, Neal returned dressed in gray sweatpants and a sweatshirt reading *Providence PD* across the front in raised navy blue letters. Then, he flashed what she had come to think of as his Magnum PI smile.

"Ready?"

She caught herself staring. He looked much younger than his forty-something years. "I'm surprised you're wearing a police department shirt. Doesn't it broadcast who you are?"

"Nah. A lot of people wear them. It doesn't mean they're on the force. Besides, Marcus isn't here to question me, so who cares?"

"Speaking of Marcus," she said, heading for the door. "He's not keen on you being in the house with us."

"Tell me something I don't already know. What guy in his right mind would be okay with another man staying in his girlfriend's house?"

She stopped and shot him a questioning look. "What makes you think I'm his girlfriend?"

Neal raised a brow. "Aren't you?"

Jeanne's cheeks flushed. "Only since you moved in."

"What do I have to do with you two being a couple?"

"It may be a coincidence. But while we were at the casino, he asked why we allowed a border based on what was happening. I reiterated your cover story, which is when he said he didn't like you being here with me. I told him he sounded jealous. And the next thing I knew, he confessed he had harbored feelings for me almost from the moment we met."

"And?"

"And what?" She raised an eyebrow." It surprised me."

"Why?"

"Because at one time, I was the one who wanted to be more than his friend. But when he never gave me any indication he wanted more, and when I saw how he flirted with all the women at work much like he did me, I changed my mind about him."

"Smart girl. It's obvious he considers himself quite the lady's man. But I have to admit. He does have a point."

Jeanne frowned. "About what?"

"I can see how my living here would present a problem for him. I'm sure he sees me as competition."

Why did his comment about being competitive release a swarm of butterflies in the pit of her stomach? Jeanne resumed walking toward the front door. "I doubt it," she said over her shoulder.

Neal held up a hand. "Let's change the subject. Your love life is none of my business. If you're ready for the run of your life, this old man plans to show you he's not as decrepit as you seem to think."

Breathing hard, Jeanne made it halfway up the circular drive before slowing to a stop. She leaned over and put her hands on her knees. The sound of her racing heart vibrated in her ears and muffled Neal's laughter.

"Still think I'm too old?" He chuckled.

Jeanne lifted her head and glanced at Neal. "You pushed me to my limit."

He took her arm. "Come on. We can walk the rest of the way so you can catch your breath."

⁓⧉⧉⁓

Fresh from the shower, Jeanne pulled a long-sleeve turtleneck over her head and was tucking it in her jeans when her cell phone rang.

"Hi, pretty lady," Marcus said before she even had a chance to say hello. "I'm barely home, and I miss you already."

"Would you please unblock your number when you call me? I can't tell if it's you or the psycho."

"You sound edgy. Has something else happened?"

"I got another call. Somehow, he knew we were at the casino. He said I should be ashamed of blowing my money when everyone who worked at FNB couldn't even afford to put food on the table. What I want to know is how the hell he could possibly have known we went to Foxwoods?"

"We? Did he mention me?"

"No."

Jeanne thought she heard him breathe a sigh of relief.

"Did you call Ray?"

"No, I—" Jeanne's hand went to her forehead. She had almost said, Neal. She crossed her fingers behind her back, something she'd done since childhood when she was about to tell a lie. In her mind, crossing her fingers reduced a lie to a fib, which wasn't a sin. "I told Phoebe, and then I went for a run."

"Have you lost your mind? Whoever is behind this is still out there. And you think it's okay to go for a *run*?"

"I didn't go alone. Neal was with me."

Marcus's irritated breath came through the line. "He sure doesn't waste any time, does he?"

"Don't read anything into it. He was going anyway, and I needed to run off the stress and didn't think it smart of me to go alone, so I asked. No big deal."

"He doesn't know what's been going on, does he?"

Jeanne recrossed her fingers. "Of course not." She paused. "Did you tell anyone we went to Foxwoods?"

"Uh…yeah. Ken called, and I told him I lost forty bucks at the baccarat table."

"Did you tell him we were together?"

"I don't think so. But with everything on my mind, I'm lucky I can remember what I had for breakfast. Hey, I've been thinking how nice it would be for you to come here and escape the madness."

"I can't leave my sisters. Especially after today's call." She momentarily thought how nice it would be to have Marcus all to herself for a few days. "On the other hand, I guess I could check with Neal and see—"

"What's he got to do with it?"

"I was about to say I could ask if he's planning to be here while I'm away. At least with him here they won't be alone."

Marcus was silent for a moment. "I'm sorry for acting like a teenager. You mean a lot to me, and I don't want to lose what's taken us so long to start."

Phoebe walked into the dining room with two cardboard boxes, one on top of the other, both marked *Thanksgiving*, and put them on the table.

"You should have told me you were getting those," Jeanne said. "I would have helped."

"I didn't think this one," she gestured to the top box with her chin. "Would be so heavy."

Jeanne took it from her sister. "Here's why." She pushed aside the bubble wrap and lifted their mother's ceramic, turkey-decorated, soup tureen from the box. "Gosh, I can almost smell her butternut squash soup." Jeanne's eyes filled with tears. "It's hard to believe she's gone. This will be our first Thanksgiving without her."

"A friend once said you become orphaned when your parents pass away. At first, her comment threw me, but the more I thought about it, I realized it was true. You lose your anchor when they're gone. Especially when it's your mother."

Jeanne wiped at a tear resting on her cheek. "There are times I feel adrift."

Phoebe hugged Jeanne and stepped back. "Come on. There are more boxes to unpack. And the last thing Mom would want is for us to be getting all sappy."

Jeanne thought about how best to let Neal know she planned to stay at Marcus's place for a few days. Did she want him to say no problem or put his foot down and tell her in no uncertain terms to stay home? She shook her head. Why did she care? After all, he was only their bodyguard.

She left her room and bumped into him on his way downstairs. "I thought you should know I plan to go to Manhattan next weekend to see Marcus."

"Not a good idea for you to be in the city, especially since the caller might be a former FNB employee, and you could be putting yourself in harm's way. Besides, your sisters will be here alone."

"No, they won't. You'll be here."

"Think again. I'll be with you."

"You can't come. I'll be staying with Marcus."

Neal shrugged. "Not my problem."

Jeanne slapped her hands on her hips. "How do you suggest I try and explain why you're with me?"

"That's for you to figure out. In case you've forgotten, I'm your bodyguard. Where you go. I go."

"But he doesn't know you're anything more than a boarder. And you're not only *my* bodyguard. You're Phoebe's and Hannah's too." She puffed out her cheeks and let the air escape between her lips. "How often do I have to tell you Marcus has nothing to do with this? I'll be safe with him. My money is far better spent having you here with my sisters, instead of playing nursemaid to me in Manhattan."

"I'm not a nursemaid. And whether you like it or not, Marcus is a prime suspect. Actually, he's our *only* suspect."

Under her breath, Jeanne called Neal a moron, turned on her heels, and walked away. "You can think what you want, but I'm going, and I'm going *alone.*"

<hr />

Marcus carried Jeanne's single suitcase up the two flights of stairs to his apartment. "I must warn you. You're about to enter some sparse bachelor digs, not at all what you're accustomed to." He unlocked the door and shouldered it open.

Jeanne stepped in and looked around. She had been unsure what to expect, but it was quite nice.

A large, flat-screen TV hung on the wall to her right, fronted by a plush, buttery soft, burgundy, leather couch. A small oval glass-topped table separating the two appeared as a catchall for neatly stacked magazines and newspapers. The kitchen stood to the right of the open space, with rich dark wooden cabinets featuring sleek metal pulls. A curved island, home to three bar stools, separated the kitchen from the large open area. While black granite countertops and stainless-steel appliances completed the space.

Jeanne gave him an approving nod. "Very nice."

He held out his hand. "Come on, let me show you the rest of the place." He led her to the bedroom, where he put her luggage on the bed. "My boudoir, or should I say *our* boudoir for the next three days." He winked at her. "And over there is the bathroom. Which I like to refer to as the library."

Jeanne coughed out a laugh. "You read when nature calls?"

Marcus laughed. "Doesn't everyone?'

"Where do you do your writing?" Jeanne asked, looking around.

He pointed to an alcove only steps from the bedroom. "Over there."

Jeanne walked over to the space. No bigger than eight by six, the area featured a narrow table, with a laptop and printer, pushed against one wall. A window on the far wall helped to brighten the room.

Jeanne eyed the immaculate work area. "My desk isn't nearly as neat as this. I expected to see more of a mess for someone writing a book. Where's all your writing stuff?"

Marcus laughed. "I shoved everything into a drawer. Didn't want you to think I'm a slob."

"Well, I have to say I'm impressed. Next time we girls do spring cleaning, I'll know who to call." A glass tank was perched on a metal stand in a far corner of the room. She squinted. "Looks like a fish tank, but I don't see any fish."

"No fish. It's home to my pet snake."

"Snake?" Jeanne ran a hand up and down her arm. "It can't get out of there, can it?"

"Only with help. Based on your reaction, it won't happen while you're here." He walked across the room and peered into the bottom of the tank. "He's harmless. Come here and take a look."

Jeanne slowly approached, eyed the snake coiled at the bottom, and shuddered.

I'm glad you agreed to go to Macy's with me," Jeanne said as they exited the subway station near the historic Manhattan store.

"What's so special about this one?"

"I guess it's the ambiance. The others are usually located in malls, so it never feels the same as when I walk into this one." Jeanne sighed. "It's one of the things I miss about Manhattan. Another is lunch at the Rock Center Café."

Marcus coughed out a laugh. "You sound like a tourist."

Jeanne grabbed his hand and led him toward Macy's revolving door. "Come on."

"I'm all in for helping you satisfy your desire to see this place," Marcus said when they arrived at the door. "But I draw the line at following you around like an obedient canine while you parade in and out of dressing rooms." He grinned. "Unless, of course, you head for the lingerie department."

"No fashion shows." She smiled at him. "And no shopping either. I only want to walk on the creaky floorboards, ride the wooden escalators, and breathe in the place."

Marcus stood beside Jeanne at the railing above the Rockefeller Center's skating rink and glanced at his watch. "I'm starving. It's only eleven-thirty, but it feels like a hundred years since breakfast. You ready for lunch?" He pointed at the Rock Center Café. "I believe you said it's a favorite of yours. And since it's early, we may be able to get a seat without too long of a wait."

"I'd love a window seat to watch the skaters."

"Let's give it a try."

Although they could've been seated fifteen minutes sooner, Marcus and Jeanne opted to wait longer for a two-top at the glass wall.

"Thanks for going to Macy's with me," Jeanne said when they sat down. "I know it wasn't at the top of your list of things to do."

Marcus covered Jeanne's hand with one of his. "I'd walk around the Fresh Kills Dump on Staten Island if it made you happy."

"Since when are you familiar with Staten Island? Or an expert on dumps?"

He let go of her hand. "I'm not. Much of the nine-eleven wreckage was taken there. I guess I remembered it from the news. I only used the analogy, so you know the lengths I'll go to make you happy."

"Aww, what a sweet thing to say." Jeanne gazed at the rink with its skaters gliding effortlessly across the ice, and the famous Prometheus statue, while snapshots of her Manhattan life marched across her mind.

Marcus tapped her arm. "Hey, where'd you go? Looks like I lost you."

"Sorry. I was thinking about how much I love this city. The sheer vitality of it. How utterly alive it is." She sighed. "I must admit there are times when I miss it."

"Then come back. I have no doubt companies would form a line to scoop you up."

Jeanne shook her head. "Never say never, but I don't see corporate America in my future anytime soon. At least not here."

<hr />

When a car door slammed, Phoebe put down the pad and pen she was using to scribe her weekly menus and went to the front door. "Jo, wait. Let me help you," she called out, then went outside to where the older woman was attempting to pull an oversized suitcase out of the trunk of her car.

"I couldn't decide what to take, so I packed more than I needed. I could stay a month with what I have in there."

"Which reminds me, we've decided to thank our trice-returning guests by offering them a free night, so maybe you can extend your stay and use the rest of those clothes you brought."

Was that relief crossing Jo's face? In an instant, it was gone.

"How generous. Are you sure?"

"You're doing us a favor."

Phoebe pulled the large luggage behind her while Jo closed the trunk.

"How so?"

Phoebe stopped. "Hannah's leaving Saturday for a couple of days, and Jeanne went to Manhattan the day before yesterday. I'm not looking forward to being alone in this big old house once Hannah leaves."

"Are you saying I'm your only guest?"

"No, Neal Jansing is here." Phoebe lowered her voice. "But he's a man and still rather new to us."

"Neal?"

"Our boarder."

"Oh, heavens, of course, you told me about him," Jo said. "I don't know where my mind is these days. I should consider myself lucky I remembered my way back."

Phoebe smiled at the woman walking beside her. "Well, we're glad you did."

Jo put her hands on her hips and looked at Phoebe. "Should I take exception with those sisters of yours for leaving you to fend for yourself while you have guests?"

"Not at all. I told them I'd be fine, and I am." Phoebe opened the door for Jo then guided her into the living room.

"Well, I won't have you waiting on me." Jo took a seat on the couch. "Maybe you'll let me do a little cooking and give you a well-deserved break. I told you I've always dreamed of donning a chef's hat."

"No need to step in. I love cooking." Phoebe took in the kindly woman's face. "We were saying the other day how much you remind us of our mother."

"What a lovely sentiment. I love coming here. My only concern is I may become a pest."

"I can't imagine such a scenario." Phoebe stood. "Since it will be only the four of us for dinner tonight, I thought we'd be informal and eat in the kitchen. If that's all right with you."

"I wouldn't have it any other way."

CHAPTER NINETEEN

Phoebe began to clear the dinner dishes from the table. "Go on and relax while I clean up," she told Jo. "You've done enough. You prepared the entrée."

"Yes, please." Hannah gathered the silverware. "Since you cooked. The least we can do is to clean up."

"I only prepared the meatloaf. Phoebe did the rest. I hope you all enjoyed it."

Phoebe gently touched Jo's arm. "It was very special."

Jo glanced at Neal. "Let's you and I catch up in the sitting room, shall we?"

Neal stood. "Sounds good. I'll be there in a minute, Jo."

"Okay, I'll watch a little of the nightly news while I wait." She left the room.

"Was it just me, or was the meatloaf as dry as a bone?" Neal whispered.

"The world's worst." Hannah giggled. "It was so dry it made the Sahara look wet."

Neal shook his head. "Thank goodness I could load up on your side dishes, Phoebe."

Phoebe stifled a laugh. "I know what you both mean. I had to force myself to finish what I put on my plate."

"I kept reminding myself not to spit it out." Hannah added.

"Meatloaf can be tricky. Maybe she couldn't remember the recipe and tried to wing it," Phoebe said.

Hannah shook her head. "Nice try, big sister, but I doubt it. From here on in, you do the cooking, okay?"

Neal raised his hand. "I second that."

Three days later, Phoebe and Jo were at the kitchen table playing gin rummy when Hannah came home from spending the weekend with Aaron.

Phoebe put down her cards. "Welcome home, Hannie. How was your time away?"

"Not so good. We're history."

"What?" Phoebe said.

Tears rolled down Hannah's face.

Jo hugged her. "What happened?"

"He's not ready. He thought he was, but when reality set in, he realized he's not."

Phoebe opened a cupboard and removed cups. "I'll make us tea. Is green okay?"

Hannah sniffed and nodded.

"Your Aaron's not ready for what?" Jo put a hand on Hannah's.

Hannah sniffed again and reached for a napkin. "Me. A relationship. From the way it sounds, he thought he'd come to terms with losing his wife and was ready to move on, but now he's unsure."

Jo patted Hannah's hand. "Well." Jo sighed. "Better you know now before things get serious."

"I'm way past *getting* serious. I told him I love him."

Phoebe held a floral serving tray fashioned with inlaid ceramic tiles in mid-air. "You did what?"

"Whoops." Jo shook her head. "Is that when he told you he wasn't ready?"

Fresh tears rolled down Hannah's cheeks. "No, but I knew something had changed as soon as the words left my mouth. He looked like he had trouble breathing. I had to stand quietly and watch as he retreated inside himself."

"Had he already told you he loved you?" Jo asked.

Hannah shook her head and wiped off her cheeks with a napkin. "No, and it wasn't as if I had planned to say it first. It just came out."

"You probably frightened him," Phoebe set the tray on the counter.

Hannah blew her nose. "I could tell I should have kept my feelings to myself based on how distant he seemed the rest of the day. Then this morning after breakfast, he said things were moving too fast, and maybe we should take a break." She gave a one-note laugh. "Then *I* was the one who couldn't breathe."

The electric teapot beeped. Phoebe put mugs, a sugar bowl, and a plate of lemon wedges on the tray. She poured the water, brought the tray to the table, and sat. "Maybe he'll change his mind. Hannah, in all fairness, you probably blindsided him. After all, you two haven't known each other long."

"I agree with your sister." Jo poured tea into their cups. "Your words probably caused him to take stock. Something he didn't see coming."

Hannah took the mug closest to her from the tray and squeezed a lemon wedge into the steaming tea. "As I said, it wasn't intentional. But even if you're both right, it seems a bit much to tell me we should take a break, don't you think?"

"Men are a strange lot." Jo's laugh sounded forced. "They don't always act the way we women expect. Sometimes they try to hide their insecurities by putting on a macho front."

Hannah picked up her mug and looked over the rim at Jo. "He doesn't strike me as the insecure type."

Jo blew across her tea. "Insecurity isn't the right word. Powerless might be better. Men like to be in control. When they aren't, they become unsure of themselves. When you said I love you first, you usurped his control. It probably made him feel like you had backed him into a corner."

"Jo has a point." Phoebe stood and put some brownies on a plate. "You put him on the spot. Made him feel like he needed to respond in kind, and he wasn't ready."

Hannah sighed. "I suppose, but now what?"

"Depends on where you left things." Jo said.

"He seemed less distant after he said things were moving too fast and we should take a break. Almost like he'd unloaded a burden." Hannah's tears fell anew. "I can't believe it's how he sees our relationship." She grabbed another napkin and blotted her eyes. "He followed me in his car to the ferry and waited with me until I drove on board." Hannah blew her nose and shrugged. "I don't know what to think."

"Those aren't the actions of a man looking to dump you, dear," Jo said.

"I agree." Phoebe took a brownie. "You talked while he waited with you, right?"

Hannah nodded. "He said he needed time and he'll call."

Jo held a brownie close to her mouth. "There's your answer. You must wait. No matter how much people think boy-girl things have changed since my day, I assure you they haven't. Let him do the calling. And if my instincts are right, it'll probably be sooner than you think."

<hr>

Weary from her whirlwind visit and train ride back from Manhattan, Jeanne wanted to jump into the shower and crawl into her bed.

Hannah's bedroom door opened as Jeanne finished climbing the stairs to the third floor. "I hope your trip went better than mine." Hannah padded barefoot across the floor, her short, pink nightgown skimming her knees.

"Why, what happened?"

"Aaron wants space. Until I hear from him, consider us history."

"You're kidding. I thought you two were on the same page."

Hannah pointed to her face. "Do these bloodshot eyes look like I'm kidding? He's not ready to commit."

Jeanne eyed her sister's face and cringed. "What is that supposed to mean?"

"He said he's not ready to move on."

Phoebe walked into the hall from her room wearing floral pajamas and a matching robe. "She told him she loved him," she said softly.

"Before he told you?" Jeanne raised an eyebrow. *Was her sister crazy?*

Hannah nodded.

"Oh, Hannie."

"I didn't mean to say it. It slipped out."

"Telling someone you love them doesn't *slip* out." Jeanne entered her room with her sisters on her heels. "You threw caution to the wind like you usually do, didn't you?"

Hannah pouted and looked at Phoebe. "I told you she wouldn't understand."

"Oh, I understand, all right," Jeanne said. "This is a prime example of you putting your mouth in gear before you engage your brain. Remember what mom always said, think twice, speak once, but for whatever reason you always seem to reverse the order."

Hannah waved a hand. "Doesn't matter."

"Of course, it matters." Jeanne sat on the edge of the bed. "You care about him. And now your heart is broken."

"Hah! You're not the one to talk about acting in the moment. I might remind you, you're the one who quit your job without a second thought."

"Enough, you two." Phoebe sat next to Jeanne and nudged her in the side. "How did your visit go?"

"We had lunch at Rockefeller Center and watched the skaters. Ate our way through Manhattan, spent a good hour at Macy's. Gosh, I love the smell of the place."

"And?" Hannah said.

"And what?"

Hannah stood by the door. "I thought you might try to get together with some of your former coworkers while you were there and help clean up our mess."

"I considered it. I even suggested it to Marcus, but he talked me out of it, saying he didn't think it was a good idea."

Phoebe put her hands on her hips. "For heaven's sake, why not? You could've told them you had nothing to do with the downfall and, like Hannah said, gotten this whole mess settled once and for all. Not to mention saving yourself money on Ray and his crew."

Jeanne picked at one of her cuticles. "He didn't think I could change Ken or his nephew's minds. And although he didn't say it, I think he was afraid I'd get my feelings hurt or worse, it would turn into a scene."

Hannah waved a hand. "Feelings, schmeelings. When someone gets bullied, the bully gets called out."

"I said much the same to Marcus, but he quickly reminded me it could be dangerous."

Neal stood in the doorway. "What's dangerous?"

Hannah stepped behind the door and peeked around it, shielding her night-gowned body from Neal.

"Jeanne considered confronting her accusers when she was in the city," Phoebe said. "But thanks to Marcus, she didn't."

Neal shot Jeanne a look. "Interesting. Don't you think?"

The following day

Jeanne walked into the kitchen and eyed the car keys Phoebe held in her hand. "And where do you think you're off to?"

"Farmers market."

"Want some company?"

"Don't think you're fooling me. I know what you're doing, and although I appreciate it, I'll be fine. Who's going to bother me at an outdoor market?"

Jeanne huffed a breath. "At least let me walk you to your car. I was going to check on those bushes we planted anyway." Jeanne followed Phoebe outside and spotted her sister's car in the driveway. "Why isn't your car in the garage?"

"I had a delivery yesterday and told them to stack it where I usually park. I haven't had time to put it away. It's all non-perishable, so it's okay."

"Hi, ladies," Neal called from the side door. "Where are you going?"

"I'm off to the farmers market, and Jeanne is going to check on the landscaping."

"I'll go along for the ride," Neal said to Phoebe.

"No need. I'll be fine." She pulled her phone from her purse. "I have my cell."

Neal stood in front of her. "Does Jeanne know where the market is?"

"Yes. It's not far and is popular with the locals. As I said, there's no need to worry."

"I can see there's no sense in trying to convince you otherwise. Be careful and pay attention to your surroundings. If something looks even remotely suspicious, give me a call."

Jeanne started a slow jog down the driveway. "Text me when you get there and again on your way home," she called over her shoulder.

"Okay." Phoebe got into her car and lowered the window. "I think I'll leave this open," she said to Neal. "It's such a lovely day. The fresh air will feel good after being cooped up in the house all week." She turned the key, pulled the gear shift into drive, and headed down the sloped driveway.

Jeanne was almost at the bushes when she sensed Phoebe's car approaching. She turned in time to see Neal crouched over where Phoebe's car had been parked.

"Phoebe, wait!" Neal yelled.

The car picked up speed. The look of sheer terror on her sister's face sent shockwaves through Jeanne.

"No brakes!" Phoebe shrieked through the open window.

Neal waved his hand and shouted at Jeanne. "Get out of the way."

The next few minutes seemed to happen in slow motion.

Neal running toward the car.

Phoebe shouting, "I can't stop!"

A group of teenagers assembled in the middle of the street scrambling to get out of the way.

"Pull up on the parking brake! Neal bellowed.

"I can't. It's stuck!"

Phoebe jerked the steering wheel to the right to avoid hitting the children. The hundred-plus-year-old stone wall fronting the property did what the brakes couldn't. The horn blared. The airbag deployed, and Phoebe's head slammed back against the headrest.

Jeanne raced to the car. "Phoebe!"

Neal yanked open the driver's door. He reached in, undid Phoebe's seat belt, and pulled her from the car. Gently he laid her on the grass, removed his jacket, and covered her with it. "Jeanne, call nine-one-one!"

Shock had Jeanne rooted in place.

"Now! Jeanne. Now!"

She fumbled in her pocket for her phone and punched in the number.

"What's your emergency?" the operator said.

"There's been an accident. My sister... Please send help."

"What kind of accident?"

"Car. Her brakes—please hurry."

"Is she conscious?"

"Neal, is she conscious?"

"No."

Jeanne sobbed. "No... no, she's not. Please stop asking questions and send help."

"I've dispatched a unit. They will be there shortly. I'll stay on the line with you until they arrive. Is she in the car?"

"No. A friend has pulled her from the car and has her lying on the grass."

"Can you tell if she's breathing?"

"Is she breathing, Neal?"

He looked at Jeanne. "I can't find— wait. There it is. We have a pulse."

Jeanne stared at Phoebe's chest. *Thank God.* "Yes, she's breathing!"

Phoebe was conscious by the time the rescue truck approached the hospital emergency room. "Where am I?" she asked Jeanne.

"At the hospital. Do you remember what happened?"

Phoebe closed her eyes and nodded slowly. "The brake pedal went to the floor. I couldn't stop. Please tell me I didn't injure those children."

But before Jeanne could respond, the emergency vehicle doors swung open, and the medics swept Phoebe inside.

⚬⚬⚬

Neal stood on the front steps as the tow truck pulled into the driveway.

"Wow, who'd you piss off?" the twenty-something, long-haired driver said when he looked under the hood.

"Excuse me?"

"Uh, sorry, mister, I meant who would be mad enough to…" He lifted one end of the brake line and ran a finger over the severed end. "This looks deliberate. You got woman troubles or something?"

Neal had no intention of discussing what had happened with a guy whose biggest worry was probably getting a Friday night date. "Any issue getting it out of here?"

"No. There's plenty of room to swing my truck around." He closed the hood. "As I said, the cut is too clean to be caused by wear."

"I heard you." After removing a small umbrella from the front seat and the registration form from the glove compartment, Neal closed the front passenger side door.

"Take it to Mike's Body Shop. But tell them not to touch it until I call them."

"You took quite a blow to your head," a young doctor said to Phoebe. "The CT scan we ran indicates you have a concussion, but there isn't evidence of a brain bleed. I want you to spend the night until we get all the test results back in the morning. In the meantime, I suggest you rest." He looked at Jeanne. "Your sister is one lucky woman. If she were on the road when it happened... Well, who knows. Assuming she goes home in the morning, can someone pick her up and stay with her for the next several days?"

"She lives with my younger sister and me. So yes, someone will be with her."

"Good. Make sure she doesn't enter into any legal agreements, and she can't drive until we know the side effects of the concussion have passed." He made a note on her chart and then looked at Phoebe. "I trust you will take it easy after you leave here, right?"

Phoebe struggled to lift her head from the pillow. "I can't. I'm the chef at the inn we own."

"I'd advise you to tell your guests to eat out for the next week."

After returning from the hospital with Phoebe, Jeanne made sure her sister was settled in her room before joining Neal who was seated in the living room.

"Don't blame yourself for what happened to Phoebe." Jeanne said to Neal as they discussed the accident and the repair of the car.

Neal shook his head and hung his hands between his knees. "I can't help but feel responsible. The only thing I can think of is the brake line must have been cut when Woody got sick during the night and had to leave his post. Although I made it a point to walk around the house a couple of times after he left. I guess when I went back inside, it gave the perpetrator the time he needed to complete his mission."

"It's no one's fault. Woody couldn't help being sick, and you couldn't be expected to stay awake all night."

The phone rang, interrupting their conversation. Jeanne reached for it. "Hi Ray, I hope you have news."

"I do. I have it from a reliable source three former FNB executives have been subpoenaed and will appear before the Congressional Oversight Committee."

Jeanne sighed. "Do you know when that will happen?"

"Not yet. I do know it won't be until after the New Year."

"I'm not surprised. Heaven forbid Congress should work like the rest of us before Christmas."

"How's Phoebe?" he asked.

"She's coming along. But with each passing day, it will be harder and harder to keep her down. I fear she'll hate me by the time this is over because I won't let her even think about cooking." Jeanne smiled at the thought of her older sister and how stubborn she was. Knowing she would be as hard to handle if the shoe were on the other foot. "I'll let you go, Ray. Please let me know if you hear anything else." Jeanne hung up and prayed nothing would happen before the hearing, but her gut said it was likely wishful thinking. If the damage done to Phoebe's car were any indication, whoever was behind the threats would continue to play out their twisted plan of revenge.

CHAPTER TWENTY

Two weeks later

"Everything okay?" Jeanne asked when Marcus answered the phone the day after Thanksgiving. "I haven't heard from you in three days."

"All's good. I got on a writing roll, and before I knew it, days turned to nights, and by then, it was too late to call. How was your turkey day?"

"Phoebe outdid herself as usual. The four of us needed to be wheeled away from the table."

"Four?"

When exactly would she learn to choose her words more carefully when it came to any mention of Neal? "Uh, yes, Neal had dinner with us."

"The last time we spoke, you said he was going to see his kids." Marcus' voice held more than a hint of irritation.

"From what I gather, his ex-wife decided at the last minute to take their daughters to her parent's house instead of him and his daughters spending Thanksgiving with *his* parents. We could tell he was disappointed, so Phoebe told him to have his ex bring the girls here for dessert.

Surprisingly, she did. They stayed a couple of hours, and Phoebe made banana splits. It was fun."

"Had to be awkward having him and his ex in the same room with all of you. Are they looking to get back together?" Irritation turned to hopefulness.

"I don't think so."

Marcus huffed a breath. "Too bad."

"It was all very civilized. I gathered she has already moved on and is seeing someone. It's sad, though, whenever a family involving children comes undone."

"I was hoping they would reunite so he would leave your house. You know how I feel about him being there doing what I should be doing."

"You can't be here all the time, and I have no intention of asking him to leave simply because you're jealous."

"Doesn't mean I have to like it." His voice softened. "I miss you."

"I miss you too."

"Why don't you come for a visit this weekend? I guarantee you won't be sorry."

"Sounds enticing, but I can't. My sisters and I are headed to Boston on Saturday and made reservations at a hotel. We can all use a break."

She intentionally hadn't mentioned Phoebe's accident because she was sure if she had, Marcus would insist on coming, which would start a civil war with Neal.

"What about the inn?"

"We purposely didn't book any guests until after the holiday, and Hannah arranged for a vet to cover emergencies for her. We plan to do Christmas shopping at Faneuil Hall." Jeanne gave a short laugh. "Believe it or not, it was my idea. Phoebe always says I'm not spontaneous, so I wanted to prove her wrong. We're taking the train. It'll be a blast."

"You're leaving Neal at the house alone?"

Jeanne crossed her fingers. "No. He's staying with friends."

───⟨⟩───

Neal strode to a waiting taxi outside Boston's South Station and opened the rear door for the sisters.

The driver got out and loaded their four overnight bags into the trunk while the three women scrambled into the backseat.

Neal rode up front. "Long Wharf," he said to the driver and closed the door.

After they arrived at the hotel, Neal unloaded the suitcases, while Jeanne paid the driver.

Phoebe looked at her watch. "I could sure use some coffee. It is already ten after twelve, which means it's been almost three hours since my morning fix."

"Sounds good to me." Jeanne nodded. "Let's take our bags to the bellman. Then we can go."

Phoebe pulled up the handle of her suitcase. "Let's check in first."

"Check-in isn't until three," Jeanne reminded her.

"Oh, of course. I forgot. It's been a while since my last hotel stay."

Jeanne laughed. "Welcome back to the twenty-first century, Pheeb. The world has missed you."

"Let's get a move on." Hannah rubbed her hands together. "The stores are calling my name."

Jeanne picked up her bag and looked at Neal. "You sure you're up for shopping with three women?"

He grabbed his duffle bag. "It goes with the territory. I've had tougher duty."

Phoebe elbowed Jeanne when Neal walked to the hotel door and held it open for them. "Wait till Marcus finds out Neal came with us," she whispered.

"I'm surprised he didn't ask." Hannah's words were sarcastic.

Jeanne nodded. "He did. I told him Neal is staying with friends while we're gone."

Hannah's eyebrows shot up. "Seriously? Miss Straight Shooter lied?"

Jeanne gave a sly smile. "Not really. We're his friends, aren't we?"

"You still have time to change your mind about tagging along with us," Jeanne told Neal after they finished a quick bite to eat, and Phoebe enjoyed a refill on her coffee. "The mall's public and no one knows we're here. How much safer can it get?"

Neal frowned. "I thought you said you told Marcus."

Jeanne grit her teeth to keep from screaming at the man. "Will you *please* give it a rest? I'll tell you what. Hannah and I have our cells with us. I promise one of us will call if anything even remotely suspicious happens. If you don't hear from us, you can assume we're fine, and we'll meet you in the lobby at five-thirty for dinner. Okay?"

Neal shook his head. "I don't like it, Jeanne. This guy's been following your every move. Without knowing who is behind this, how do we know he doesn't somehow know where you are?"

"Impossible." She put up a hand. "And don't you dare bring Marcus into this again."

⚬⚬⚬

"You ladies sure do look fresh-faced and ready for the day ahead." Neal leaned back in his chair at The Paramount restaurant after they ordered breakfast the following day. He sniffed the air. "Somebody smells good."

Hannah smiled. "It's probably the lavender glycerin soap I bought yesterday."

"I bought some, too." Phoebe's cheeks took on the color of the pink carnation rising from the table's bud vase.

Neal gave them a soft smile. "Well, I'd say it was worth the cost."

Jeanne scooped up the remaining bits of her tomato and basil omelet. "How nice it is to truly relax and not worry about waiting for another shoe to drop."

"I certainly feel the difference." Hannah finished her breakfast and placed her napkin beside her plate. "Since our train doesn't leave until one. I was hoping we could check out Beacon Hill before we leave."

"Sounds good," Phoebe looked at Jeanne and Neal. "What about you two?"

"Sure," Jeanne said.

Neil smiled. "I'm only along for the ride."

Jeanne drank the last mouthful of her coffee and put her cup down. "I'll get the check and meet you all outside." She looked at Neal. "And please don't argue with me about it. Paying for your breakfast is the least we can do after you treated us to dinner last night and decided to follow us around Faneuil Hall yesterday."

Neal gave her a salute. "You're the boss."

※

Sunday afternoon, Phoebe unlocked the side door and entered the house alarm's security code.

Jeanne rubbed her arms. "What did you lower the thermostat to before we left? It feels chilly in here."

"I set it at sixty-five because it takes too long to bring the temp up if I set it much lower. But you're right. It does feel cold."

Neal headed for the hallway. "I'll check the downstairs thermostat."

"I'll do the same upstairs." Jeanne left the room.

"I'm off to the clinic to check on things there," Hannah said.

A few minutes later, Neal and Jeanne returned to the kitchen.

"The thermostat says fifty-eight, but as Phoebe said, it is set to sixty-five."

"Same upstairs."

I'd better check the furnace," Neal said.

Phoebe frowned "But it's new. We had it installed a week before we opened."

Neal headed for the basement. "Maybe they messed up the installation."

"I guess it's possible since this is the first time we have needed heat since the installation."

Jeanne tapped her forehead. "I'll be right back. I should have grabbed us both a sweater while I was upstairs."

A few minutes later, Neal returned and reached for a paper towel. "The furnace is as cold as a day-old corpse."

Phoebe put a hand on her hip. "Well, that's a new one."

"Uh, sorry, cop-speak." He shrugged. "I guess some habits are hard to break. I think it's time to pull out the paperwork."

"Jeanne has it. She keeps track of all our purchases."

Jeanne walked in and handed Phoebe a sweater. "What's this about a purchase?"

"The furnace died while we were away." Phoebe shivered and pulled on her sweater.

"But it's brand new," Jeanne said.

"Apparently, the furnace forgot. It's colder than a day-old corpse."

Jeanne's eyebrows shot up. "Phoebe Stanton Milner, where the hell did that come from?"

Phoebe smiled and tilted her head toward Neal.

Jeanne chuckled. "Sir, you're warping my sister's mind. Why am I not surprised?" She sighed. "I'll call the company who installed it."

Marcus sat on his couch, feet propped on the coffee table, watching the Giants football game. As he brought his bottle of beer to his lips his cell phone rang. He glanced at the phone lying next to him. *Guess you're back, Jeanne.* He put the bottle down and ignored the call. *Time to feed Balboa,* he sauntered to the snake tank. *I'll tell her I was working hard on my book and didn't want to break my concentration like I did last time.* He picked up a box resembling Chinese take-out.

"Hungry, buddy?" He peered into the tank, opening the box he had taken from the freezer an hour earlier, and dumping a dead, newly thawed, rat into the tank.

The snake slowly moved toward the rodent.

"Chow time."

Neal started a fire in the sitting room fireplace, stood back, and rubbed his hands together. *This should warm things up until the repair man gets here.*

The sisters joined him a few minutes later, wrapped in heavy sweaters.

Jeanne picked up the remote and turned the TV on, then sat beside Phoebe on the couch.

Hannah settled into one of the wing-back chairs.

Neil glanced from the remaining chairs to the couch, then gestured Jeanne aside and sat next to her, giving her one of his Magnum smiles.

Jeanne's cell phone vibrated. She picked it up from the coffee table and looked at the screen.

Neal leaned in to read it.

Blocked Caller.

"Put it on speaker," he said.

"It's probably Marcus. I left him a message earlier."

"Humor me. Put it on speaker."

Jeanne pressed the button. "Hello?"

"Cold?" The caller said. "Now you know what it feels like to be without heat, like many former FNB employees." *Click.*

For the last six and a half months, insomnia had become Marcus's constant companion. Falling asleep wasn't a problem, but after about an hour of peaceful sleep, he would waken and remain bug-eyed until dawn. His thoughts sprinted from one land mine to the next, often making him wonder how much longer he could hold things together. One thing he knew for sure. Jeanne would soon be a memory—a sweet one, but a memory, nonetheless. Of course, he would do his best to sway her thinking once she learned the truth, but he knew her well enough to know his chances of her forgiving him were, at best, slim. He lay on his side facing his bedroom window, watching night turn into day, his mind finally shutting down out of pure exhaustion and allowing sleep to take him as the sun climbed higher in the sky.

At nine-fifteen, Marcus's cell phone jolted him from much-needed slumber. He slapped his night table to find his phone, opened one eye, and hit the green button.

"What?"

"Things are heating up. We need to talk and fast."

CHAPTER
TWENTY-ONE

The next day Jeanne and Phoebe sat in the kitchen over cups of coffee.

"I'm glad we have heat again," Phoebe said to Jeanne shortly after the repair man left. "How on earth did the water get in the oil?"

She did not intend to tell her sister the technician found no evidence of a cracked pipe. And his best guess was someone had inserted a garden hose into the outside entry point. Jeanne shrugged. "An old house thing, I guess."

"Regardless of what caused it, I'm glad there will be heat for our incoming guests and us."

"Speaking of guests," Jeanne said. "Since our next group arrives Friday, we should get the Christmas decorations out and put them up before they arrive."

Phoebe grinned. "Already on it. Mom always hired someone to put the outside lights up. But since we can't afford it, I asked Neal if he would mind helping us."

Jeanne's jaw dropped open. "You didn't."

"Of course, I did. Why are you so surprised? It's no big deal." Phoebe smiled. "He said he would if I make him what he calls my famous blueberry pie. But I had to promise we'd check the lights first."

Jeanne shook her head and smiled. "You're too much, Pheeb. What about a tree? A real one or Mom's enormous artificial?"

"Mom liked real. She only employed the fake a couple of times. Like two years ago, when she visited her sister in Florida the day after Christmas and didn't want to worry about a real one drying out before she made it back. And last year, probably because she wasn't feeling well enough, although she never let on it could be the reason. I vote for real. The house should smell like Christmas." Phoebe shrugged. "After all, what stately Colonial inn doesn't have a real tree at Christmas?"

Neal carried the ladder to the front of the house and leaned it against the porch roof.

"These have been tested, right?" He put his arm through the loop of lights Jeanne held out and pulled them over his shoulder.

"Of course. You think I'd let you climb up there without knowing they'll work?"

Neal flashed a grin. "Thought I should ask. My ex didn't the last couple of times simply to tick me off."

"The last thing we want is our bodyguard to be upset with us." Jeanne pointed to the porch roof. "Hannah said the clips to attach to should still be there from last year."

Neal scanned the area. "I see them. I'll have this place glowing Christmas before you know it."

An hour and a half and five ladder moves later, Neal called down. "Okay, plug them in."

"Come down first. I'm not letting go of the ladder until you do."

Neal descended to the second rung and jumped off the rest of the way to the ground. "Worried I'd hurt myself?"

"We can't afford a lawsuit."

Neal put his hand to his heart. "Now *that* hurt. Here I thought you cared about me."

"I didn't mean..." Jeanne's face warmed. "Of course, I don't want you hurt. I mean... Oh, never mind. I'm plugging in. Watch this." She held up the remote she'd bought. "Is this a great invention or what? We won't have to come outside every night to light them."

Neal chuckled. "Why am I not surprised you thought of it?"

Jeanne plugged the cord into the remote and backed up, her eyes on the porch's roofline, her hand on the remote. "Ready to be impressed?" She looked over her shoulder at him.

He waggled his eyebrows. "I already am."

"Stop with the eyebrows!"

"Why, it's fun. And the view from back here is amazing."

Jeanne's face grew warmer.

"See? The eyebrow thing works. You're blushing."

"I am not. Are we going to do this?"

"We are."

Jeanne pushed the button, and all three hundred and fifty lights came to life. "Oh, Neal. Look at how pretty it is. Thank you."

"You're welcome, but you handed me the strings and manned the remote. I'd say it was a team effort." He offered up the smile she had secretly come to adore. "And I'd further say we make a good one."

A week later

Jeanne picked up the ringing phone at the registration desk. "It's a wonderful day at The Inn at Napatree."

"Jeanne?"

"Jo. How are you?" she asked, immediately recognizing the older woman's voice.

"Good. How was your Thanksgiving?"

"Very nice. Phoebe earned another gold star."

"I'm sorry I missed it. I'm sure everything was beyond wonderful."

"I hope you had a good day."

"Oh, yes. I cooked the main course, and my daughter brought the pies."

Considering all she'd heard about Jo's meatloaf, Jeanne wondered if the turkey had been edible. "Can we expect a visit soon?"

"I wanted to come this past weekend, but when I called Saturday morning, your answering service said you were closed. It worried me, so I thought I'd better check and ensure everything is all right."

"How sweet of you to worry. We're fine. We seized the opportunity to get away for a few days and went to Boston for Christmas shopping. As it turns out, it's good we had a lull in bookings because our furnace decided to take a break, too."

"Oh, that's a shame, but I'm relieved you girls are okay. I hope you enjoyed Boston. It's such a fun city."

"We did." Jeanne clicked on the reservation calendar. "When are you thinking of coming?"

"I know it's short notice, but I hope you can accommodate me this week. Thursday and Friday. Please tell me it isn't a problem. My daughter, son-in-law, and grandson got here Wednesday night, left Friday afternoon, and wore me out. The boy is quite a handful. As you once pointed out, it's time to refill my bottle."

Jeanne checked the online calendar to confirm what she thought was true and frowned. "Oh, Jo, I'm sorry, we're booked solid from Thursday through the weekend."

"Well, I'm disappointed. But it's my fault for calling so late. Maybe next—"

"Wait. We could put you in a room on the third floor with us. It's not as big as the one you've had, but it's nice."

Jo paused. "You girls have spoiled me with such a wonderful space, but my main reason for wanting to come is to relax and spend a few days with all of you before Christmas. Any room will do."

"Good. It's settled, then. You can have mine."

"Oh, I don't want to take your bed."

"No problem. I may go to New York to see Marcus anyway. If I don't, I'll bunk with Phoebe." She laughed. "It's not like we haven't done it before."

"Are you sure?"

"Absolutely."

⁓⊱⋆⊰⁓

Marcus ran his hands through his hair after dialing Jeanne's number. He hoped the excuse he had come up with for not calling her back sooner would work. *Here goes nothing.*

"Have fun in Boston?" he asked when she answered her phone.

"It was good to get away and do something different. Did you get my message? I called when we got home."

"I did. I'm sorry. I got caught up again in this book and lost track of time. I even forgot to take a break to eat dinner.

When my stomach started sending distress signals, I ran out to the neighborhood deli before they closed, and by the time I got back and finished eating, it was too late to call."

"I wondered if maybe something had changed. We hardly spoke last week, and then when you didn't return my—"

"Don't be silly. Nothing's changed. If I remember correctly, you're the one who gave me the brush off in favor of shopping. You're still coming at the end of this week, right?" His voice took on a sexy tone. "I bet I can outdo the fun you had in Boston."

<hr />

Neal drove the sisters to a Christmas tree farm in nearby Charlestown.

Jeanne sat up front when her two sisters claimed the backseat. "I'm so excited." They pulled into the farm's parking lot. "I haven't been here since the year before I left for college."

"Probably not much in the way of tree farms in Manhattan, huh?" Neal gave her a sideways glance.

"Hardly."

"Mom always wanted a Douglas fir." Hannah opened her door. "I think we should get one too. They smell the best."

They went straight to the Douglas section and deliberated over a dozen pre-cut candidates before Phoebe called from a few yards down the row.

"I found one!" She shook out the tree she'd pulled from the rest, her head almost buried in its branches.

"That's at least ten feet." Jeanne tipped her head back trying to see the top.

"So?" Phoebe shook needles from her hair. "It'll be fine. The ceiling in the sitting room is twelve."

Hannah smiled. "I like it."

"Me, too," Neal said.

Jeanne gave a small smile. "Since when do you get a say?"

"Since I fell in love with you." He waggled his eyebrows again.

"Stop. You're not in love with me. And you know it."

"Maybe not yet, but I'm working on it."

"What?" Jeanne asked Hannah, who'd been glancing from Neal to Jeanne since they returned home.

Hannah faced Neal. "Are you really falling in love with my sister?"

"Hannah!" Phoebe said. "He was joking."

Neal bounced his eyebrows again at Jeanne.

Her face reddened. She spun around and marched to the stairs. She stopped and glared over her shoulder. "Hannah, we need to talk. Now!"

Neal put his car keys in his pocket. "I need to go to my room and make a phone call." He strode toward the stairs while Jeanne stepped aside. "Go easy on your sister," he whispered in passing then bounded up the stairs.

"You're acting like you're sixteen," Jeanne told Hannah when she heard Neal's door close.

"You know you like him."

Jeanne grit her teeth. "For goodness' sake, I barely *know* him."

"Girls." Phoebe joined her sisters. "Let's get the table set. I have a turkey casserole in the oven."

Hannah grinned. "Sounds good. And during dinner, I can tease Jeanne some more."

⁓◦✕◦⁓

Twenty-five minutes later, Neal walked into the kitchen. "Smells wonderful, and by the looks of it, Jeanne's gotten past my earlier comment, so at least we have that going for us."

Jeanne put a hand on her hip and glared.

"Maybe I was wrong. Hannah, I think we might owe your sister an apology. Since I started it, I'll go first." He directed his attention to Jeanne. "I'm sorry."

Hannah hesitated.

"Hannah?" Neal said.

"Yeah, so am I," Hannah said begrudgingly.

Neal raised a finger and smirked. "But I don't take it back."

Jeanne's face turned as red as a Valentine's heart.

While they dug into their casserole, Phoebe did her best to center the conversation around tree decorating and Christmases past. While Neal contributed some of his own stories to help break the tension. Before long, everyone was laughing, even Jeanne.

"After we clean up, let's decorate the tree," Hannah suggested.

"Tell you what." Neal forked up the last of his blueberry pie. "I'll handle the cleanup as long as I can have another slice of this."

Phoebe grinned. "You've got yourself a deal."

Phoebe stood back from the tree. "Okay, that's the last of the fourteen strings of lights. Let's plug it in and see how it looks."

Hannah pushed the plug into the outlet, and a collage of red, blue, green, yellow, and white lights emerged. "Perfect." She stepped back to admire it. At one of two card tables stacked high with a mountain of unwrapped, decades-old ornaments, she held up a small box with three glass teddy bears. "Remember these?"

"Mom's baby bears." Jeanne's face softened. "I remember when she had them hand blown for each of us." Jeanne took the one wearing the gold hat from the box. It stood the tallest. "This one is yours, Phoebe." She handed it to her older sister.

Hannah held out the red-hatted bear. Beans, this one is yours, and this little guy," she put the last glass bear against her heart. "Mom gave him a purple hat because it's my favorite color."

"Doesn't seem so long-ago Dad sat in his chair and smoked his pipe while Mom and all of us decorated the tree."

Phoebe sighed. "Yeah, he called us his four little women."

Jeanne looked at the spot where her dad's chair still stood. "Remember how we would leave the angel at the top of the tree for him to put on?"

Hannah chuckled. "As I recall, mom wouldn't let him do much else because he had no sense of where things should go." Her eyes welled. "Gosh, how I miss them."

Phoebe squeezed Hannah's hand. "Thank goodness, we have hundreds of good memories. Not everyone is so lucky."

⁓⟶⟿⟵⁓

After the sisters finished decorating the tree, Phoebe continued to deck out the sitting room with Victoriangarbed carolers and a dozen pots of pink, red, and white poinsettias.

Jeanne covered the dining room table with a Christmas holiday-themed tablecloth and matching napkins, then removed the existing candles from their holders, and replaced them with red, cinnamon-scented ones.

Hannah strung light-embedded garland down the banister in the hallway and placed pots of Christmas holly against the wall at the bottom of the stairs and alongside the registration desk.

The house was ready for the holidays.

CHAPTER TWENTY-TWO

A riot of tangled emotions rummaged through Aaron's mind as he paced around the room, causing a triangle of hope, fear, and guilt to rise to the surface. He stopped and took a deep breath. "Okay, let's try this again. Hi Hannah, it's me, Aaron." He shook his head. "Too chipper. Jerks shouldn't sound chipper." He took another deep breath and shook his head. "Hannah, it's me." He used a more somber tone. "I deserve it if she's moved on."

He ran his hands down his face, pulled in a third deep breath as if diving into a pool's deep end, picked up the phone, and punched in her number before he lost his nerve.

She answered on the second ring. "Hello, Aaron."

He exhaled. All the words he carefully practiced erased the instant he heard her voice. "How are you?"

"Okay. And you?"

Aaron sat on the edge of his bed. "Better now. I worried you wouldn't answer, or worse, you'd hang up. Oh, Hannah, where do I start? I was a jerk. I'm sorry. I miss you. I think I'm falling in love with you. No, wait. I know I am."

Silence.

"Hannah?"

"Did you say you're in love with me?"

"Yes. I don't know why I haven't told you sooner."

"I didn't think I'd ever hear from you again," she whispered.

He raked his fingers through his hair. "I'm so sorry."

Silence.

"Hannah?"

"I'm here. I didn't expect…."

"You've met someone, haven't you?"

"Are you kidding me? I don't fall out of love this fast and move on."

Aaron smiled. "Good. You had me worried there for a second. I guess I needed a little time. I've been kicking myself for not making my thoughts clearer. Would it be okay if I came up for a few days? I need to see you. And apologize in person."

"Of course. As far as I'm concerned, the sooner, the better."

"I'd come this minute if I could, but I must arrange to cover the pharmacy. How does Saturday sound? It's only three days from now. I'll get the early ferry and stay until Monday morning, assuming you have room."

"We'll make room. A guest is staying in Jeanne's room for two nights, but she's checking out Saturday, so it'll be fine."

Marcus looked at his watch. *12:20*

Enough time to straighten up, shower, and get to the train station by one-thirty.

The phone rang. Marcus looked at the screen, rolled his eyes, and answered it.

"You have everything you need?" the caller asked.

"Almost."

"You're still going to Rhode Island, right?"

"No, Rhode Island's coming here."

"She doesn't have any idea about—"

"Of course not." He punched the end button.

<hr />

Jeanne stepped off the train.

Marcus was leaning against a column, arms crossed, wearing a wide grin. He walked toward her and held out his arms. "Gee, it's good to see you."

She hugged him. "You, too."

He kissed her and stepped back. "Hungry? We can stop and grab something to eat if you are."

Jeanne shook her head. "I'm good for now."

Marcus grabbed her hand. "Then let's get out of here."

<hr />

After making love with Marcus, Jeanne gazed at the ceiling. Why was Neal in every one of the images flying across her mind? She closed her eyes, hoping to get rid of the images, opened them, and turned to Marcus. "*Now* I'm hungry."

Marcus reached for her. "You'd put food before another round?" His eyes twinkled.

She pulled the sheet around her and slid her legs off the bed. "*My* next round is a sandwich."

He ran a hand down her back. "Are you sure?"

The touch of his hand on her bare skin sent shivers of desire down her spine, almost making her want to slip back beneath the sheets with him. But instead, she held firm. "Quite."

"Okay." He got out of bed and pulled on his trousers. "Let's go to the grill down the street. It's Thursday. Their special will be pastrami."

Jeanne laughed. "Phoebe would be *so* not happy if she knew you have the specials memorized. If I told her, she might start sending you homemade care packages."

Jeanne felt the effects of the two glasses of wine she'd had since arriving at the restaurant. Marcus had ordered a second round before she had finished the first one. Counting the glass at the apartment, this made for three in four hours, not something she was accustomed to. Her buzzed brain made it hard for her to concentrate and even more challenging to erase visions of Neal from her mind. She pushed her empty glass away. "Wow, I shouldn't have had the second one on an empty stomach. I'm feeling a little loopy."

"Just my luck. You're loopy, and we're in a public place." Marcus motioned for the waiter. "Let's order, so I can get you back to my apartment before it wears off."

A few minutes later, she eyed the two-inch thick, pastrami sandwich on dark-seeded rye the waiter put in front of her. "This looks delicious."

"It's their specialty. In my humble opinion, it's by far the best around."

Jeanne took a bite and closed her eyes as her tastebuds luxuriated in the savory flavor. After swallowing, she opened them. "You're right. This is beyond good."

"Remember where we used to go for lunch when we worked at FNB?"

"Don't tell me. Let me see if I can remember." She snapped her fingers. "Duck Soup, right?"

Marcus nodded. "Theirs was good, but this is so much better."

"Definitely." She took another bite.

"Speaking of FNB, if you don't mind, my book needs some questions answered." He put down his sandwich and removed a small recorder from his pocket.

Jeanne took another bite and motioned for him to go ahead while she chewed.

"First of all, when did you first become concerned about the future of the bank?"

Jeanne swallowed and took a sip of her water. "I'd say about three months before I left."

"What exactly snagged your attention?" He briefly shut off the recorder. "I can research a lot, but you're the only one I know who suspected the company was headed for trouble before it tanked. I won't mention your name, but an approximate timeline of when and what would help. I'm at somewhat of an impasse."

"Isn't the demise the crux of the book? If you're at an impasse." The wine pushed her to ask. "What have you been working on?"

"Office politics, the overall atmosphere at the bank."

Jeanne wrinkled her nose. "I hope you have more planned because as a reader, I find what you described slows the action."

Marcus looked away.

"I'm sorry." She reached for his hand. "You know more about writing a book than I do."

He returned his attention to her. "You're probably right. Which is exactly why I need your help."

Jeanne put down her sandwich. "Here's what I recall."

Marcus turned the recorder back on. "Shoot."

CHAPTER
TWENTY-THREE

Phoebe decided a dinner buffet would be a nice change from the traditional sit-down for their latest group of guests. Plates, soup bowls, silverware, and napkins headed the food parade. A soup tureen, featuring soft shades of blue embellished with vibrant green leaves and colorful butterflies, was filled to the brim with creamy lobster bisque. Perched on the top of the cover was a ceramic blue bird acting as a handle. Next in line were two large salad bowls of assorted greens, tomatoes, olives, diced beets, and cucumbers, followed by warming trays of Beef Braciole, Chicken Piccata, and Jumbo Stuffed Shrimp. And if this weren't enough to make everyone's taste buds water, a large wicker basket of freshly baked aromatic bread and rolls anchored the buffet's far end.

"This looks amazing," one of the women guests said after entering the dining room.

Phoebe smiled. "Thank you. Please help yourself and have a seat at the table. You'll find an assortment of beverages on the sideboard."

"I hope this is as good as it looks." Another woman carried her heaping plate to the table and stopped by Jo. "Do you mind if my husband and I sit beside you?"

"Please do. And I guarantee you'll love every morsel. If there is one thing I've learned while staying here, is you'll never leave the table hungry."

The man leaned around his wife. "You've been here before?"

"Oh, my yes. Several times. I fell in love with this place and these girls almost from the first moment we met."

"Well, I can see why," the diner next to Jo said. "The location is to die for, and the accommodations are nothing short of five-star."

Phoebe stood beside Jo and rested her hand on the older woman's shoulder. "Does anyone need anything?"

"What else could we possibly need?" Neal said from the end of the buffet line. "You could feed a small country with what you have here."

Phoebe smiled and clapped her hands. "Please, everyone be sure to leave room for dessert. Tonight, we're having mile-high lemon meringue pie."

Jo was on her way to her car when Aaron pulled into the driveway. She waited for him to park and get out. "Well, hello, Aaron." She extended her hand to him. "You probably don't remember me."

Although the quizzical look on his face betrayed his words, he said, "Of course I do." He squinted his eyes as if trying to put a face with a name. Then his face brightened. "Jo." He took her hand. "How are you?"

"Fine, thank you." She leaned in as if to impart a secret. "Rumor has it you will be staying in the room I vacated. I expect Phoebe is changing the linens as we speak. I *so* hate to leave." She looked at the house and sighed. "Such an inviting place to come to ease our weary minds and bones."

"It is."

"Too bad you weren't here yesterday. You missed out on a wonderful dinner last night."

"What did Phoebe serve this time?"

"She outdid herself. The buffet she prepared was of near epic proportions." She laughed and patted her midsection. "I'm still full." She lowered her voice. "I'm embarrassed to say I made quite a pig of myself."

"Not hard to do when it comes to Phoebe's cooking. I ate light before coming knowing what would be in store for me."

She giggled. "I didn't dare ask what's on the menu tonight. If I had, I'd probably forsake my budget and beg to stay another night."

"From what Hannah told me, the place is booked solid. I'm glad she was able to make room for me."

Jo touched his forearm and gave him a wink. "Oh, I'm sure she didn't have to think twice."

Hannah looked up from what she was doing at the registration desk. At the sight of Aaron walking through the front door, her face went hot. She rounded the desk and put her hands on his shoulder. "It's so good to see you. I can't believe you're here." When she hugged him, he relaxed into her.

He stepped back and gazed into her eyes. "I'm glad you're so forgiving. I guess it explains why I'm falling in love with you."

She swallowed hard, momentarily closed her eyes, and let the potency of his words sink in.

"I bumped into Jo outside. It sounds like this place is buzzing."

Hannah rolled her eyes. "No kidding. Phoebe's running around like sheep who spotted the clipping crew. I've offered to help her countless times, but she keeps saying she has everything under control." She leaned toward him and whispered. "I think I get in her way, but she's too nice to say it."

Aaron took his wallet out and handed Hannah his credit card.

Hannah pushed his hand away. "You're not paying."

He scoffed. "What? Don't be silly. Of course, I am."

"You're my guest and not even staying in a regular guest room." She held up a hand. "There's nothing to discuss. Just say thank you."

Aaron smiled. "Thank you. But I'll only accept your offer if you let me take you to dinner tonight. You choose the restaurant."

"I know just the place."

⎯⎯⎯⎯⎯⎯

Aaron drove across the Newport Bridge. "It's been a long time since I've been to Newport. My father was a sailing enthusiast, so we came here once to watch the *America's Cup* races. Young as I was, maybe nine or ten, I remember thinking how ritzy it all seemed. Then before we went home, my mother insisted we tour one of the mansions. I can't remember the name, but I do remember the bathrooms."

"Really?"

Aaron took a right at the end of the ramp. "I was fascinated to learn the tubs had hot and cold running *salt* water piped in from the ocean." He laughed. "Funny, isn't it, the things we remember?"

"No doubt the Newport mansions are gorgeous." Hannah sighed. "It blows my mind how anyone could've afforded one, let alone use them only as a summer retreat."

Aaron pulled up to a light and came to a stop. He glanced at Hannah. "Well, your house is nothing to sneeze at. Not to say it isn't now. But I bet it was quite the place in its day."

When the light changed, Aaron followed the signs toward Bowen's Wharf.

Hannah reached into her purse, took out a box of breath mints, popped one in her mouth, and offered the pack to Aaron. "Mint?"

"Thanks."

"I know what you mean, and you're right. It sure drew its share of attention back in the day." She tilted the box into Aaron's hand and returned it to her purse. "For one thing, the nine bathrooms all had working toilets. Which I'm sure was unheard of at the time except for the mega-rich like the Vanderbilts. After my mom passed, we reviewed some of her keepsakes and found a folder filled with newspaper articles handed down over the years."

"What did they cover?'

"The one I found particularly interesting was about the grand open house party in eighteen-ninety-six shortly after our ancestors moved in."

"Sounds interesting. I'd like to see them sometime."

Hannah pointed to a building. "There's the restaurant over there on the right."

Within minutes they were escorted to a table next to a window overlooking the harbor. "This place isn't full, but close." Aaron held out her chair. "I bet you can't walk in here and get a table like this during the summer."

Hannah shook her head. "No way. Even reservations are hard to come by. Although the warmer months are quite nice, I find the traffic and crowds overwhelming, which I think takes away some of the fun."

Aaron scanned the wine list and ordered a bottle.

A few minutes later, the waiter returned. He poured a small amount into Aaron's glass. "Will this do, sir?"

Aaron twirled the pale golden liquid in the glass, brought it to his nose, sniffed, and nodded. He sipped, seemingly letting the wine linger on his tongue before swallowing. "Very good. You may pour."

After the waiter walked away, Hannah leaned toward him and grinned. "I'm impressed. I didn't know you were a wine connoisseur."

"I'm not. I know just enough to make it seem like I am."

Hannah gave him a mischievous grin. "How did you come upon your knowledge? Are you a closet wine drinker?"

He chuckled. "Hardly." He glanced out over the bay. "Gillian taught me everything I know about wine. Her father owned a Long Island vineyard."

"She sounds like quite a woman." She reached across the table and cradled his cheek with her hand. "I can't imagine losing someone you love as much as you obviously did her."

Aaron nodded. "It has been more than hard. But deep down, I know Gillian wouldn't want me to be lonely. If she could whisper in my ear right now, she'd tell me to live life to the fullest."

Hannah took her hand back and smiled. "Sound advice. My mother always used to say we should live each day as if it were our last."

"Sometimes it's easier said than done. I think, in part, it's why I was shocked to hear you say you were in love with me. I'd been living in the past, and it caught me off guard, so I didn't know how to respond. Your words made me realize, though, that I had to decide whether I wanted, or was ready, to move on. The truth is, I wasn't sure. But life without Gillian hasn't been much of a life."

"I'm sorry. I didn't mean to push you."

He took her hand. "Please don't apologize. You only said what I should have said sooner. I knew I wanted there to be a you and me, an us, but it took me time to come to terms with it." He shook his head. "I'm sorry it took so long, and in the process, I hurt you."

"Some things take time," Hannah said softly.

A moment passed.

"This may sound crazy, but I believe in some small way Gillian helped."

Hannah raised an eyebrow.

"I've dreamt of her a lot since she died. But until recently, seeing her in my dreams only made me miss her more. This last time was different."

"How so?"

Aaron eased his hand from hers. "In the past, she would stand at the foot of our bed. I would try to reach out to her. To touch her. But I never could seem to move my arms. But then, before I left for the pharm con— the pharmaceutical conference in New York, something changed." Aaron gazed across the dining area.

Hannah rested her forearms on the table. "If you feel comfortable sharing it, I'd love to hear about it."

His face softened. "For the first time, she seemed at peace." He turned his attention to Hannah. "And before long, I felt a degree of comfort myself. It was such a vivid dream that as silly as it may sound, I expected her to be there when I woke up." His eyes glistened. "Regardless of how brief, her visit made me feel better. So much so the next morning, before I left for the city, I called Goodwill and asked them to send a truck to pick up the nursery furniture and baby clothes. Then I called a realtor."

Hannah's eyes went wide. "You're selling your house?"

"As much as I love the house it belongs to my life there with Gillian. If I truly want to start over, I think the best thing I can do is step away from the yesterdays. I've also decided to sell my business."

Hannah flopped back in her chair. "That's an awful lot of change. Are you sure you're ready?'

Their waiter came to the table. "May I take your order?"

"We need a few more minutes," Aaron said.

The waiter nodded. "Of course."

Aaron drew in a lungful of air and slowly blew it out. "I hope what I'm about to say won't make you think twice about getting involved with me."

"I always want you to be comfortable telling me what's on your mind."

"I want," he paused. "No that's not right, I *need* to make a fresh start, and I think Rhode Island might be the place."

Hannah shrieked and covered her mouth with her hand. "Sorry." She lowered her hand. "My emotions sometimes get the best of me. Where in Rhode Island?"

"Somewhere close to you. I could never afford Watch Hill, but maybe somewhere else in Westerly or something nearby like Kingstown."

"How exciting. Do you know what you will do once you get here? Maybe buy another drugstore?"

"I'm not sure. I have thoughts of returning to school. I think I'd like to study pharmaceutical compounding."

Hannah's face clouded. "I'm familiar with compounding. My mom tried a holistic alternative when conventional cancer meds stopped working."

"Although I've always believed holistic medicine has its place, like anything else, it isn't the answer to everything." He shook his head. "Anyway, it's something I'm thinking about. For all I know, I might easily end up at one of the big conglomerates."

"Do you plan to look for a house to buy, or will you rent for the time being?"

"Rent."

"As thrilled as I am with your decision, Aaron, I want to ensure you have thought this through. Selling your house and business and moving to another state is a lot. Long

Island is what you know. Rhode Island will be an adjustment. I don't want you to feel you have to walk away from all you know for me. I mean, I think you should. I mean…"

Aaron smiled. "Do you always blurt out what you think?"

Hannah ran her thumb up and down her wineglass' stem.

Aaron cupped her chin. "It's okay if you do. Better than always having to guess what's on your mind. It's one of the things I like about you." He lowered his hand, picked up his wine glass, and raised it. "What shall we toast to?"

"How about fresh starts?"

"Fresh starts." He grinned and tapped his glass against hers.

<hr />

"Did you and Aaron have fun last night?" Phoebe asked when Hannah came into the kitchen the following day.

"We had a great time."

Phoebe held up a hand. "No TMI, please. You're still my baby sister."

Hannah laughed. "No chance. I do have news, though." She took a mug from the cupboard and poured herself some coffee.

"Are you going to tell me? Or do I have to pry it out of you?"

"He's selling his house and business and moving to Rhode Island to be close to yours truly." She jabbed a finger into her chest.

Phoebe's eyes widened, and her mouth dropped open. "You're kidding."

Hannah beamed. "I still can't believe it. He said it's time to put his past behind him."

"Well, who knew? I never thought of him as the impulsive type. But from the sounds of it, he's as headstrong as you." Phoebe chuckled. "Maybe you two were separated at birth."

<hr />

"Has everyone checked out?" Neal asked Phoebe when he walked into the kitchen.

"Everyone except Aaron. He's not leaving until tomorrow."

Neal took an apple from the bowl on the kitchen table and polished it against his shirt. "When's Jeanne coming back?"

"Tomorrow afternoon. She called last night to find out when Aaron's leaving so she can have her room back. Why?"

"I hope Ray doesn't stop by. He'd have my head if he knew she's in Manhattan without me." He took a bite of the apple.

"Why? She's with Marcus."

"Exactly"

"Uh-huh. Couldn't be you miss her, now could it?"

He lowered his eyes. "Maybe."

"So, it's safe to assume your concern isn't just business."

"Well, not *strictly* business."

<hr>

"Are you sure you have to leave today?" Marcus nuzzled Jeanne's neck.

"I don't like being away from my sisters too long based on what's been happening. And besides, Aaron's leaving today, so my room is all mine again."

"I'll miss waking up next to you."

Jeanne ran a hand through Marcus's hair. "Christmas is only a few weeks away. Why not come to Rhode Island and spend it with us?"

"I'd love to, but I'm not sure my schedule will permit me such a luxury. I should finish this book so I can get back to looking for a job."

"You can work on it at my place. I helped you the other day, didn't I?"

He laughed. "Are we still talking about the book?"

She swatted his shoulder. "Stop it."

"Stop isn't what you said last night."

Jeanne's face reddened. "Can we please get back to Christmas?"

"But this is much more fun. You're right, though. You did help. Now the onus is on me to get it into something I can hand to a publisher. And time's running short."

"So, what if you miss your self-imposed deadline by a week? What's the big deal?"

"The big deal is I need to pay the rent. Unlike someone else I know. I wasn't bright enough to sell my stock before the bottom fell out."

Jeanne threw off the covers and swung her legs over the side of the bed. "I told you back then what I thought you should do. It's not my fault you didn't listen. You know what they say on Wall Street. Bulls and bears make money, but pigs get slaughtered."

Marcus pushed his nose up with his finger. "Oink. Oink."

CHAPTER
TWENTY-FOUR

"You just missed Aaron," Hannah told Jeanne after Neal brought her home from the train station.

Jeanne placed her rolling luggage in the hallway and sat on the third step. "Oh, too bad. I was hoping to say hi. I take it things went well this time."

"I think so, considering he's selling his house *and* pharmacy and moving too little ol' Rhody."

"You can't be serious. He's only known you for slightly more than two months."

"Love isn't a math quiz, Beans." Hannah sat beside her sister, wrapped her arms around her knees, and giggled. "Two and two don't always equal—"

Jeanne shook her head. "Heaven help us. And here I thought he was the level-headed one of the two of you."

"He is. He's not doing this *just* to be close to me." Hannah preened. "Although I'd like to think so. He may go back to school, and he's considering URI. I think it will prove to be a welcome change. While he lives in the town Gillian died in and slept in the bed, they, well, you know what I mean."

"But to sell a well-established business his father started decades ago and move from the town you've called home your whole life after only knowing someone for just two months." Jeanne shook her head again. "Sounds crazy if you ask me."

Hannah let out a breath. "For your information, I would've considered moving there if it wasn't for what's going on with you. But we all know I can't leave now even if I wanted to."

Phoebe joined them. "Hannah's right. We must stick together until we figure out who is behind this lunacy."

"Who knows, we may have to shut down for a while if we don't figure this out soon." Hannah shrugged. "I don't want to but . . ."

"We are *not* shutting down." Jeanne pounded her fist on her knees. "End of story."

Phoebe coughed out a laugh. "Not to make light of such a serious situation, but can you imagine if we had to tell Jo we were closing? Where would she run to after her grandson's next visit? As much as she loves him, she finds it hard to handle his visits. From what she said, it gets so loud even her cat runs and hides under the bed."

"I do recall her saying he's a handful." Jeanne chuckled. "I'm not sure I could handle the boy."

"When Rob was close in age to his, I would have sworn an alien had invaded my sweet boy's body. Thankfully, it didn't last too long. So, I completely understand what Jo means."

Hannah's face grew serious. "I think there is more to her coming here. Seems to me she's lonely since her husband died."

Phoebe looked at Hannah. "You're probably right. Mom said she didn't know what to do with herself after Dad died, even though by then you'd taken over the clinic and moved back in here."

"Do either of you know where her daughter lives?" Jeanne asked.

"No. Her daughter and family stayed at Jo's a few nights over Thanksgiving, so I suspect they're not on Staten Island. Or maybe they are and stayed to keep her company."

"Well, it's none of our business. I was just curious. Did she say if she'll be back before Christmas?"

Phoebe nodded. "Maybe for a day or so. But not much longer."

Jeanne yawned, grabbed the banister, and hoisted herself up." I'm exhausted. I think I'll take a nap."

Phoebe gave Jeanne a sly look and mused. "You might try telling Marcus to let you get some sleep next time."

<hr/>

"I thawed out the rest of the leftover turkey and made a big pot pie," Phoebe told Neal.

"How did you know it's one of my favorites?" He gave her a dimpled grin.

"It's Jeanne's too. Eating out as much as she did in New York, I thought I'd surprise her with a nice home-cooked meal."

Jeanne walked into the kitchen. "Surprise who?"

"You." Phoebe slapped a potholder against her palm. "I was telling Neal how much you love pot pies."

"Yours. Not the frozen so-called gourmet ones."

Phoebe's digital timer dinged, and she opened the oven door. "Where's Hannah? This is ready."

"I'll get her." Neal stood. "She's out back playing Frisbee with Fenway."

After he left, Phoebe whispered to Jeanne. "Tell me, did Neal give you the third degree about your trip?"

"No. Why should he?"

"All kidding aside, I think he likes you. Hannah and I sensed he didn't appreciate you being with Marcus."

"I'm sure he didn't. He thinks Marcus might be involved. If I were you, I wouldn't read too much into it."

"I don't know. I was right about Marcus, wasn't I?"

"If you're right and Neal *is* interested, he's out of luck."

"Beans, it never hurts to have a backup pitcher."

After dinner, the sisters and Neal went to the sitting room to watch the news. The nightly news anchor's eyes were somber. "Good evening. We are following breaking news. Let's go right to David Sadler for the details."

Pictures of Richard Alvarez, Ken Marshall, and Dan Bradbury flashed across the top of the television screen like a row of playing cards.

"Former executives of the now defunct First National Bank here in Manhattan are expected to be called to Washington to testify," the reporter said. "It's rumored the Justice Department may also be involved. Although not a high-ranking officer of the company, Dan Bradbury is a prime suspect in the securities investigation."

"Sounds like you had him pegged," Phoebe said.

Jeanne put up her hand. "Shush, I want to hear this."

"According to our sources, an unnamed informant will also testify. From what I've heard, the informant is a former employee who has cooperated with authorities and has provided reliable information regarding the bank's past business practices. Now back to the studio."

"At least our maniac is half-right." Jeanne changed the channel. "Looks like someone *did* report them. Hopefully, once they find out it wasn't me, things will return to normal."

Marcus checked the caller ID, muted the news story, and answered his cell on the second ring. "Hi, beautiful."

"Have you heard the latest about FNB?"

"And hello to you, too," Marcus said.

Before he had a chance to say anything else, Jeanne continued. "The top story was Alvarez and Marshall have been subpoenaed to appear before the Senate Judiciary Committee along with my little friend the slime bucket."

"Jeanne, slow down."

"With those big guns involved, they must have some solid reason or even evidence of wrongdoing. Maybe a disgruntled client—"

"A client?" Marcus scoffed. "Don't be ridiculous."

"It's not so far-fetched. Even though Dan and others thought their clients followed them with blind faith, it wouldn't be hard for one or more to put two and two together and come up with three when all the talk of the failure came to light, and people suddenly found their life savings vaporize."

Marcus paused. "Uh, sorry, Jeanne, I have to go. I've got another call coming in. It's Ken. I need to take it. I'll call you back."

Marcus hung up and pressed the talk button. "Hey, buddy. Just heard the news."

<hr />

Neal sat in one of the wing chairs in the room he called the parlor and picked up the evening newspaper.

"Where is everyone?" Jeanne came into the room.

Neal lowered the paper. "The last time I saw Phoebe, she was in the kitchen, and Hannah has left for the clinic."

Jeanne sat on the couch and laid her head against the back of it.

"Something wrong?"

"More like odd."

"Something I should know about?"

Jeanne lifted her head. "I called Marcus to see if he'd seen the news, and we weren't on the phone for more than a few minutes when he abruptly said he had to go."

Neal arched an eyebrow. "Why do you find it odd? Maybe he had something to do."

"His reason rubbed me the wrong way. A call from Ken Marshall was more important than speaking to me."

"Doesn't Marcus consider Ken a friend?"

"I never thought so. From what I recall he and Ken weren't more than coworkers."

"When Woody returned from Manhattan, he told Ray and me it seemed to him they were buddies." Neal didn't share Woody had also told them Marcus hadn't come to her defense once during the get-together.

"If they're so friendly, why hasn't Marcus set him straight about me?"

Finally! "You'll have to ask him. But don't forget you told me yourself Marcus met with him several times when Ken needed someone to talk to. Something not usually done unless the talker considers the listener a friend."

"Marcus is too nice to let Ken think otherwise. He probably just goes along with it."

Oh, brother.

CHAPTER
TWENTY-FIVE

The deafening sound of the fire alarm shattered Jeanne's fitful sleep. For a split second, she wondered if she were dreaming. But the sound of the shrieking alarm and the eerie jack-o'-lantern's glow filling the room confirmed she was awake. She rocketed out of bed, ran to the window, and gasped. The entire left side of Hannah's clinic was ablaze, and Neal was trying to quell the flames with a garden hose. She pulled on her robe and yanked open her door.

Hannah tore past her, terror etched across her face. "The clinic's on fire! There are two dogs in there!" She raced down the stairs.

When Jeanne reached the second floor, Phoebe was shepherding their guests from their rooms. The lights of the approaching fire engines splayed across the walls as she flew down the stairs behind Hannah. "Phoebe, can you get everyone outside?" she called on her way past her sister. "I'm going to help Hannah and Neal."

Phoebe gave Jeanne a shooing motion. "Go. The guests who boarded their pets are already outside. I'll evacuate everyone to be on the safe side."

"Neal, there are dogs inside," Hannah yelled when she got outside.

"Hold this, and keep it aimed at the back section." He handed over the hose to Hannah. "Do you have the keys?"

She tossed them to him. "Here."

Neal caught the keys, unlocked the door, and dashed inside. A few minutes later, he appeared carrying a silver-colored schnauzer and laid it on the ground. He handed her a stethoscope. "Here this was hanging on a hook near the cages. Give the hose to Jeanne." He ran back inside.

Jeanne grabbed the hose. "Hannah take care of the dog. I've got this."

The helpless owner ran to Hannah, clearly distraught. "Will he be okay?" she cried.

Hannah put her stethoscope against the dog's chest. "He'll be fine."

Moments later, his face dark with soot and his left sleeve and pant leg singed, Neal exited the clinic carrying a black lab and deposited him next to the schnauzer.

A fireman who had jumped off the truck, ran toward the clinic. "We'll take over now."

Before Jeanne could turn off the hose, Hannah shouted, "Jeanne, keep an eye on this one, while I check on the lab."

The lab's owner bent over her dog, who began to cough. Her eyes wide, the owner's face was pale with worry. "Breathe baby, breathe for me, please!" She glanced up at Hannah. "It's a good sign he's coughing, right?"

"Besides inhaling some smoke, he's frightened. But he'll be okay."

Half an hour later, Neal walked over to Jeanne after the firefighters had successfully extinguished the blaze.

The owner of the schnauzer kneeled on the ground next to her dog. "How can I begin to thank you? If it wasn't for you," The owner gazed at her dog. "I might have lost Hans."

Jeanne's knees cracked when she stood. "Yes, Neal, thank you." She looked at his singed sleeve and pant leg. "Are you okay?"

"Don't worry about me. I'll be fine."

"How did this happen?"

He leaned down and whispered so the owner couldn't hear. "I'd say the perp just added arson to the list."

⸎

The harsh smell of burnt wood permeated the air around the inn. After the fire department ensured the flames were out, had their questions answered, and announced the structure was safe to enter, they left. The sisters went into the scorched building to see what could be salvaged. Thanks to Neal, the fire did not have time to spread to the entire structure. The left side where supplies were primarily housed bore extensive damage, and was most likely where the fire had started. Except for smoke damage, the small medical area for the pets who were hospitalized or boarded was largely unscathed.

"I checked the dogs at midnight." Hannah turned from one of the crates. "Everything was okay then."

Phoebe lifted a red ceramic treat jar fashioned after a fire hydrant. "This looks like it can be saved."

Hannah pointed to a stack of other items near the door. "Put it over there."

"Thank goodness for Neal." Jeanne picked up a soot-covered leash. "Who knows what could have happened if he hadn't awakened, seen the fire, and sounded the alarm."

"Neal saved those dogs' lives." Hannah bit back a sob. "I hate to think what—"

Phoebe stepped around a murky puddle. "Not only did he save the dogs, but he's also responsible for keeping the flames under control until the fire department got here. If he hadn't thought to hose down the fire, it could have easily spread. As dry as it is, it could have been far worse. Not only did he save the clinic from being destroyed, but he also saved our home too."

"Thank goodness we decided to have the alarm monitored. It saved us precious time." Hannah's eyes glistened. "I feel bad for the owners and their dogs. I'm so thankful no one was hurt."

"Talk about poor timing." Phoebe shook her head. "The owners only arrived last night."

Jeanne held a blackened, green ball. "I'm glad Neal's burns aren't too bad. I made sure the EMTs checked him out before they left. They bandaged his arm and leg and instructed him on what to do until it heals."

Hannah continued to sift through the remains of the supply closet. "I'll have to find a temporary location until the damage can be repaired. Which will put a sizable crimp in my income." She looked at Jeanne. "As much as I hate to admit it, this wacko is winning the war."

CHAPTER
TWENTY-SIX

"Are you coming here for Christmas?" Jeanne tried to keep sarcasm from her voice when Marcus finally called the week before the holiday.

"If I do, I can't stay more than a day or two. I'm in the final stages of wrapping up my book."

"Are you sure it's the book you'd be rushing back to?"

"What do you mean?" His voice sounded suspicious.

"Maybe it has more to do with your best friend, Ken."

"Come on, Jeanne. He's hardly my best friend."

"Could've fooled me. If he's not, then what exactly is he? It's surprising because I never thought you two were close when I was at FNB."

"We weren't. It happened after you left."

"And it's continued?" *Why was she acting like this toward him? Were Neal's suspicions rubbing off on her?*

"Why wouldn't it?"

"Because we haven't excluded him as the perpetrator, that's why."

"You may consider him to be on the shortlist, but I don't. And second, I wouldn't have been able to set up the meeting for Ray if he didn't think of me as a friend."

Oooh. He was being irritating. "How can you be sure he doesn't have a hand in all this? Did you ask him?"

"I don't have to."

Jeanne entered the kitchen and caught Phoebe swiping at her cheek with the hem of her apron. She draped an arm around her sister's shoulders. "Hey, what's wrong?"

Phoebe shook her head and waved a hand as if shooing away a pesky fly. "Don't mind me. I'm having a pity party."

"This is so unlike you. Tell me what has you in the dumps?"

"Even though my ex was a jerk, this will be my first Christmas as a single woman. You and Hannah have someone. I don't."

"You won't be alone. What are Hannah and me? Chopped nuts?"

Phoebe gave her sister a wobbly smile. "Of course not. Thank goodness I have you both. But you're my *sisters*. It's not the same."

Jeanne suspected Phoebe's sadness had less to do with being without a man for the holidays and more to do with her son, Rob, choosing Christmas at a ski lodge with his girlfriend and her family instead of coming home to her.

"Rob's not even coming. He only met the girl over a month ago and wants to be with her instead of me." Phoebe's eyes welled. She pulled a tissue from her apron pocket, wiped them, and blew her nose. "Maybe his father was right when he said I was the problem in our marriage."

Jeanne turned her sister toward her. "Nonsense. The demise of your marriage had nothing to do with you. The truth is, you're better off without such a poor excuse for a human being, and you know it. And as for Rob, this is his first year away from home. He's testing his wings. I bet he'll call to say he's changed his mind before the week ends."

"Oh, I don't know." Phoebe tossed the tissue into the trash. "He's excited about meeting her parents. And you know how he loves to ski. I won't be surprised if he doesn't even call on Christmas."

Hannah stopped at the registration desk and looked over the papers Jeanne was studying. "What're you doing?"

"Seeing how far off budget we are," Jeanne said. "With the comps we've handed out and are about to, coupled with the food bill, it's tilting our finances into the red."

"Aaron's paying for his next visit which will help. And I suspect Marcus will too."

Jeanne looked at her sister. "I thought we were comping them."

Hannah shrugged. "Aaron wouldn't hear of it. He insisted on paying."

"Well, Marcus won't be a paying guest."

"Why not?"

"Hannah, unlike Aaron, who has a job. Marcus doesn't."

"Whose fault is that?"

"A publisher wants his manuscript as soon as possible before another author beats Marcus to the punch. So, he's under the gun to complete it."

"Why can't he write *and* look for a job at the same time?"

"Writing isn't easy. I think because he's never tackled something like this before. It's a full-time job."

"Since he told you a publisher has picked him up, I assume they gave him an advance."

Jeanne stared at her sister. *Interesting.* "He didn't say anything about getting any money."

"Then he probably didn't because I would think he would have mentioned it. What I want to know is, even though it sounds like his book will be published, what will it get him in terms of income? If he expects it to be a bestseller, he'd be better off writing a thriller than some dry old business book. Who cares about FNB?"

"Books written by insiders do very well. I guess time will tell."

⁓⟨≫◦≪⟩⁓

"Oh, Jo, you shouldn't have." Phoebe took the gift-wrapped box from Jo when she arrived a week before Christmas.

Jo placed her suitcase next to the registration desk. "It's nothing. Just a little something for dessert."

"Does it need to be refrigerated?"

"Not really, but I think it tastes better cold, so you might want to."

"You've piqued my curiosity. What is it?"

"Open it." The corners of Jo's mouth turned up.

Phoebe pulled off the paper and lifted the cover. "A fruitcake. How lovely. It looks delicious." If there was one thing none of the Stanton's had ever acquired a taste for, it would be a fruitcake. But since Phoebe knew Jo meant well, she gave her a wide smile. "Thank you."

"It's a family recipe handed down from my great-aunt. It's always been a favorite of ours. I hope you will all enjoy it."

"I'm sure we will," Phoebe lied. "We can sample it tonight after dinner."

Jeanne came down the stairs and opened her arms. "Jo, how nice to see you."

The women hugged.

"I'm sorry I missed you last time. We'll have to catch up while I'm here. I want to hear all about your trip to Manhattan."

"Look, Jeanne." Phoebe held out the box. "Jo brought us this delicious-looking fruitcake. It's a family recipe. I was saying we'll have some after dinner tonight."

Before Jeanne could respond, Jo linked her arm with Jeanne's. "Is it all right to leave my suitcase here for a while? I'd love to sit and chat with you girls. Please say you're not too busy to spend time with an old woman."

"You're hardly old, Jo." Phoebe laughed. "I bet you're not even sixty-five."

Jo's cheeks pinked. "Why thank you, dear. But I'm afraid sixty-five was seven long years ago."

Jo put her plate of fruitcake on the table beside her in the sitting room, picked up her coffee cup, and looked at Hannah. "I take it things between you and Aaron are going well."

"Better than well. It's more like fabulous."

"I'm glad you two maneuvered through your rocky patch." Jo leaned forward to pet Fenway, lying on the floor between them. "You're a good boy, aren't you?" Jo glanced at Hannah. "Thank goodness he wasn't near the fire Phoebe told me about. We have them for such a relatively short time as it is. When my cat Rocky goes, I'm sure I will be devastated." Jo petted Fenway again and leaned back in her chair. "Let's talk about something more pleasant before I dissolve into tears. Tell me about your Aaron. I want to know *everything* about where things stand with the two of you."

Hannah burst out laughing. "As if you don't already. Phoebe probably gave you every detail within five minutes of your arrival."

Jo gently blew into her cup to cool her tea, then gave Hannah a sly smile. "Well, not *every* detail. Did he say anything about how he felt when you told him you loved him?"

"It surprised him."

Jo nodded. "See, I told you, boy-girl, things haven't changed much since my day. So now what?"

Hannah grinned. "He's selling his house on Long Island and moving here."

"Really?"

"I'm over the moon."

"Well, I'm happy for both of you. Somehow, I knew it would all work out. And although it doesn't matter what I think, for the record, you make a very cute couple."

"Thank you. How are things with you, Jo? Will you be spending the holidays with your family?"

"Oh, yes. It will be a fun time. I always enjoy seeing my grandson. He's a good boy, a handful sometimes, but worth the effort."

CHAPTER
TWENTY-SEVEN

"It'll feel more like Christmas if we get the snow the weather geeks are predicting." Jeanne smiled at Marcus when he stepped off the train on Christmas morning. "Especially for the children."

Marcus pulled his coat collar up. "It's colder here than in the city."

"This is New England, remember?"

Inside the car, Marcus pulled Jeanne to him and kissed her. When their lips separated, he looked into her eyes. "I've missed you."

"What a nice Christmas present."

"Speaking of gifts, I didn't know what—"

"Don't worry."

"I'll feel like a jerk when everyone opens presents. I have nothing for you."

"Would you feel better if I give you yours when we're alone?"

Marcus slapped his forehead. "Now I feel horrible. Why did you get me something?"

She placed her left hand beside her seat and the door and crossed her fingers. "It's nothing much." *Only a cashmere sweater.*

⁓◦◦⁓

Aaron stood at the bottom of the stairs and gestured to Hannah to join him.

"What're you doing over here? Jeanne will be back with Marcus in a minute, and then it'll be time to open presents."

Aaron kissed her cheek. "I want to give you yours in private." He reached into his pocket and took out a small blue velvet box. "Sorry, I'm not good at wrapping."

Hannah's face reddened and her hands shook. She looked from the box to Aaron's face. "Aaron...."

"It's not a diamond, but I hope you like it."

Her eyes welled when she opened the box. "It's beautiful."

"Here, let me put it on you." He took the black and white pearl ring set in white gold with a small diamond separating the two from the box and slipped it on her ring finger. "Take this as a sign of how much you mean to me."

Hannah fingered the tears from her cheeks. "Oh, Aaron. I love it." She threw her arms around his neck and kissed him. "I'll never take it off."

⁓◦◦⁓

"Hurry up, you two," Jeanne yelled when Hannah and Aaron strolled into the sitting room arm-in-arm. "We're ready to open presents."

Hannah held up her right hand. "I already got mine. Isn't it beautiful?"

Jeanne took her younger sister's hand and held it to the light. "Look, Phoebe."

"Aaron, you did *good*." Phoebe grinned. "It's gorgeous."

"I'll go first." Hannah picked up a seven-inch-long rectangular box and handed it to Aaron. "Merry Christmas."

Aaron sat cross-legged on the floor next to Fenway, tore the paper off the box, opened it, and widened his eyes at the watch inside. "Wow, Hannah, this is a very expensive gift."

Marcus let out a long low whistle. "Very nice."

"This is a great gift, but I feel guilty accepting it. It's extravagant."

"No more extravagant than the ring you gave me. Please think of me every time you wear it. I even had it engraved. Read it."

Aaron slid the watch out of the box and turned it over. "Thank you."

"Read it out loud," Hannah said.

"Really?"

She nodded.

He looked around the room, a blush creeping into his cheeks. "You have my heart and love, Hannah."

"Aww." Phoebe's eyes sparkled.

"Who wants to go next?" Neal looked at Marcus as if allowing him to step forward. When he didn't, Neal volunteered. "I'll go."

The room quieted.

He moved his eyes from sister to sister. "Living here has allowed me to see how hard you all work at making the inn a success. I thought it would be nice if someone did something for each of you for once." Neal waggled his eyebrows. "A masseuse is waiting for each of you at the Seaside Manor."

Phoebe giggled. "Now *that* I can use. Maybe with a little luck, I'll get a young stud with magic fingers." She slapped her hand over her mouth, and her eyes went wide. "Did I say that out loud?"

Everyone laughed.

"Pheeb-Meister." Jeanne shook her head. "Sometimes you slay me." She looked at Neal. "I thought you quit wiggling your eyebrows."

"He only does it for you." Hannah gave him a playful look before hugging him. "Thank you."

Phoebe stood and hugged him, too. "Yes, thank you. You're a good friend."

When she stepped away, Neal smiled at Jeanne and held out his arms. She hesitated momentarily, trying to decide what to do so she wouldn't anger Marcus. Then tossed caution to the wind and walked into his arms. "Thank you." She started to pull away, but he held tight and rocked her from side to side before letting her go.

Marcus glowered. "A masseuse, huh? It would have been good if you had spoken to me first. I gave Jeanne a whole *day* at a *Fifth Avenue* spa, which she can use when she stays with me." He looked at Jeanne. "Sweetheart, you should have told me we would exchange our gifts in front of everyone. I thought we decided to do ours in private." Marcus moved over and put an arm around Jeanne's waist. "To be clear, my gift is in no way an indication she needs any help to look her best."

"We'd have to be blind to think otherwise." Neal didn't smile at Marcus.

Jeanne's cheeks warmed.

Marcus narrowed his eyes at Neal and pulled Jeanne closer. "Let's not forget the lady belongs to me, buddy."

Jeanne pulled away and fired him a look. Since when had he learned to lie so effortlessly? Hadn't he told her on their way to the house he hadn't gotten her anything? She did her best to hide her irritation, walked to the tree, and picked up a blue-ribboned box wrapped in silver foil paper. "I believe Santa left something under the tree for you, too. "Here." She handed it to Neal. "This is from the three of us."

Phoebe looked at Jeanne, her face a roadmap of confusion.

Jeanne turned her head so only Phoebe could see and touched her lips with her forefinger.

"The four of us," Hannah said, playing along. "Don't forget Fenway."

A moment later, Neal pulled a navy-blue, turtleneck sweater from a plastic bag. He looked at the label. "Cashmere. This is *very* nice. Thank you."

"Wow, what an awesome gift," Marcus said. "I guess they like you."

Hannah shot Marcus an icy look. "We do."

"We're glad you like it," Phoebe said. "We didn't know what to get you, and uh, we talked about it, and uh, well, we decided on the sweater."

Jeanne winked and gave her a small smile. "We weren't sure what size to get." She took the sweater from him. "Turn around." She held it up across his shoulders. "Oh, this is too small. You need at least the next size."

"I'm an extra-large."

"And this is a large. I'll exchange it. Jeanne picked up an envelope from under the tree and handed it to Marcus. "Since you already announced your gift to me, here's yours. Merry Christmas."

Marcus opened the envelope. He pulled out a one hundred-dollar gift card originally intended for Neal. "Thanks, Jeanne, you shouldn't have."

You took the words right out of my mouth.

They had been seated for Christmas dinner for about ten minutes when the doorbell rang.

Phoebe started to get up, but Neal stood and dropped his napkin onto his chair. "Stay where you are. I'll get it."

A minute later, he stood in the dining room's arched doorway, his size seeming to half-fill the tall space. "Phoebe, looks like you have company."

Phoebe stood, napkin in hand. "Company? Are you sure?"

Rob stepped out from behind Neal, his face covered in a grin. "Looks like you didn't hold dinner for me."

With open arms, Phoebe ran to him. "Oh, sweetheart. I thought you weren't coming. You said—"

"I wanted to surprise you, and Aunt Jeanne told me to use my girlfriend as the reason and embellish it with the ski lodge thing. She said you wouldn't let me off the hook for less."

Phoebe dropped her arms and swatted Jeanne's shoulder with her napkin. "So, you had something to do with this?"

"Guilty as charged."

Rob rubbed his stomach. "I hope I'm not too late. I'm starving."

Hannah laughed. "When has your mother not had enough to feed the French Foreign Legion?" She looked down the table at Jeanne and Marcus. "Scoot down a little, you two. We need to make room for Rob."

Phoebe set Rob's place and brought a chair from its temporary spot against the wall. "How did you get here?"

Rob sat. "I drove."

"You trusted your old VW bug to get here?" Jeanne took a roll from the breadbasket.

"It's not so bad."

Phoebe looked up from cutting her meat. "But what about your girlfriend?"

"I spent the last three days with her. We exchanged gifts last night. I said goodbye this morning and drove non-stop."

Phoebe raised an eyebrow. "This morning?"

"Chill out, Mom. We were at her parents' house." He smirked. "You didn't think I wouldn't be here on Christmas, did you?"

"She did." Jeanne grinned at Phoebe. "She's been in the dumps the last few days. I felt so bad not telling her, I almost caved."

"Well, I'm glad you didn't. The look on her face when she saw me standing there was worth the long drive."

"Rob," his mother said. "Let me introduce you to our guests. This is Aaron, Aunt Hannah's boyfriend, and Marcus, Aunt Jeanne's, and you met our newest friend, Neal Jansing."

Rob nodded while simultaneously piling three slices of ham on his plate. "Nice to meet all of you." Then he looked at his mother. "Would you please pass the potatoes?"

Phoebe gave her son a soft smile. *Merry Christmas, baby.*

CHAPTER
TWENTY-EIGHT

Phoebe got up from the couch on New Year's Eve, took her son's hand, and pulled him off his chair. "Come on, everyone, it's one minute to midnight. We've got pots to bang."

Rob winced. "Seriously?"

"Does the box of pots and pans by the front door your mother had me drag up from the cellar look like she's kidding?" Neal asked.

Phoebe clapped her hands. "Time to pick our instruments! Too bad Hannah and Aaron decided to go out. They're going to miss all the fun."

Jeanne nudged Rob toward the front door. "Come on. Indulge your mother. Who's going to see you?"

Neal picked up two saucepans, handed them to Jeanne, and waggled his eyebrows.

"Nothing I can say, huh?" Jeanne raised one of her own at him.

"Nope, they do it by themselves."

She laughed. "I bet."

Neal opened the door, and they went out to the porch.

The MC's voice at the New Year's Eve television show at Times Square filled the air through the open door. Three, two, one! Happy New Year!

After the countdown, they banged their pots.

With a twinkle in her eye, Jeanne pivoted toward Neal and hit the saucepan in her right hand against one of his.

He bent forward and kissed her cheek. "Happy New Year, Jeanne."

Phoebe stopped banging. "Ah, come on, Neal, you can do better."

"You're right." He pressed his lips to Jeanne's.

<hr>

Two days into the New Year, Phoebe and Jeanne were undressing the tree when the phone rang.

Jeanne put down the box she held in her hand. "Let's hope someone is calling to make a reservation."

"We can certainly use the money."

Jeanne picked up the phone at the front desk. "It's a great day at The Inn at Napatree."

"Fire, fire, pants on fire." The caller snickered. "You're lucky Hannah escaped harm. And your nephew made it back to school without a scratch. After all, his Volkswagen is practically vintage."

Click.

Neal was right. The fire was arson. She took a deep breath and let it out slowly. *Calm down. Rob's okay. I would know if he wasn't.* She rolled her shoulders, crossed her fingers behind her back, and returned to the sitting room.

"Who called? "Phoebe asked.

"Someone wanting our rates. I told them they could get the information online."

"I thought you said not to say that. It's too impersonal and would make people think it's the level of service they should expect."

"I didn't like his tone. We don't need any more problems." Jeanne took an ornament off the tree and put it in a box marked 1975 ornaments. "By the way, have you heard from Rob? I take it he made it back to school, okay? I worried about how his car would hold up."

"He called last night. He's fine. According to him, his car was fine, despite itself. I sometimes think kids with old cars have angels under their hoods. He said his only problem was a streaky windshield and having to watch for speed traps. Thank goodness it rained only briefly before he made it back."

<hr />

Neal came around from the back of the house midway through his third daytime surveillance and stopped. Jeanne was sitting on a bench near the bluff's edge, looking out toward the Atlantic. He pulled his coat collar up around his ears and walked toward her.

"What're you doing out here? It's freezing."

"Cabin fever." The wind blew off the water, and Jeanne hugged her midsection. "I thought a walk would help."

"You're not walking. You're sitting. And it's what? Twenty-two degrees?"

"Doesn't bother me much. I'm used to it."

"Yeah, right. Don't give me any bull about cabin fever. Tell me what's on your mind."

"What makes you think it's anything more than what I said?" Jeanne snapped.

"I can tell when someone's not telling the truth. I was a cop for twenty years, remember?"

She granted him a smile. "Sorry, I didn't mean to bite your head off. You're right. It's not cabin fever. I needed a place to think without anyone hovering."

"Not about Rob, I hope. I told you I called the campus police, explained why we were concerned, and asked them to monitor his dorm. They said they would. He'll be fine."

"I've decided to attend the hearings and plan to ask Marcus to accompany me."

Neal sat down next to her. "Now that's a surprise. I thought you finally saw through him at Christmas. You hired me to keep you safe. I can't do my job if you're floating around DC with him. It's bad enough I let you go to Manhattan."

"You didn't *let* me go anywhere. I keep trying to tell you you're too preoccupied with him. Which explains why this person is still on the loose."

"And *I* keep trying to tell you your lover-boy isn't all you think he's cracked up to be."

She stood and glared at him. "Marcus isn't the problem, damn it!"

Neal stood and gently touched her arm. "I'm not the enemy, Jeanne. Shouting at me is not going to change things."

Jeanne blew out a lungful of air. Her shoulders sagged. "I didn't mean to yell."

"You've been under a lot of stress. This guy has done his homework which makes for a challenging case. I'm not used to dealing with a virtually invisible perp, so my stress level is amped up too."

Jeanne nodded, and after looking at the ground momentarily, she raised her head. "I do not plan to change my mind about DC or going with Marcus."

"Why is this trip so important?"

"I want them to see me and know how foolish they were not to listen to what I had to say."

He put his hands on her shoulders. "I get it, but you could be putting yourself in danger. This is a great example of why being right is not always worth the battle."

"Marcus will be there. I'll be safe."

He let his hands drop. "Jeanne, whether you like it or not, Marcus is our number one suspect. I can't let you go with him."

"You can't stop me."

"Oh, I beg to differ, Miss Stanton. I most certainly can. And will. After the crap he pulled at Christmas, I thought you wouldn't want to be anywhere near him. I hoped you finally came to your senses."

"His behavior at Christmas has nothing to do with this. Not being able to afford a gift doesn't make him a suspect."

Neal looked at her for a moment before speaking. "He's a con man and a good one. He's taking advantage of you."

Jeanne looked away.

"The sweater you gave me was intended for him, wasn't it?"

"How did you know?"

"You're not hard to read. And I could tell Phoebe was as surprised as I was."

"You only thought so because the size was wrong."

"Oh, please give me a little more credit. When was the last time you ever saw me in cashmere?" He held up his hand. "Before you say anything, the answer is never. But the same doesn't hold true for pretty boy, does it?"

CHAPTER
TWENTY-NINE

Jeanne put on her blue, snowflake, flannel pajamas, got into bed, and pushed the power button on the TV remote.

"Our network will cover the First National Bank hearings live starting Tuesday, January twentieth," the local news anchor said.

She hit the off button on the remote, tore out of bed, and ran down the stairs without bothering to pull on a robe.

As she reached the bottom step, Neal walked in the front door after his final surveillance round for the day. "Don't you look cute," he said, removing his coat.

"The hearings start next Tuesday."

He hung his coat on the coat tree. "When did you hear that?"

"A few minutes ago, on television."

Phoebe walked in, stifling a yawn. "What are you doing here in your pajamas?"

"The hearings start next Tuesday," Jeanne said.

"What does that have to do with you standing here wearing your pajamas?"

Jeanne ignored her sister's comment while her heart pounded in her ears. "I've decided I'm going to attend."

Phoebe shook her head. "You can't."

"I can. And I will. Someone has threatened to destroy everything important to me and been bold enough to follow through on his threats. I suspect that someone will be in DC. When it's clear I'm not the informant, I want him to regret the damage he has caused and be there to hold him accountable for his actions."

Phoebe frowned. "Have you considered this maniac could attack you?"

Jeanne held up her hand. "He doesn't want to hurt me directly. If he did, he already would have."

"If you go. I go," Neal said. "End of discussion."

"I told you I'm going with Marcus. He knows all the players and is familiar with my situation. Besides, if you go, when he sees you, it'll blow your cover."

"I don't care about my cover, and have you considered Ray will most likely drop the case if he finds out."

"He'll only find out if you tell him." She turned on her heels, climbed the first four steps, stopped, and looked at Neal and her sister over her shoulder. "Do what you have to do. Tell him. I don't care. Not you or anyone else will dictate where I go and who I go with."

"I take it you saw the news and know the hearings start on Tuesday," Marcus said when Jeanne called.

"Yes. I thought I would catch the train Sunday, spend the night at your place, and we can leave for DC Monday afternoon. Sound good?"

"Sorry. I'm already in DC."

"Why didn't you tell me you were going? You knew I would want to go."

"Not a good idea, Jeanne."

"You sound like… Ray Grossi." She cringed after almost saying Neal.

"Maybe you should try listening. After all, you are paying him to keep you safe."

"Forget it." Jeanne huffed. "If you don't want to go with me, I'll go alone."

"Do what you want. I don't have time for this."

Jeanne was stunned. "You don't care if I go alone?"

"Of course, I do, but I already told you my thoughts."

"Why are you in DC already?"

"Come on, Jeanne I told you I don't have time for this."

"Why?" she pressed. *What was wrong with him?*

"Why does it matter?" His words were clipped as if he were on the verge of shouting.

"Because it does."

"Give me a break."

"Give *you* a break? My life has become a *Dateline* special, and you expect *me* to give *you* a break?"

⌒≫◦≪⌒

Neal looked over the rim of his tumbler as Jeanne walked into the sitting room, this time wearing a white and navy-striped robe over her pajamas.

"Is that alcohol?"

"Bourbon. I bought a bottle and put it in the butler's pantry the other day. Want one?"

"I prefer wine."

Neal put his glass down on the side table. "I'll get it." When he returned, he handed her a glass of chardonnay. "Are you still thinking about DC?"

"You'll be happy to know Marcus won't be going with me."

"I'm glad you came to your senses."

She took a sip of wine and swallowed. "It has nothing to do with my senses. Marcus is already there."

Neal sat and picked up his drink. "You didn't tell him you plan to go, did you?"

"What do you think?"

"Damn it, Jeanne." Neal slammed his glass on the table. "Why do such a thing?"

"The last time I checked, I've been over twenty-one for thirteen years. Therefore, I am quite capable of making my own decisions. Good decisions, I might add. Thank you very much."

"If going to DC is one of them, you could've fooled me."

The next day

Neal knocked on Jeanne's bedroom door. "Phoebe said to tell you dinner will be on the table in fifteen minutes."

"I'll be right down," Jeanne called out.

"Can I come in?"

Jeanne opened the door. "I'm packing. I'll be down in a second."

Neal eyed the open suitcase on her bed. "Since you still plan on going, I'll start packing, too."

"You don't have to make the trek to DC to watch over me. I'm a big girl. Besides, I can't afford to pay for your trip, and I don't want to leave my sisters alone in case something else happens while I'm gone."

"Don't worry about footing the bill. And as far as your sisters are concerned, I'll speak to Ray about covering for me."

Jeanne sighed. "Really you don't—"

"I need to do my job if I want Ray to keep me on the payroll. Which, in case you've forgotten, means keeping you safe."

CHAPTER
THIRTY

After dinner, Phoebe climbed the stairs to Jeanne's room. "Beans, can I come in?"

"Sure, it's open."

Phoebe pointed at the box of quart-size baggies. "I was wondering where the box went."

"Airport security rules. You can't take liquids or gels in carry-on luggage in containers larger than three ounces. They must be in a see-through quart bag. One more reason not to want to fly."

"Why not check your luggage? Then you don't have to worry about it."

"The airline charges for checked baggage, and it's only for a couple of days, my suitcase should easily fit in the overhead compartment."

Phoebe sat on the corner of Jeanne's bed. "Neal said he's going with you. Where are you two staying?"

Jeanne told her.

"What about Marcus?"

"Who cares?"

Phoebe arched a brow.

"I'm still upset he decided to go to DC without me."

Phoebe frowned. "Why would he do that?"

"Good question."

"Does he know Neal is going with you?"

"No."

Phoebe narrowed her eyes. "Are you and Marcus—"

"I don't know how I feel lately. Or what I think about us."

"Have you told him?"

Jeanne closed her suitcase. "I think he suspects it."

Phoebe chuckled. "I'd buy tickets to see his reaction when Neal walks in with you."

Jeanne shrugged. "Not my problem."

"You know, Beans, regardless of what you think of him, he might have done you a favor by going alone. I get why you want to go, but it could be dangerous."

"For goodness' sake, the hearings will be held at the Rayburn Building. How much safer can it get? Besides, Neal will be with me."

Phoebe sighed. "I'm thankful, but still."

"I'll be fine. Who knows, the television in the hotel lounge might be as close as we get. I'm sure the hearing room will be quite crowded."

"You're having breakfast before you go tomorrow, right?"

"Yes, but no need to set your alarm clock. We won't be leaving until nine-thirty. And Ray will arrive about nine and stay until we return."

Jeanne parked her suitcase at the foot of the steps. She went to the registration desk to check the inn's schedule for the next several days, followed her nose to the kitchen, and found Phoebe scrambling eggs mixed with turkey sausage crumbles.

"Good morning. Breakfast will be ready in a minute." Phoebe gestured to the oven. "Do me a favor, will you, and take the pancakes I'm keeping warm out and put the glass dish on the table."

"Sure." Jeanne did so, then poured herself some coffee. "I see Jo's coming back. When did she call?"

Phoebe emptied the pan of sausage-filled scrambled eggs onto a platter. "Last night."

"I didn't hear the phone."

"She called after you said you were going to shower. Between you and me, I hesitated about telling her we had an opening."

"Why?"

"I plan to watch the hearing and didn't want to be rude. You know how she loves to talk."

"She'll be good company for you." Jeanne arched an eyebrow. "Unless you're looking for a little private time with Ray."

"For heaven's sake. He's not at all my type."

"I think he's sweet in a gruff sort of way. For all you know, he might sweep you off your feet if he ever gets the chance and figures out how to string more than three words together at a time."

Neal guided Jeanne through the terminal at Reagan National Airport with his hand on the small of her back. "Nervous?"

"I didn't think I would be, but yes, as much as I hate to admit it, I'm glad you're here."

"Good."

"I know you're still unhappy about me coming, but it means a lot. I want to be there when they grill Rick Alvarez and Ken Marshall, not to mention Ken's nephew Dan. It'll take every ounce of control not to scream out I told you so."

"Probably not a good idea if you want to be allowed to stay in the hearing room. Outbursts are not tolerated."

She sighed. "I suppose it will have to be enough that once the truth comes out, it will finally put this nightmare to bed, and none of us will have to worry anymore."

"Assuming the people testifying are the ones lobbing the threats."

Neal was waiting in the hotel lobby when Jeanne stepped off the elevator with her coat slung over her arm and wearing the same gray wool pants and mint green sweater she'd worn on the plane.

"I asked the concierge what he suggested for a first night in DC. He recommended a limousine service which gives private nighttime tours of the city. I thought it might take the edge off things, so I made reservations. It's been years since I've been here, and since this is your first, I wanted you to see our capital in style. The hearing doesn't start until nine-thirty tomorrow morning, so the night is ours."

"How thoughtful," Jeanne said. "I'm not dressed for dinner, though."

"You're fine. From what they told me, it's nothing fancy. By the way, have you heard from Marcus?"

"No."

⁓✎✎⁓

Two days later

"Crappy weather, huh?" Hannah said to Phoebe when she walked into the kitchen. "Looks like yesterday's rain turned to sleet. "Glad I only have to walk out the back door to go to work. And even that could be treacherous."

The phone rang.

"Maybe it's Jeanne," Hannah said.

"I doubt it. She called last night. I'll get it, though, just in case." Phoebe returned to the kitchen a few minutes later. "Someone wanting to sell something."

"Did Jeanne mention the hearing delay Ray told us about?"

Phoebe nodded. "Uh-huh. Typical Washington. I wish those Congress people would get their act together. Thank goodness she's not alone, especially since she will be there longer."

"Neal will keep her safe."

"I'm sure. She told me they intend to play tourist during the downtime."

"Good, she deserves a break. Maybe it won't be too much longer before we don't have to worry about every phone call or what will happen next."

Phoebe grinned. "Something tells me she won't be anxious for Neal to leave."

"You know something?" Hannah asked.

"Not really, but she said Neal arranged a limousine tour of the city last night, and later they had dinner at a lovely bistro. Jeanne doesn't gush, and from the sounds of it, she was gushing."

"I bet it feels good knowing all this should be behind you soon," Neal said to Jeanne during breakfast on the first day of the hearings.

Jeanne raised a forkful of Brioche French Toast to her mouth. "My biggest regret is I didn't do more to try and save FNB when I had the chance. If I had, maybe none of this would have happened."

"You did all you could. You went to the top with your concerns. What more could you have done?"

"I should have followed through with my threat to go to the authorities." Jeanne swallowed, obviously savoring the bite. "Maybe if I had, they would have stepped in and saved the company from ruin. And we wouldn't be living in fear."

Neal used the side of his fork to cut into his omelet. "No sense second guessing. Look how long it took them to investigate Bernie Madoff, who perpetrated the biggest Wall Street fraud in US history. In my opinion, their practices should come under scrutiny if companies can commit fraudulent activities without being caught."

"It's no excuse, but the number of qualified people they lost over the last few years hasn't helped. The financial landscape has done a one-eighty recently, and no one, including the FNB auditors, raised a hand to what they had to suspect was going on. There's a lot of blame to go around." Jeanne sighed. "Unfortunately, what happened at the bank can happen again. And it probably will."

Neal drank some coffee and put his cup down. "Dirty hands sometimes develop a conscience and become an informant."

"I can't imagine the informant is anyone from FNB. All the people I spoke to thought I was a nut case." Jeanne wiped her mouth with her napkin. "If it *is* someone from the bank, I'd put my money on it being someone from the accounting department."

"That would take a lot of nerve." Neal shook his head. "Talk about putting your job on the line."

CHAPTER
THIRTY-ONE

After passing through the security checkpoint, Jeanne and Neal headed down the hall to the hearing room at the Rayburn Building.

Neal gently poked her in the rib with his elbow. "There's your friend."

She nodded and walked toward Marcus.

Neal followed.

"Jeanne, what are you doing here? I told you to stay home."

Neal chuckled. "And you seriously thought she'd listen?"

Marcus glared at him.

Jeanne turned to Neal. "Will you excuse us, please?"

He pointed toward the hearing room door. "I'll be right over there if you need me."

"What's *he* doing here?" Marcus said through clenched teeth when Neal walked away.

Jeanne poked a finger at his chest. "What I expected *you* to do. Support me. What the hell's going on?"

"Nothing."

"Since when are you Ken Marshall's nanny?"

Marcus blew out a bunch of air. "Jeanne, this isn't the place—"

"It's as good as any. Unless you've forgotten." She poked him again. "My sisters and I have had our world knocked off its axis." She dropped her hand. "Your friend Ken, on the other hand, is only getting what he deserves." She exhaled and shook her head. "What a fool I've been. All this time, I thought you cared about me."

"You're no fool. You know I care. I always have."

"Last call," a portly guard announced from the entrance to the hearing room.

"Jeanne, I have to go. The door's about to close."

Jeanne waved her hand in the air. "Go. Before you do, though, there's one more thing."

Marcus's shoulders slumped. "What?"

"We're finished."

***

Neal watched Marcus narrow his eyes at him as he brushed by.

"He's not a happy camper," he pointed out when Jeanne approached. "What the hell did you say to him?"

"I told him what we had is over. Finished. Come on, let's go inside to get a seat." She stomped toward the hearing room.

As Neal followed her, he couldn't contain the grin exploding across his face. "Sure thing, boss."

Phoebe looked up when Jo walked into the sitting room.

"What are you watching, dear?"

"A Washington hearing." Phoebe patted the couch cushion next to her. "The company Jeanne worked for is under investigation. Want to join me?"

Jo's mouth dropped open. "What on earth for?"

"It collapsed, and a few executives are going to testify."

Jo made her way to the couch. "Was it a shady place?"

Phoebe shook her head. "Not at all. It had an impeccable reputation. In large part, it's why Jeanne accepted their offer when she graduated from Harvard."

"Harvard? I had no idea."

"She's not one to brag. She graduated in the top one percent of her class."

"Such an accomplishment."

"Yes, Bean's flair for numbers is amazing."

Jo raised an eyebrow. "Beans?"

Phoebe put a hand to her mouth. "Oh, please don't let on I let it slip. She'll kill me if she finds out. It's a sister thing."

"Bean's is such an odd nickname. I'm curious about its origin." Jo lowered her voice. "Does she have a gastric problem?"

Phoebe laughed. "No. Which is exactly why she doesn't want anyone to know about it. It came to be because she's a whiz with numbers. Beans as in bean counter. I hope you will keep my slip a secret?"

Jo made a zipper motion across her mouth. "My lips are sealed."

"Is there anything I can get you before this starts? I plan to watch a good deal of it, which I'm afraid means I won't be much of a hostess."

"I don't expect you to wait on me. Please think of me as family. If it's okay, I'll make us tea and bring it in. Then we'll watch it together, at least until my soaps start. I try not to miss an episode of my favorite one. I've followed it for years. I used to watch a number of the sagas, but—there I go rambling. I better go make the tea before I talk your ear off."

Phoebe smiled. "Tea will be lovely. The tea bags are in a canister on the counter."

"By the way, where *is* Jeanne? In Manhattan with Marcus?"

Phoebe hesitated. "Uh, no, she's attending the hearing."

Jo frowned. "Please tell me she isn't under investigation."

"Heavens no. She worked at FNB for ten years. She saw the direction it was headed and tried to warn several people. Including some of the top brass. But no one would listen to her."

Twelve, high-backed, leather chairs stood side-by-side behind the imposing, raised, paneled dais. A cascade of red velvet drapes provided the backdrop. At floor level stood a six-foot-long mahogany table home to two microphones and dual trays of bottled water.

Television camera operators readied their equipment on the floor between the dais and the table.

Jeanne eyed the sweating water bottles. *I hope the FNB executive's brows will soon look the same.*

A side door opened, and a line of Congressmen and women filed in and took their appointed seats.

Jeanne took a deep breath and let it out slowly.

Neal put his hand on hers.

She closed her eyes for a moment, exhaled, then swallowed around the lump in her throat. Her stomach flipped like she'd been on a fast carnival ride.

The committee chairman seated in the center of the raised dais pounded a gavel on a small block of wood. "Order, please. We're about to begin." The gavel sounded again. "Order."

The room quieted.

"I have a few housekeeping items for the gallery. First, talking will not be tolerated. You will be escorted from the room if you cannot control yourself. Second, it's nine-thirty. We'll break for lunch at eleven-fifteen. Until then, I request you remain in your seats. If nature calls, you may leave, but you will not be allowed to return until we reconvene. If you can't abide by these rules, please feel free to leave now." The chairman briefly scanned the room.

No one moved.

Jeanne leaned back in her seat.

Neal gently squeezed her hand.

The room buzzed with excitement.

The gavel sounded.

"Order, please," the chairman said.

The gallery hushed.

"Okay," the chairman said to the guard at the side door. "Please ask our first witness to come in."

Ray came downstairs to find Phoebe and Jo watching television.

"Hi, ladies, what's so interesting?" Ray looked at Phoebe, trying to silently remind her with his eyes of his guest status.

"Executives from a New York bank are about to testify in Washington, DC." Jo's eyes sparkled. "It's all so exciting."

"My sister worked there," Phoebe said, playing along with Ray. "The bank went under last summer."

"Unfortunately, not at all uncommon these days." Ray shook his head.

"It's about to start," Phoebe said.

Ray took a seat next to her. "Mind if I join you?"

CHAPTER
THIRTY-TWO

Jeanne's heart raced when the side door of the hearing room opened. The doorway remained empty for what seemed a lifetime. Jeanne craned her neck to get a better look. Two men slowly entered the room. Jeanne let out an audible gasp.

Neal turned to look at her.

Several people stirred and murmured.

The chairman banged his gavel. "Order."

Jeanne clamped a hand over her mouth.

The room quieted.

The chairman directed his attention to the men. "Is this your counsel?" he asked the witness.

"Yes."

Please state your name for the record," the chairman said to the lawyer.

The man did so.

The Chairman then directed his attention to the witness. "Please state your name for the record."

A muted response.

"Please press the button on your microphone, sir, so we can hear you," the chairman said, "Now, please restate your name."

This time the man's voice filled the air."Marcus Reynolds."

"Proceed with the oath," the chairman ordered.

Jeanne's eyes welled. *What are you doing here?*

Marcus stood and took the oath, then sat and briefly glanced at the man seated to his right, who was clad in a thousand-dollar-looking blue, pin-striped suit.

"Mr. Reynolds, I understand you have a prepared statement you would like to read before we begin our questioning," the chairman said.

"I do."

"Please proceed."

Marcus opened a binder on the table before him and flipped to the first page. For the next twenty minutes, he spoke of meeting with federal authorities to further their case against FNB. He confirmed high-ranking officials had bolstered their borrowing ability by inflating asset values to advance their borrowing position when investments they held lost significant weight.

Without naming her, he told of a former colleague who had attempted to warn management before the financial institutions' demise and ended with an in-depth timeline of events, in his opinion, had ultimately led to the failure of the bank.

Is this why you grilled me about my suspicions? There really wasn't a book, was there?

"Thank you, Mr. Reynolds. Is there anything else you'd like to add before we proceed?" the chairman asked.

"No, sir."

"All right, I'll start the questioning. Mr. Reynolds, when did you first learn what you have outlined for the committee?"

Marcus leaned toward the man seated next to him and whispered something.

"Mr. Reynolds?"

Marcus directed his attention to the chairman." May I have a moment to confer with my attorney?"

"Yes."

Why do you need an attorney? What have you done?

After briefly speaking with his lawyer, Marcus addressed the chairman. "April two thousand and twenty-two."

"And when did you first speak with the authorities?"

"Early summer of twenty-two.

"Did you approach them?"

Marcus fiddled with the papers in his binder. "No."

"Why did they contact you?"

"May I have a minute?"

"Yes."

Marcus spoke to his attorney in a hushed tone, then responded. "They questioned me about a stock sale."

"A personal stock sale?"

"Yes."

"When did this transaction take place?"

Marcus looked at his attorney, returned his attention to the dais, and took the Fifth.

The chairman frowned. "Let me ask you this. Were you friendly with any of the corporate executives during your employment?"

"Not initially."

"When did your relationship change?"

"In May of two thousand twenty-two."

"Who exactly did you count as a friend at the bank?"

Marcus hesitated. "Ken Marshall."

"What was his position there?"

"Chief financial officer."

"Were you considered an insider?"

"No."

"Mr. Marshall's position made him one, didn't it?"

"Yes."

The chairman flipped through several pages of text and returned his attention to Marcus. "How did you learn about what you outlined in your opening remarks?"

"From Mr. Marshall."

"When was that?"

"Shortly after we became friends. I think somewhere in the June time frame."

"Before or after you sold your stock?"

Marcus took the Fifth.

"Did Mr. Marshall know you owned stock in the company?"

"Yes."

"Did he advise you because of the information he disclosed, you would be considered an insider?"

Marcus conferred with his attorney and again took the Fifth.

Frustrated with Marcus's lack of cooperation, the chairman glanced at the other panelists. "I'll reserve the balance of my time. The Chair recognizes the gentlewoman from New Jersey."

"Thank you, Mr. Chairman. Mr. Reynolds, I'd like to return to the former employee who attempted to warn management. Did your colleague share their concerns with you?"

"Yes."

"Did your colleague go to the authorities?"

"No."

"Do you know why?"

"My colleague left the company shortly after expressing concerns to the CEO."

"I take it those concerns were ignored?"

"Yes."

The congresswoman jotted a note. "Were they valid?"

"In hindsight, yes."

"When did your colleague leave the bank?"

"Several months before the collapse."

Jeanne clenched her hands into fists. *Was her name going to come up?*

Neal took one of her hands in his. "It's going to be all right," he whispered.

"Did you report the concerns when you met with the authorities?"

Marcus nodded. "In part, yes."

"Were you able to verify the information before you reported them?"

"Yes."

"How?"

"During conversations with Ken Marshall."

"So, your colleague shared concerns with you, and you were able to verify them, yet you didn't report them to the authorities until after they approached you, correct?"

"Yes."

"Why?"

"I believed Mr. Marshall when he told me the bank practices weren't out of the ordinary."

You believed him but not me? Jeanne's eyes stung from hurt and anger.

The congresswoman narrowed her eyes. "To what did you attribute your colleague's comments?"

"I thought she was upset when no one acted on her concerns."

Jeanne had to restrain herself from jumping out of her chair.

"This former colleague is a woman?"

"Yes."

The congresswoman bit her bottom lip before going on. "Did you only think of her as upset because of her gender?"

"Not exactly."

"Well, what *exactly* did you attribute it to, Mr. Reynolds?"

Jeanne's stomach clenched as Marcus turned on the charm. The same charm she'd fallen victim to.

"Wordsmithing is not my forte. I may be many things, but a chauvinist is not one of them. When she warned the corporate executives, and they dismissed her concerns, I took her comments as a result of a blow to her pride. *Anyone* in the same situation would be emotional. My former colleague is one of the brightest people on the planet, but I didn't think she was right. I considered her approach as others did, old school."

The woman shook her head. "If we had more so-called old-school approaches, maybe we wouldn't find ourselves here today."

Marcus nodded and reached for his water bottle.

The congresswoman flipped through several pages of documentation. Then held up an index finger and looked at the chairman. "May I have a moment, please?"

"The gentlewoman from New Jersey is allowed one minute."

She scanned through the papers. "Here it is. I want to revisit the timing of your conversations with the authorities. If I remember correctly, you testified the SEC contacted you in early summer. Correct?"

"Yes."

"Tell me this, Mr. Reynolds. How many FNB stock shares did you own then?"

Marcus looked at his attorney and took the Fifth.

"Was your relationship with Mr. Marshall prompted because of valuable stock you owned at the time?"

Marcus turned to his attorney. They spoke in whispers.

"Mr. Reynolds, please answer the question," the chairman said.

Marcus returned his attention to the dais and took the Fifth.

The congresswoman tapped a pen on her notes. "Have you been offered immunity from prosecution related to insider trading? Did you make a deal to avoid prosecution in return for information regarding the business practices at FNB?"

Marcus turned back to his attorney.

His lawyer stood. "May I address the panel?"

"You may," the chairman said.

"Thank you. In an effort not to waste the committee's valuable time, I should tell you I have advised my client not to answer any questions regarding stock transactions or immunity." The attorney sat.

The congresswoman huffed. "I'll reserve the remainder of my time, Mr. Chairman."

"Thank you. The chair recognizes the gentleman from New York."

"Thank you, Mr. Chairman. Mr. Reynolds, is it fair to say the authorities enlisted your help to build their case?"

"Yes."

"And you were a willing participant?"

"Yes."

"Were you able to supply them with the requested information?"

"Yes."

"From first-hand knowledge?"

"No, from conversations with my former colleagues."

"The colleague who left the company and Mr. Marshall?"

"Yes."

"Were *they* willing participants?"

"Yes and no."

The congressman looked over his reading glasses at Marcus. "Which is it, Mr. Reynolds? Yes, or no?"

"They participated in conversations with me but didn't know my reasons for asking."

"Why did the colleague who left the company think you were asking?"

"I told her I was writing a book about the company's demise and needed help to fill in the blanks."

Jeanne gasped loud enough for the chairman to hear her.

He shot her a look and banged his gavel.

Jeanne mouthed, *sorry*.

"So, the press had it wrong when they reported a whistleblower. You didn't go to the authorities, they came to you, and you ultimately became an informant to save your skin. Because in return for your information, I suspect you have been granted immunity from prosecution for selling your shares. Shares you sold and profited from based on the information you received from Mr. Marshall and the colleague who left the company. Correct?" The congressman held up a hand. "Don't bother to take the Fifth. The answer to my question is clear." He leaned his forearms on the dais and locked his gaze on Marcus. "Can I assume these two people considered you a friend?"

"Yes."

The congressman shook his head. "Let me conclude, Mr. Chairman, by simply saying this." He took off his reading glasses and glared at Marcus. "Mr. Reynolds, I don't know how you sleep at night, knowing you have benefited from a disastrous situation which has financially crippled thousands of innocent people and contributed to an economic, financial mess." He leaned back in his chair, shook his head again, and sighed into the microphone, the sound echoing in the room. "Your actions, sir, are not only criminal. They are nothing less than disgraceful. Thank you, Mr. Chairman. However, I request Mr. Reynolds be subject to recall."

Marcus turned for a moment and looked at Jeanne, his face devoid of all emotion.

"Thank you, Mr. Reynolds," the chairman said. "You are free to go at this time but are subject to recall following the testimony of the former FNB executives."

"Ladies and Gentlemen, this committee will meet in closed session this afternoon to review Mr. Reynolds's testimony. We will reconvene tomorrow at nine-thirty to hear the testimonies of the former executive staff." He rapped the gavel on the wooden block.

Jeanne leaned toward Neal. "I'll see you at the hotel. I want to be alone." Before Neal could stop her, she stood and left the room without another word.

Jeanne broke into a run down the marble-floored hallway, oblivious to the staring eyes surrounding her. She felt like she was going to be sick. How could she have so badly misread Marcus? Outside, she pulled in as much air as her lungs could hold, put her hand on one of the building's imposing stone pillars to steady herself, and fought to keep the nausea in her stomach from erupting.

CHAPTER
THIRTY-THREE

Hannah joined Ray, Phoebe, and Jo, who were huddled in front of the television while they watched the committee meeting room empty. "My last patient took longer than expected," she rolled her eyes. "Mrs. Manning wanted to tell me every detail about her trip to the Galapagos Islands. What'd I miss?"

Phoebe pointed at the television. "Look who's leaving the room."

"What the hell?"

"Can you believe it?" Phoebe looked at her sister. "Marcus used Jeanne and Ken Marshall to save his skin."

Hannah sat down hard on the couch between her sister and Jo. "I knew something about him didn't seem right."

"My heart goes out to Jeanne," Jo said. "Phoebe tells me she had no idea what Marcus was up to. If he were here right now, with the things he's said, you girls would have to hold me back."

Hannah frowned. "What's he been saying?"

"Jeanne was too emotional to be believable when it came to her concerns about where the bank was headed." Phoebe clicked off the TV. "He made it sound like it's why no one listened to her. And they also considered her concerns old school. And get this. You were right about the book he said he was writing. There was no book." She shook her head. "He used it as an excuse to pump her for information so he could feed it to the authorities. He used Ken Marshall, too."

Hannah bit her bottom lip. "But what did he have to gain?"

"It sounds like he dumped his stock once Marshall confirmed what Marcus had heard from Jeanne," Phoebe said. "The problem is the information he got from Marshall made Marcus an insider. He didn't volunteer to speak to the SEC out of any sense of duty. He did it to avoid wearing a striped jumpsuit."

"Poor Jeanne. That man!" Hannah wiped her damp eyes. "She must feel like such a fool."

Jo jumped in. "If you ask me, she should dump him like a red-hot coal. But first, I think he deserves a good swift kick."

"And to think he cried poorhouse every time he stayed here." Hannah slapped a fist into her palm. "And used it as a lame excuse not to get Jeanne a Christmas present, while all the time he must have a small fortune stashed offshore somewhere."

"And when I think of the times we let him stay here for free," Phoebe clenched her teeth. "It makes my blood boil. I have a good mind to send him a bill."

Aaron sat on his couch, unable to move for a full five minutes after watching the FNB congressional hearings. He picked up a file folder filled with news articles he had been collecting about the bank's collapse from the coffee table. He thumbed through them and tossed the folder back down. "It's not fair," he said aloud. "My life has been destroyed not once but twice. Not only did I lose Gillian, but I also lost her entire inheritance all because of greed. Marcus shimmied into friendships to break the law and make a fortune. And what happens to him? Nothing. Ken Marshall will probably get more of the same tomorrow. The only people paying the price for their actions are me and thousands of others like me." He swept his forearm across the coffee table, sending the folder across the room, its contents floating in the air. "*Arrgh!*" he roared.

Two hours after leaving the Rayburn Building, Jeanne sat on a bench across from the White House in front of the bronze statue of Andrew Jackson in Lafayette Park. She shivered and looked at her watch. One thirty.

Her phone rang, startling her. She pulled it from her purse and looked at the screen filled with missed notifications. "Yes."

"Where the heck are you?" Neal's voice rose to near yelling.

"In Lafayette Park, commiserating with Andrew Jackson."

"I'm on my way."

Neal jogged toward Jeanne, who was seated on a park bench. Her shoulders hunched, head bowed, clutching her purse in her lap. "You're shivering."

Her breath curled in the air like a puff of smoke.

"Come on. Let's get you back to the hotel. Have you eaten?"

"No."

"There's a hotel across the street. They must have a restaurant."

"I don't feel like eating."

"All right. We'll catch a cab and head back to our hotel. Maybe by then, you will."

"It's only a few blocks. We can walk."

"Are you nuts? If you were any colder—"

Jeanne gave him a shaky smile. "I know. I'd be a day-old corpse."

Seated at a corner table in the hotel café, Neal gently squeezed Jeanne's hand after they ordered coffee and cups of minestrone. "I'm concerned about you. You look like someone whose dog died."

"It's been a rough day."

"I know. Maybe you should take comfort knowing at least Marcus brought your concerns to the authorities."

"He didn't *bring* anything. He only volunteered information to save his skin." She fingered the napkin holding the silverware. "He did nothing to make Ken realize I was not responsible. He could have set him straight, and none of what my sisters and I have been through would have occurred. He's a coward. And a greedy one, too."

The waitress brought their soup.

"I'm not sure I'll be able to keep this down. My stomach is doing jumping jacks, and I've got a splitting headache."

"Probably from not eating. Try a little. It'll warm you and hopefully calm your head and stomach."

Jeanne raised her spoon to her lips. "He certainly turned on the charm with the congresswoman, didn't he? But unlike me, she saw right through him."

"We often turn a blind eye to friends and family. Has he called?"

"I don't know. Every time the phone rang, it was you, or I thought it was. I ignored all the calls. How many times did you call?"

"Five."

"Seemed like there were more." She opened her purse and pulled out her phone. *Nine missed calls.* "Yours aren't the only messages.

"The others are probably from him."

"I have no intention of speaking to him. For all I know, he's the one who's behind the—"

"I don't think so. His working with the authorities explains a lot."

"Like what?"

"I knew he was hiding something, which is why I kept him on my radar. He always said he'd stay if you wanted him to but was quick to leave when given the opportunity." Neal reached across the table again and put his hand on hers. "Think about it, what man in his right mind would be so anxious to leave a woman like you?"

Jeanne sat on the edge of the bed in her hotel room and listened to the slew of messages Marcus had left.

"Jeanne, I can explain—"

Delete.

"Give me a chance to ex—"

Delete.

"You can't walk away without—"

Delete.

She clicked off the phone and tossed it on the bed. Tears spilled down her cheeks. "All this time, I thought you cared about me. How could I have been so blind?" She curled into a fetal ball and sobbed into her pillow.

Neal took Jeanne's arm when she stepped off the elevator into the hotel lobby. Her eyelids were swollen, and her face blotchy. "You've been crying."

"I thought I'd covered it with makeup."

"Not much you can hide from an ex-cop. I spoke to Ray. He said everything is okay at home, so that can't be it. Marcus didn't come by, did he? I told you to call if—"

"I haven't seen him, but I listened to parts of his messages. Why'd you ask me to come down? Have you heard something?"

"No. I thought you could use a drink. Maybe a glass of wine will help soothe you."

They went to the lounge and sat in round-backed upholstered brown chairs, a small square table separating them.

"What would you like?" Neal asked.

"A glass of red."

Neal got their drinks and returned to his seat.

"Do you want to tell me what Marcus said?"

Jeanne rested her head against her fist. "It's what he didn't say. He wants to explain. What's to explain? How can he justify setting the fire or cutting Phoebe's brake line?"

"I don't think he's guilty of those things. More than likely, he wants to try and win you back."

"Why does him being the informant, change your mind about his involvement?"

"Because his actions make more sense now."

Jeanne dabbed at her eyes. "I feel like such a fool."

"You're no fool. Now tell me what he said."

"I only listened to the first few and deleted what I heard." She reached into her purse, pulled out her cell, clicked on her voice mail, and handed the phone to Neal. "I didn't delete all the messages. I'm not interested in anything else he has to say. If you want to listen, be my guest."

Neal put the phone on speaker. The first two were from Neal. The last from Marcus. "Jeanne, please pick up. I can explain if only you'll give me—"

Jeanne took the phone from Neal's hand. She hit the delete button. "See what I mean? Nothing of substance. He's only thinking of himself. He thinks he can talk himself out of this."

"I can't blame the guy for trying."

"I already told him I never wanted to see him again, and that was *before* I knew what he'd done."

"I gather you have no intention of talking to him."

"And say what? Hi, Marcus. I know you didn't mean to endanger our lives to save your ass and, in the process, add another notch to your bedpost." Jeanne brought a bar napkin to her eyes. "What is there to say?"

Neal paused. "I changed our return trip. We're on the nine-fifteen back to Providence in the morning."

"You changed our flight without asking me?" She tossed her balled-up napkin on the table. "Well, change it back.

I'm not ready to leave. I want to hear what those idiots have to say tomorrow and be there to watch them squirm."

"You can do the same at home. I agree with Ray's assessment that it's best to leave DC and get away from Marcus and the others as soon as possible. We don't know his state of mind right now. It's not a chance worth taking."

"I thought you said you don't consider him a suspect."

"I don't. Doesn't mean I trust him. It wouldn't be out of the realm of possibility for him to take his frustrations out on you. He's probably so low right now he could crawl under a pregnant ant."

"More cop-speak?"

"Not really."

"How will I face my sisters?"

"There's nothing to face. You've done nothing wrong. They love you."

"I should have listened to Hannah. She doubted him almost from the start. I bet she can't wait to throw her I told you so's at me. And I deserve it."

"She's not likely to do that."

Jeanne gave a half-hearted laugh. "You don't know Hannah." She looked at the ceiling for a moment and sighed. "I guess you're right about leaving. Why should I give these jerks one more minute of my time?"

"That a girl."

CHAPTER
THIRTY-FOUR

Jeanne settled into her seat across the aisle from Neal on the Providence-bound jet, put her head back, and closed her eyes. The events of the last two and a half days swirled through her head like a nor'easter. She opened her eyes, looked at Neal reading the newspaper, and smiled. *Thanks for being there when I needed you.*

After a relatively short flight, the plane bumped hard and rolled along the tarmac when it landed at the TF Green airport.

Neal stood when the plane came to a stop at the gate. He reached overhead for Jeanne's luggage, then retrieved his own. "I called Phoebe before we left and told her you'll need space for a few days."

"You think of everything, don't you?"

Neal smiled. "She told me Jo Reasoner left early to give you your privacy."

"That was very thoughtful. I'll have to thank her next time I see her. At least there will be one less person I have to dodge. On the other hand, I might drive myself nuts." She gave Neal a sad smile. "And I'm afraid it would be a rather short trip in my current frame of mind."

Phoebe opened the front door and threw out her arms.

Jeanne went into them and let her sister hold her. After a moment, Jeanne stepped back. "Thanks, Pheeb."

Phoebe glanced at the grandfather clock in the hallway. "It's five to twelve. Why not settle yourselves, and I'll have something to eat waiting when you're ready."

After taking her bag to her room, Jeanne found Phoebe in the kitchen, taking a cast iron pan sizzling with chicken quesadillas from the oven.

"Phoebe don't fuss. I don't have much of an appetite."

"Not eating isn't going to change things. Besides, these are leftovers." Her face was etched with concern. "So, how are you?"

"I need some time."

"It's a good thing Marcus isn't here because I'd be tempted to give him a piece of my mind."

"Trust me. He's not worth the effort."

Jeanne reclined on the chaise lounge in her room and was reminded of how she had taken Marcus into her confidence and allowed him into her bed. Tears clouded her vision. She wiped at the tears and glanced out the window. "I sure hope Neal is right. If you are behind the threats, I'm not sure how I will handle that," she whispered to the empty room. She shook her head. "Sad to think all I ever was to you was a get-out-of-jail-free card and a handy piece of a—"

Jeanne's cell rang. She got up, yanked it from her purse, and looked at the screen.

Blocked.

"You don't give up, do you?" The ringtone persisted. She pushed the talk button. "Stop calling me!"

Marcus let out a breath. "Thank God you finally answered. We need to talk."

"About what?"

"I want you to know how important you are to me. I want to explain. I miss you. Let me make things right between us."

"You want to make things right? Are you crazy? This isn't some mea culpa you can gloss over. There is only one thing I want to hear from you."

"Ask me anything."

"For once, I want the truth. Do you have anything to do with the incidents here?"

"No."

"Are you sure?"

"Of course. I'm telling you the truth."

"Do you even know what the truth is?"

"I said I'm not involved. If it's any consolation, Ken and Dan cornered me after they got the stuffing kicked out of them at the hearing and let me have it. I accused them of threatening you. I could tell by the expression on their faces they weren't involved either. It's someone else. I've been trying to figure out who, and I have a couple of ideas. Let me come up there, and we'll talk. I'll explain why I had to do what I did, and we'll work through you and me. Give me a chance. Please."

"You don't get it, do you? I told you we were through in DC, which was before I knew what you did."

"It's Neal. Isn't it? He's been filling your head with crap about me, hasn't he?"

"Don't go looking for someone to blame. Neal has nothing to do with this. I suggest you look in the mirror if you're looking for who's at fault."

"I see now. You slept with him in DC, didn't you?"

"How dare you?" She tried to control her voice so her sisters wouldn't hear her yelling.

"You've been attracted to him long before this week. If I remember correctly, you gave him one heck of an expensive sweater for Christmas."

"The sweater was meant for *you*." She took a deep breath to steady herself so she wouldn't cry. "Don't call me again. There's nothing more to say."

Click.

Jeanne threw the phone onto her bed, went to the bathroom, and turned on the shower. She undressed. The devastating images in the hearing room flashed before her, joining forces with Marcus's gut-punching betrayal. She stepped into the shower, and let her emotions go.

CHAPTER THIRTY-FIVE

"I have a contract on my house, and the two brothers interested in the store came back today to review my financials again," Aaron said when Hannah answered the phone. "My agent thinks they'll probably make an offer."

"Things are moving right along, aren't they?"

"Yeah, and the house buyers want a quick closing. If the brothers decide they want the pharmacy, my agent said they will want to move fast, too. They already have a loan approved."

"Are you still okay with this? As I've said before, these are two big changes."

"I'm looking forward to it."

"What's next?"

"I have to find a place to live and start packing. Will you have room at the inn next weekend?"

"The last time I checked, we only had one room reserved."

"Good. I will check online for rentals as soon as I hang up. Keep your ear to the ground, too. Something close to the inn would be nice. Preferably a small house."

"I'll ask my clients. Many of them have lived here forever and know everybody and everything."

⚜

Two suitcases lay atop Aaron's bed. The one not closed awaited one more thing. He sat on the bed, stripped to its mattress cover, reached over to his nightstand, and picked up a silver-framed photograph of him and Gillian on their wedding day.

He had put it in a dresser drawer each time Hannah came and put it back in its rightful spot when she left. He slid the back off the frame and took out the black and white sonogram. *How often I have thought about you and grieved your loss these past two years. I wish I had gotten to know you. I bet you would have been one terrific kid.*

Aaron tucked the sonogram behind the wedding picture and turned the picture over. He ran a finger over Gillian's face. "Honey, the movers will be here any minute now. I think you'd like the couple who bought the house. They've only been married a year and a few months, and she's pregnant. They are having a girl. They seem excited about our house." He sighed and put the photograph face up in his suitcase. "No matter what the future holds, I will always love you, sweetheart." Aaron closed the lid.

⚜

Alone with her thoughts, Jeanne stood at the edge of the bluff behind her house, listening to the waves hurl themselves against the shore as Hannah approached with Fenway. "Is Aaron excited about his new place?" Jeanne asked, exiting the thoughts which continued to haunt her.

"Yes. And it sounds like the owners of the beach house I told him about are excited too. I guess they usually rent to a gaggle of college kids, which makes for a lot to repair when the semester ends. I'm sure they are relieved their newly renovated house will be well cared for this time. He called this morning and asked me to drive to Misquamicut and do a fast walk-through with him. I couldn't make it because minutes before I was ready to close for the day, Mrs. Otero rushed her cat in to see me for what turned out to be an infected paw." Hannah checked her watch. "He's picking me up in about a half hour. I can't wait to see it."

"Well, you sure can't beat the location."

Hannah grinned. "Best of all, he'll be less than five miles away!" She dropped Fenway's leash, threw her arms around Jeanne, and hugged her. "If you hadn't come up with the idea of turning Mom's house into a B and B, I never would have met him."

─────◦◦◦◦◦◦─────

The bungalow on Montauk Avenue wore a fresh coat of blue paint. Four blocks from the ocean, the salty air permeated the area. With two bedrooms, a single bath, a galley kitchen, and an open living-dining room, it was all Aaron needed. The furnishings would be sparse since he'd only taken his sofa, bedroom set, and kitchen table, the rest being sold to a neighbor's soon-to-be-married daughter.

"Home sweet cottage." Aaron slipped the key into the lock.

Hannah looked around the neighborhood before entering. "This was an excellent find."

"Yes. Thanks to your cat client." Aaron pushed open the front door and stepped inside. "The street's named Montauk, like the town in Long Island. I guess what they say is true. A part of our past always travels with us."

Hannah followed him inside. "Oh, this is cute. Cold though." She pointed to the stone slab between the living and dining area. "When is the woodstove the owners bought being delivered?"

"Tomorrow."

Aaron took Hannah's hand. "Let me give you a tour."

The walls were painted a pale green, and each room was accented with white chair rails. The white kitchen cabinets matched the color of the appliances. Although Hannah preferred stainless steel, white was less expensive and fit well with a rental.

"You'll feel like you are always on vacation in this little bungalow."

"I like it. I know it's small, but it's all I need."

"I agree."

"Hey, I saw an old-fashioned soda shop in the middle of town," Aaron said, after they completed the tour. "What do you say we grab a sundae or something?"

Hannah rubbed her arms. "I prefer hot chocolate."

"Sounds good. I need to use the bathroom before we go. I'll be right back."

Aaron closed the bathroom door. A recent edition of the New York Times, along with a folder lay on top of the sink. The newspaper headline reading, *First National Bank Executives Testify Before Congress*. Thank goodness Hannah hadn't seen this during the tour. He picked it all up and slipped everything under a stack of towels in the vanity below the sink. The last thing he wanted was for Hannah to question why he had it.

⸻⟡⸻

A month later

After sliding into a red leather booth at Chop Sticks in East Greenwich, Jeanne and Neal ordered moo goo gai pan, spring rolls, and Chinese tea.

Jeanne spooned duck sauce onto her plate. "You said Chinese food is one of your favorites. What are some of your others?"

"Well, I like to read."

"What genre do you like most?"

"Anything about the Roman era, Russia, the Orient, or this country's political beginnings. I even enjoy the smell of an old book. I've been collecting dusty classics since college. What about you?"

Jeanne took a spring roll from the basket. "I'm not a big reader, but I do enjoy plays."

"Another thing we have in common. I am a season ticket holder at Trinity."

"I love that theater." She cut into the crispy spring roll. "Tell me, what do you think you'll do now since the Stanton case has been put to bed?"

"Ray isn't happy with your decision. He wanted to ID the perp so you could prosecute. He thinks you are pulling the trigger too soon."

"It's been quiet for over a month. Whoever the culprit is, they now know I had nothing to do with the collapse of FNB. The Fire Marshall is investigating the fire, and the insurance company is working on the car incident, so it's not like no one is investigating. And since you're still at the house until you find someplace else to live, you still have our backs. "Will you stay on with Ray?"

Neal spooned another serving of moo goo gai pan onto his plate. "I like Ray. He's one of the good guys. And policing is pretty much all I know, but there's something else I've been toying with since my mid-twenties. I talked to Jim Bigelow about it the other day."

"The same Jim Bigelow who owns the bookstore in town?"

Neal nodded. "Uh-huh. His wife wants them to retire and move to Florida. He says she's had enough of the New England winters."

"I know both the Bigelow's. Mindy was a friend of my mom. I remember when they opened the store. It was small then, but when the tearoom next door moved to a bigger location about two or three years later, the Bigelow's seized the opportunity to expand their space. They converted the front of the tearoom into a small coffee cafe and created a reading nook in the back."

"Jim said Bigelow's is a Watch Hill cornerstone."

"It is. They opened in the winter, so as you might suspect they didn't have the tourist traffic needed to jolt them into immediate success, but the locals adored the place and kept it going during the off-season months and still do. Mrs. Bigelow is always hosting book events for local authors." Jeanne nodded. "I agree Bigelow's is a Watch Hill institution."

"I spoke to Jim about buying it."

Jeanne set down her fork. "You want to own a bookstore?"

"Yes. You seem somewhat surprised."

"I am, but I think it's great. I would never have guessed a bookstore would interest you."

"Law enforcement will always be a part of who I am. But I think it's time for a change, and owning a bookstore is what I want to do." Neal snapped open his fortune cookie, wiggled his eyebrows and chuckled. "I'll take this as an omen. You are well suited to what lies ahead."

"I guess it's true about March coming in like a lion," Jo said when Phoebe answered the phone. "The weather here is dreadful and probably colder still where you are, dear."

"It's thirty-eight today, not bad for a winter day, but tomorrow it's supposed to drop into the high twenties, and they're calling for snow."

"That's what I heard too. I was hoping to come and see you girls this weekend, but I'm not up for driving in the snow. I think I'll wait until the end of the month when March traditionally turns into a lamb."

Phoebe chuckled. "Would you like to make your reservation now?"

"Yes, maybe it will help guarantee the suite I've come to consider mine."

Phoebe checked the dates Jo gave her. "All set, and I was able to secure the suite you prefer. We will look forward to seeing you. Anything special you'd like to see on the menu?"

"Everything you make is beyond wonderful, but I especially enjoy your pork roast. It's always so flavorful, and your gravy is to die for."

"Consider it done."

CHAPTER
THIRTY-SIX

On the anniversary of their mother's passing, the sisters visited their parents' grave at the Swan Point Cemetery with a dozen calla lilies, their mothers' favorite flower.

"I can't believe it's been a year." Phoebe put the flowers in the pop-up vase embedded in the headstone. "Doesn't seem possible."

Hannah wiped tears off her cheeks. "So much has happened since she's been gone."

"I'm glad she didn't have to witness what happened." Jeanne put her hand on the headstone. "She would've worried herself sick."

Phoebe put an arm around her middle sister. "She would've wanted to take out a contract on the jerk who tried to hurt her girls or vandalize her property."

Jeanne smiled. "She could be feisty when she wanted to, couldn't she?"

Tears streamed from beneath Hannah's sunglasses. "Especially when it came to protecting her three baby bears."

"Jeanne, when you get a chance, I'd like to talk to you," Neal said when the sisters returned home.

"Now's good. She slipped off her coat and hung it on the coat tree in the hallway. "What's up?"

"I want you to be the first to know I have purchased Bigelow's."

Jeanne hugged him. "Good for you. Do you plan to keep the staff, or will you try and run it yourself?"

"I will hang on to the two most experienced, but the rest of the efforts must fall to me. I thought maybe...."

"What?"

"Maybe you might consider helping me with the budget."

"Sure. Anything. Just let me know."

Phoebe walked into the hall. "Anyone up for lunch?"

"When have I ever said no to one of your meals?" Neal grinned.

"Guess what?" Jeanne said when Hannah joined them. "Neal has a surprise."

Hannah rubbed her hands together. "Tell us. After what we've been through, we can use a surprise."

"I bought Bigelow's."

"The downtown Bigelow's?"

"One in the same." Neal rolled back on his heels and grinned.

Hannah beamed. "Cool. You can continue living here and see Jeanne whenever you want."

Jeanne fisted her hands and brought them to her hips. "Hannah!"

⌒⌒⌒

Ray drove up and down the street near Neal's store twice before spotting someone pulling out. "I should have called," he muttered.

Neal smiled from behind the counter when Ray walked in. "Hey, buddy, what brings you down this way?"

Ray eyed the surroundings. "Had to see your new setup for myself." He whistled. "You sure got yourself a boatload of books."

Wooden bookcases stood three-quarters of the way to the ceiling along each wall. Eight-by-ten black and white framed photos of well-known authors, celebrities, and politicians who had once visited the store paraded above them. A tiger-maple rectangular table stood inside the front door topped with stacks of books and a sign rising from the center announcing *thirty percent off*. A small café stood off to the right. Filling out the rear of the store was a seating area with four well-worn overstuffed chairs encircling a pine cocktail table.

"Never saw you as a bookman. What's with the name?"

"It's been Bigelow's for almost two decades. I figured, why mess with success?"

"I'm impressed. This is quite a place." Ray chuckled. "Even has a musty museum smell you find in a good bookstore."

Neal gestured toward the café. "Coffee?"

"Sure."

A customer approached the register. Neal held up an index finger. "Go on. I'll be with you in a minute, Ray."

After ringing up the sale, they brought their coffees to a small table in the far corner.

Neal wrapped his hands around his coffee cup. "All right. What made you drive down here?" He made a stop motion with his hand. "And don't tell me it's because you had to see the store."

Ray turned his cup in a circle. "The Stanton case."

"What about it? Jeanne told you to drop it."

"I know, but it didn't feel right to turn my back on it. I finally found a way to ID the cell towers where the calls pinged from." He mimicked Neal's earlier stop motion. "Don't ask how. That way it will only be *my* ass in a sling. I felt I owed Jeanne something more than the protection we provided. She deserves to know the truth." He lowered his voice. "I thought I should talk to you before approaching her with what I have found."

"Where are the towers? Manhattan?"

"Here's where I need your help." He pulled a small notebook from his shirt pocket, flipped a dozen pages, and pushed the open notebook across the small table to Neal. "Does Jeanne know anyone from there?"

CHAPTER THIRTY-SEVEN

Hannah snuggled into Aaron as they sat on his living room couch. "Nothing much good on TV tonight, is there?"

Aaron shook his head. "I know, right? How could I have all these channels, and not have anything worth watching?" He turned off the television and gazed at her. "Have I told you how much I love having you here?"

Hannah nestled closer. "Only three times so far tonight, but it never gets old." She glanced at the clock on the wall and gave him a quick kiss. "Unfortunately, it's getting close to ten, though, and I have cats and dogs to see tomorrow and a few patients I should check on tonight."

Aaron picked up his car keys from the coffee table. "If you must. Are you ready?"

Hannah willed herself off the couch.

As they walked to the car he asked, "I've been meaning to ask if you think Jeanne will return to the city since the inn is up and running?"

Hannah knew this was as good a time as any to choose her words carefully. Unlike her usual mode of operandi of speaking once and thinking twice, the last thing she wanted was to put her foot in her mouth and have to listen to her sisters after they agreed not to tell anyone what had been happening during the last several months. "I doubt it. I think she likes where she's at."

"I haven't seen Marcus around for a while. Is she still seeing him?"

"No. Which probably plays a part in her not wanting to return to the city. Although the likelihood she might run into him is slim, I don't think she wants to take the chance."

"I take it the breakup was hurtful?"

"Let's say he wasn't the guy she thought he was and leave it at that."

"What about Phoebe?" Aaron opened the car door for her. "Will she continue on as the chef?"

"Are you kidding? She's as close to heaven as she can get and still take a breath. She loves cooking and taking care of everybody."

Aaron slid into the driver's seat and started the engine.

"What about you?" she asked. "Are you still okay with your decision to leave Long Island?"

He squeezed Hannah's hand. "Thanks to you, I am. But I'd be lying if I said I don't think about it, especially every time I drive down Montauk Avenue, but I guess like Jeanne I'm content with my move."

Jeanne had just exited the garage when Jo pulled into the driveway. She quickened her pace. "Jo, let me help you with your luggage."

"Oh, thank you, dear." Jo hugged Jeanne.

"We've missed you." Jeanne wheeled Jo's bag toward the front steps and checked her watch. "Hannah will finish up at the clinic soon. She is so looking forward to seeing you again."

"I couldn't sleep last night, rolling my trip around in my mind. I want to hear all about how she and Aaron are getting along. Do you think there's a ring in her future?"

Jeanne lifted Jo's suitcase up the stairs to the porch. "I guess time will tell."

"And how are you? I've been concerned ever since I watched the hearing. Please tell me you aren't still seeing Marcus."

"No." Jeanne opened the front door for her elderly friend.

"Have you found someone else?"

Jeanne paused. "Not really, but I have struck up a friendship with Neal."

"Is that so."

Knowing Jo could get every last detail out of her and not wanting to go there, Jeanne quickly added. "Now, let's get you registered."

"I'm glad to hear about you and Neal. He seems like a very nice man." Jo scanned the hallway leading to the stairs. "You can't imagine how much I've missed being here. I'm so looking forward to the next few days."

"Dinner will be served at six. Which should give you plenty of time to rest after your drive."

"Resting is the last thing on my mind. There is so much I want to do. Like catching up with Phoebe over a nice cup of tea. By the way, I assume Neal will join us for dinner."

Jeanne shook her head. "I don't know if he will be able to make it. He recently bought a bookstore in town. It keeps him on his toes."

"Well, how will you know for sure unless you ask?"

Jo passed the bowl of mashed potatoes to Neal during dinner. "I'm so glad you were able to join us. I hear you are the proud owner of a bookstore."

Neal took the bowl. "I am."

"How is it working out for you?"

After plopping several spoonfuls on his plate, he passed the potatoes to Jeanne. "So far, so good."

"Have you been in retail before?"

"Not even close. But I've always had an affinity for books."

"Neal's an avid reader," Jeanne said. "Owning a bookstore has been a longtime dream."

Jo looked at Neal. "My husband was fortunate to realize his dream as well." She looked around the table. "My memory isn't what it used to be. Have I told you what he did for a living?"

"I don't think so." Hannah put a piece of roast on her plate.

Jo's face brightened. "He was a decorated member of the NYPD."

"Oh, we knew you and Frank were Staten Island natives," Phoebe said. "But we had no idea he was a policeman."

"So, you're from Staten Island." Neal eyed Jo. "When it comes to that borough, the only thing I know is Bruno Lombardi, the famous crime boss, lived there."

"In his role as captain, Frank was in charge of the task force responsible for investigating him and ultimately bringing him and his criminal family to justice."

Neal brought his fork to his mouth. "Interesting."

"As I said, my husband loved his job." Jo took a slice of pork roast from the platter Phoebe passed to her. "But once he left the force, his zest for life seemed to escape him."

"I'm sure that would be quite an adjustment," Jeanne said handing over the gravy boat.

Jo breathed out a sigh. "Especially when you find your health failing and the future doesn't seem as bright as it once did."

<hr />

Two weeks later

"I accepted the job offer from Bonardi's Drugstore," Aaron said to Hannah one night during dinner at his house.

"What made you decide on Bonardi's?"

"The owner is offering to let me run the pharmacy while he concentrates on getting his compounding venture up and running. By being by his side, it will kill two birds with one stone. Not only will I collect a paycheck, but I'll be able to see if holistic is something I want to pursue. It's a win-win."

"Owning your store probably played a big part in helping to land the job for you."

"I think so." Aaron added sour cream to his baked potato.

Hannah raised her wine glass to her lips. "When do you start?"

"Next week, thank goodness, because not having much to do every day isn't all it's cracked up to be."

CHAPTER
THIRTY-EIGHT

Jeanne had been anxious ever since Neal texted her and asked for her to come to his store. Why would he do so when he would see her in a few hours at the inn? Had he intercepted a new threat and wanted to tell her without being overheard by her sisters? Then again, maybe it had nothing to do with her and everything to do with Neal's new venture. Had he had a change of heart and decided to sell? When she arrived at Bigelow's, she prepared for what she had convinced herself could only be bad news. She palmed the door handle, took a deep breath to fortify herself, and pushed it open.

Neal was inside the front door unpacking books.

"Hi."

He put a book back in the box. "Thanks for coming. Sorry to drag you down here, but there is something we should talk about, and I didn't feel comfortable discussing it on the phone."

Hadn't that been precisely what she had said the day she telephoned Marcus after receiving the first threat? She said a silent prayer hoping it didn't have anything to do with what she had started thinking of as her former situation. In a Hannah-like burst, she plunged forward. "Let me guess. This place isn't working out." The words tumbling from her mouth in quick succession. "You've decided to sell and will be moving back to Warwick."

"No. But if I did, would it bother you?"

Jeanne lowered her eyes. "Well, yes. I guess it would."

"Then, it's fair to say you have nothing to worry about. You're stuck with me for the foreseeable future. Come on. Let's go to my office." Once there, he motioned for her to sit, closed the door, and settled into the chair behind the desk. "I wanted to let you know Ray stopped by yesterday with something you should know."

This couldn't be good. "About the case?"

"Yes."

"He isn't working for me any longer, so why would he have something new?"

"He felt obligated to finish what he started, regardless of whether he was still on the payroll or not. I think it grated on him that he hadn't figured out a way to trace the calls without involving the police. Although he wouldn't go into detail as to how he accomplished it, apparently, he recently found a way around it." Neal paused. "Jeanne, he located the tower where the calls pinged from. He asked me if I'd ever heard you or your sisters mention anyone who lives near there. Although he said there is still more work to do, he wanted you to know what he found out."

Jeanne called Hannah and Phoebe and asked them to meet her at Neal's store, knowing the information she would soon be imparting had to be done in person and not where they might be overheard.

Ten minutes later, Hannah followed Phoebe into the store. "What's going on? Tell me this isn't bad news."

"I'm afraid it could be."

Neal pulled over two folding chairs in his office and motioned for them to sit.

"This looks serious. What's going on?" Phoebe ran a hand over her arm. "You're giving me goosebumps."

"Neal, tell them what you told me."

"Ray stopped by the other day to say he never stopped working the case."

"Even though Jeanne told him not to?" Hannah raised an eyebrow. "Which, if you ask me, was a mistake."

"You got your wish," Jeanne said. "He didn't listen."

Phoebe nodded. "Good. Maybe now we will finally know who was behind the threats and be able to bring the person to justice."

"Remember the adage be careful what you wish for? Well, it may apply here because Ray knows where the calls came from."

Phoebe leaned forward in her chair. "He does? Where?"

"Staten Island."

"So, what." Hannah huffed a laugh. "Half of FNB probably live or used to live there."

Jeanne nodded. "True. But it is also where Jo lives. Neal didn't know where she was from until she talked about her husband at dinner."

"But didn't Ray do a background check on Jo?" Hannah asked. "Surely her address would have come up."

Neal toyed with a pen on his desk. "Neither Ray nor I ever did a search on her because, by the time he was involved, you had already checked her out."

"Just because Jo lives there doesn't mean she has anything to do with what happened." Hannah's voice shook. "She's a seventy-two-year-old woman for heaven's sake."

"You're right. It's still possible it could be someone else, but Ray ran down all the FNB names he had and couldn't get a location close to the tower on any of them. And if there is one thing you learn in law enforcement, coincidence and crime usually don't go together."

"Her residing on Staten Island is not a strong enough reason for me to suspect Jo."

Phoebe pursed her lips and folded her arms over her chest. "I agree."

"There is only one way to know for sure and that's to confront her," Neal said.

"*Confront* her?" Phoebe was clearly horrified. "Slow down. This is our friend you're talking about."

"Unfortunately, I think Neal is right." Jeanne put a hand on Phoebe's arm. "We will never know for sure unless we lay out the situation and see how she responds."

"You both have lost your minds." Hannah raised her voice. "I would rather have Ray do a full investigation before we say anything to her."

"I understand your hesitation." Neal drummed his fingers on the desktop. "But from what Jeanne told me, I think we have the perfect opportunity coming up. If we let it pass, we may come to regret it."

Hannah glared at Jeanne. "I can't believe you are on board with this."

"I'm not in love with the notion she could be the one who has caused us such grief either, but I think Ray's finding should be followed up on. If we don't, I for one, will always wonder about whether she could have been involved."

Neal stepped in. "From what Jeanne told me Jo plans to spend Memorial Day weekend here. I say we approach her then."

Phoebe shook her head so hard, her dangling earrings hit the side of her face. "No way. We are fully booked that weekend, and the last thing we need is to create a scene."

"I understand. But I think I have a workaround. Besides if we were to ask her to come sooner it might tip our hand."

"How do you plan to handle this without creating a scene?" Hannah folded her arms across her chest.

"I told Jeanne we can confront her here. I'm closing early that Saturday because of the downtown food festival. By doing so we can contain any commotion. If there is any."

"And how do you propose we get her here?" Phoebe asked clearly as perturbed as her younger sister.

"Jeanne can tell her I want to show off my store."

Hannah tightened her lips. "And *what* exactly do you plan to say when she gets here? Hi, Jo. We want to know if you planted a dead rat in our pantry and reported it to the health department. Cut Phoebe's brake line and set fire to the clinic." She shook her head. "She will think you've gone stark raving mad. And who could blame her?"

"Hannah's right." Phoebe nodded. "Like Hannah said, this is a seventy-two-year-old woman we are discussing. It can't possibly be her. Why not have Ray find out who the number belongs to before we go anywhere near accusing her?"

Neal shook his head. "No dice. The phone used was a disposable. He traced the purchase to a drugstore on Staten Island. The transaction record indicated the buyer used cash, and the surveillance film is no longer available. He questioned the clerks, mostly kids, who couldn't remember anything. According to them they sell a lot of burners, so no one stood out."

"Where on Staten Island was the drugstore located?" Phoebe asked.

"Willowbrook."

Hannah gasped and side eyed Phoebe. "Willowbrook is where she told us she lives." She stood, looking like she wanted to pace, but having no room, sat back down. "This makes no sense. Why would she, of all people, want to hurt us?"

"If she is guilty," Neal said. "My question is why does she continue to visit?"

"Because she has nothing to hide." Hannah grinned triumphantly. "She watched the hearing. She knows Jeanne didn't cause the collapse."

Jeanne looked at her sisters. "On the other hand, if she has had a part in this, maybe she thinks she has to cover her tracks."

The sisters sat in silence for a few minutes after Neal left the office to assist a customer. Jeanne rubbed her palms on her khaki-colored capris. "I certainly want your opinions, and I'll consider them, but I'll be the one who makes the ultimate decision. After all, we are in this mess because of me. Plus, I'll be the one to speak to her. If it turns out, she's innocent. I'll be the bad guy."

"I can't believe we are even discussing this." Hannah swiped her hair from her face. "A lot of people live in her town."

Phoebe nodded. "I agree. "I can't wrap my head around this either. With the number of times she has visited, she never once hinted at anything sinister. Quite the opposite."

"I don't want to believe it, but let's think about what happened and when. The inspector showed up shortly after one of her visits. She could have easily put the rat poison in the pantry during the night." Jeanne looked at Phoebe. "And I specifically remember you told her what you planned on doing for Halloween. She even gave you some suggestions, as I recall."

Phoebe nodded slowly. "But what about the brake line? She wasn't here the day it happened."

"No. But you didn't use your car until the day after she left."

"I keep asking myself, *why*?" Hannah picked at a loose thread on her shirt. "It doesn't add up. What could she possibly have to do with FNB?"

"Hannah's right. What could she possibly get out of doing something like this?"

"I don't know." Jeanne's voice showed her frustration with her sisters. She didn't want it to be Jo, either. "Maybe she took the plight of the FNB people to heart. She's soft-hearted. Maybe she felt someone had to speak up for them."

Hannah shook her head. "Nah. Her husband passed away a month before she first came here. Why would she care about some abstract company after she just lost him? I'm telling you. It doesn't make sense."

"We *think* her husband passed away, but only because it's what she told us." Jeanne looked at her sisters. "What if none of it is true?"

"Oh, come on. Now you think she's a pathological liar, too?" Hannah narrowed her eyes. "This whole thing is bizarre."

"I'm simply pointing out that we only know what she wants us to know."

Phoebe held up a hand. "Let's say it *is* her. Why on earth would she target you? How would she even *know* you worked there? It's not like you made the papers after the collapse."

Hannah leaned forward and pounded the desk. "Yeah, why you? The CEO, maybe. He's someone she could have read about. But you? No. It's a long shot."

"She watched the hearings with us. Even if she *thought* it was you, the outcome would set her straight." Phoebe slapped her knees. "It just can't be her."

"Maybe it did, which is why nothing has happened since the hearings. Unfortunately, we'll only know if we ask her."

"Okay, and say we do, and she confesses." Hannah frowned. "Then what?"

"Yes, then what?" Phoebe added.

"We'll have to report it to the arson inspector and the insurance company after we turn her over to the police which will take it out of our hands. They will be the ones to take the appropriate action."

Hannah stood and glared at her middle sister. "If you ask me, Neal and Ray are living in a crime drama. The only thing I know she's guilty of is making cardboard like meatloaf and reminding us of Mom. And the last time I checked neither is against the law."

CHAPTER
THIRTY-NINE

Jeanne flipped from side to side for the umpteenth time since going to bed and looked at the clock.

She would be glad when the confrontation with Jo was behind her. Phoebe had reluctantly agreed she and Neal should question Jo but made it clear she did not want to be there to witness it. Hannah tried to talk Jeanne out of it, but finally gave up. Jeanne hoped she would find Jo innocent and preferred facing the fallout instead of thinking the woman who had so captured their hearts could be the culprit. She knew the confrontation would be like walking a tightrope. One misstep could easily break the bones of a friendship they had all lovingly cultivated.

Finally, after three hours, Jeanne threw back the covers, got out of bed, reclined on her chaise, and hoped the new location would help lull her to sleep. She leaned her head back, and somewhere along a mental journey that went fuzzy, her eyes grew heavy, and she finally dozed. She woke at five-thirty, stiff from sleeping on the old sagging chaise, put on a pair of jeans, pulled a t-shirt over her head, and went to the kitchen.

Despite being booked to capacity, the house was quiet. Even Phoebe, known for being an early riser, wouldn't be down until six-thirty. Jeanne flipped on the small lamp by the door, turned off the automatic start her older sister had programmed into the coffee maker, and hit the brew button. The aroma of Phoebe's unique blend wafted through the room.

"Couldn't sleep, Jeanne?" Jo said from the doorway.

Jeanne's hand flew to her chest. "Jo, you startled me. What are you doing up so early?"

"I've had trouble sleeping since Frank passed away. I miss having him next to me, or then again maybe it's another chapter in the advancing age saga. What about you? I don't recall you having a sleep problem."

Jeanne looked at the well-intended woman who could easily pass as her mother's sister. *How would she be able to proceed with the plan?*

Jo walked across the room and put a hand on Jeanne's forearm. "Are you okay, dear?"

Jeanne stepped back. "Yes, I'm fine. I've had so much on my mind lately. I can't seem to turn off the thoughts."

"I understand. Do you mind if I join you for a cup of coffee?"

Jeanne's insides churned. It wasn't her nature to back away from a situation, but she and Neal had agreed on an approach, and she didn't want to pull a Hannah-like explosion of emotions in a moment of anxiousness and change things. On the other hand, could she sit idly by and make small talk when she would be accusing Jo of something criminal in a few short hours? The mere thought made her cringe. "Not at all. Please do."

Jo reached for a mug and poured. "I, too, find my mind racing at times. Let's enjoy the solitude and use the time to catch up."

Jo gently squeezed Jeanne's hand. "Jeanne, what is it? I can tell something's bothering you. If I'm right, is it something you would like to talk about?"

The elderly woman was so kind, it made her want to scrap the plan. What had she been thinking? How could Jo possibly be involved?

Jo's eyebrows drew together, and a single vertical wrinkle erupted in between. "Is that bum Marcus causing problems for you?"

Jeanne shook her head. "No. I guess I'm overwhelmed with what it takes to run this place."

"Please forgive me. I don't mean to pry. I know it's none of my business. But you girls have come to mean the world to me, so I'm here for you if you change your mind and want to talk. In the meantime, let's find something of no consequence to discuss before this old house comes alive. Shall we?"

Relief washed over Jeanne. Thank goodness Jo had stopped pushing because she had come close to spilling what was on her mind in the dimly lit kitchen. "I don't know if we have mentioned it, but our mom used to host huge Memorial Day and Fourth of July celebrations. At times, the crowds grew so large there were people in attendance none of us recognized. She not only invited friends and neighbors but *their* families as well. So, Phoebe suggested we uphold the tradition but on a much smaller scale. She has been busy preparing food all week for this weekend. I'm glad you will be here to enjoy it."

Jo lifted her cup to her lips. "You don't suppose Marcus will decide to crash the party, do you?"

"No chance. He knows we are finished."

"Good." Jo put her cup down. "Speaking of young men, Rob is such a joy, isn't he?" She giggled. "God bless his appetite."

"Phoebe did an outstanding job raising him."

"Well, it shows. I suppose, though, to be fair, her former husband probably played some part in his upbringing, wouldn't you say?"

Jeanne shook her head. "He was more of a bit player. She was always the star of the show."

"Hannah's closing her clinic early because of the holiday weekend," Jeanne said when she called Neal to review their plan. "Jo and I will follow her to Aaron's at about three because Jo wants to see his house. Hannah talked about what a great find it was, which piqued Jo's interest. The only thing up in the air right now is if Hannah will wait for Aaron to come home before returning here to help Phoebe prepare for tomorrow. She's still not on board with us confronting Jo, so she wants to stay far away from the fallout."

"What about you? Are you having second thoughts?"

"No. But I almost got into it with her this morning."

"Glad you didn't. It would not have been a good idea. So, you still plan to bring her to the store a little before five today, right?"

"Yes. But I pray your instincts are wrong about her."

"I know how hard this is for you and your sisters. But the only way we'll know is to follow the plan."

Jeanne let out a long stream of air. "I hope we can do this in a way so we don't torpedo our relationship if it turns out she is innocent."

"There is no nice way to accuse someone of being a criminal."

"Exactly. Which is why I don't think we *should* accuse her. I stayed awake all night coming up with a version which would avoid wrecking our friendship."

"You're pipe-dreaming."

"Hear me out. What if we use the good cop, bad cop scenario? I'll be the good one by making her think I'm confiding in her about what's been going on."

"And where am I during all of this?"

"I don't know, keeping yourself busy nearby, rearranging books or something. When you hear me tell her what has been happening, you walk toward us wearing a stern expression. If she's guilty, she'll react. She's not stupid. She'll figure it out. But if she's innocent, she'll probably keep on listening."

"You've been watching too much television. It doesn't work that way. Let me lay it on the line as we discussed. I'll be the bad cop, as you put it, while you can act surprised and try to make her think you are coming to her defense. If it's not her, I'm the one she'll be upset with."

After giving Jo and Jeanne the grand tour of Aaron's small beach house, Hannah stopped in the kitchen. "Well, that's it."

"This is charmingly cozy." Jo turned in a circle and smiled. "I'd say it's a little love nest."

Hannah's cheeks colored. "I don't live here. At least not yet." She hadn't intended to snap at Jo, but her level of anxiety was at an all-time high knowing what the woman would soon be dealing with.

Jo paused as if trying to pick her words more carefully. "Tell me, how does Aaron like his new job?"

"So far, so good. It has freed the owner up to work on launching a compounding section which is why he went looking for someone like Aaron in the first place."

"Pardon my ignorance, but what is compounding?"

"It's a more holistic approach to medicine." Hannah avoided eye contact with Jo as she handed her the glass of iced tea. "Excuse me while I get the sugar and lemon." A minute later, she put the sugar bowl and a plate of lemon wedges on the table. "Aaron says the owner is nearing seventy, and once his new venture is up and running in a year, he plans to sell the store and move to Georgia to be close to his children."

Jo brought her glass to her lips. "Is he married?"

"His wife died seven years ago of breast cancer. Which spurred his interest in the alternative to conventional drugs. There was not much traditional meds could do for her after her diagnosis. So, after she passed, his goal was to make holistic alternatives available to the community in her memory."

Jo nodded and looked off for a moment as if lost in thought.

Jeanne put her iced tea down on the table and looked at Jo. "We better get going."

"Let me get the dip Aaron made for tomorrow out of the refrigerator." Hannah walked across the kitchen. "I plan to hang out here and wait for him to come home, so I told Phoebe I'd send it home with you."

⁓⧉⧉⁓

When Jeanne and Jo returned to the inn, they found Phoebe in the kitchen, looking frazzled.

"Are you nervous about your party?" Jo asked.

Phoebe closed her eyes and sighed. "A little. Mom's parties ran so smoothly. I don't want my first to be a flop."

"Mom also had help." Jeanne reminded her. "Which you keep saying you don't need."

Jo hugged Phoebe. "You shouldn't worry. I'm sure your event will be a spectacular success and make your mother proud."

"Thank you, Jo."

Jeanne checked her watch. "I know we just got here, but we must get to Neal's before he closes."

"It's not a big deal if we don't go. I could see it some other time. Maybe I should stay and help Phoebe get things ready."

"Everything is about done." Phoebe made a shooing motion. "Go ahead. Neal's expecting you."

"Okay, if you're sure, but give me a few minutes to freshen up."

Hannah paced in Aaron's small living room after Jeanne and Jo left. She hadn't been able to psych herself up to return to the inn with them. It felt to her like Jeanne was marching Jo off to the gallows. She wanted no part in it. Hannah glanced at the time on the cable box. She was way too anxious to sit and watch television. "It will be forty-five minutes before Aaron gets here. He said he did laundry last night. I bet it's still in the dryer." She went to the louvered door closet where the stackable duo was stored and opened the dryer door. "Leave it to a man." She started to take the clothes out, saw how wrinkled they were from being in the machine overnight, closed the door, and turned the dial to air dry.

After washing the iced tea glasses, she returned to the dryer, folded the clothes, took the stack to Aaron's bedroom, and put them on his bed. "Okay, let's see where he puts what." She pulled open the middle drawer of his bureau. A manila folder peeked out from beneath a pile of briefs. She cocked her head to read what it said. 'FNB.'

"What the hell?" She pulled the folder out and opened it. Inside were more than a dozen newspaper articles about FNB's demise, the hearings, and the investigations. "What is he doing with these?" She grabbed the bedpost to steady herself and sat on the edge of the bed. Her hands shook as she tried to grasp what stared back at her.

"I have to get to Jeanne before it's too late." She ran to the kitchen, grabbed her cell phone, and dialed the inn. "Damn it," she said, when the answering machine picked up. "Where the hell are Jeanne and Phoebe?" She tossed the folder on the counter and bolted to her car. She had to get to Jeanne before she and Neal ruined everything.

⌘

On the way to the inn, Hannah's thoughts swirled like an F-five tornado. *Why does he have those articles? Please let there be a reasonable explanation. He can't be involved in what has happened here, can he?* She glanced at the dashboard clock. She couldn't let Jeanne and Neal drag the woman she had come to care so much for through the wringer. Toss a net over her and see if she could wiggle free. Hannah eyed the speedometer and pressed down on the accelerator. Eleven minutes later, she pulled up the driveway, too nervous to recall the trip, and spotted Phoebe and Jeanne coming out of the garage carrying food trays from the overflow refrigerator. She slammed on her brakes and shoved the gear shift into park while simultaneously opening the door.

"Jeanne! Phoebe!"

They stopped.

Jeanne frowned. "You're back. I didn't expect you until later."

"There's something you need to know," she yelled, raced across the driveway, and skidded to a halt in front of them. "You haven't spoken to Jo yet, have you?" Bent over, she rested her hands on her knees, trying to catch her breath.

"No. Why?"

"I found a file folder in Aaron's underwear drawer."

Phoebe jerked her head back. "What were you doing in Aaron's underwear drawer?"

"I was putting his clothes away, but that's not important. Jeanne, the folder contained newspaper articles about FNB."

"FNB? Why would he have those?"

"I don't know." Her eyes brimmed with tears. "I didn't hang around to find out. I had to get to you before you spoke to Jo."

Phoebe looked at Jeanne. "This could change things. It would be best if you tell Neal. Maybe hold off on the Jo thing until you do."

Jeanne glanced up at Jo's window.

Jo smiled down at them and gave them a small wave.

<hr>

"Surprising. He never entered my radar," Neal said when Jeanne called to tell him about the articles. "Let's think about this. It seems unlikely he'd travel from the eastern tip of Long Island to Staten Island to make the calls. It's at least a three-hour drive."

"I hope for Hannah's sake you're right. But why else would he be collecting information about the bank? There's no logical explanation that I can think of."

"I say we continue as planned. Hopefully, we will find she's innocent."

<hr>

Jeanne and Jo walked down the hill, past the carousel, to Neal's store.

"This is such a pretty area," Jo said. "I'm so glad I found your place."

"It is. I never appreciated it growing up, but now I can't think of anywhere I'd rather be."

Jo linked her arm with Jeanne's. "Tell me, are you and Neal an item?"

Unlike Hannah, who seemed to share every thought with virtually anybody, especially Jo, Jeanne preferred to keep personal matters personal. "There's a lot about him I respect, but we're not, as you say, an item."

"Oh, Jeanne, this is me you're talking to, not some stranger. I've seen the way he looks at you, and I've seen the way you seem to study him when he's not looking. I never saw you do so with Marcus."

"I knew Marcus a long time."

"Yes, and I'm sure it was easy to fall under his spell when you were so vulnerable."

"What makes you think I was vulnerable?" Jeanne's antenna engaged.

"Your mother had recently passed away. A loss leaves a deep vacuum, and our nature seeks to fill it as quickly as possible. If you ask me, you were ripe for the picking. I believe he took advantage of you. And if you must know, I have to say I never liked him."

"Why?"

"The man is enamored with himself. I've seen his kind before. My daughter married someone like him."

"You seemed to get along fine with him."

"It wasn't my place not to. But if you were my daughter, I would have spoken up and told you what I thought in no uncertain terms." Jo paused. "Neal, on the other hand, is a book of a different cover, isn't he?" She laughed. "No pun intended."

"Here we are." Jeanne opened the door to Bigelow's.

CHAPTER
FORTY

"Hi," Jeanne called out when they entered the store.

"Glad you could make it, Jo." Neal swept an arm out to encompass the space. "Welcome to Bigelow's."

"What a cozy place." The older woman closed her eyes and inhaled. "I love the rich smell of books. Conjurers up thoughts of a rainy day and a cup of hot chocolate."

"I think I mentioned Neal is something of an admirer of classics. The books in the glass cabinet you'll pass on the way to the café are from his personal collection."

Jo went toward them. "Are they for sale?"

"No. They've been in storage over the years. I figured, why not break them out and maybe inspire this generation's readers to try one? I stock the titles."

"Do you have a favorite author, Jo?" Jeanne's smile wobbled with nerves.

"I'm not much of a reader, although I read Rebecca and Wuthering Heights as a young woman. Doesn't every girl? And, of course, some of the Nancy Drew mysteries. As I grew older, though, I got caught up in dating and pretty clothes and never seemed to have the time."

"Reading has always been one of my passions," Neal said, "I recall enjoying all the Hardy Boy adventures when I was eleven or twelve."

Jo smiled. "Like the time I spent with Nancy."

"If you ladies will excuse me, I have to secure the back door and set the alarm before we leave. After Jeanne shows you around, tell Mia, our café manager, coffee is on me."

Jo leaned into Jeanne. "If it's all the same with you, I'd prefer tea."

Mia filled Jo and Jeanne's order, and the women sat at a nearby bistro table. "Neal is quite a different breed from that alley cat Marcus, isn't he? I never understood what such an intelligent woman as yourself saw in him. As I said on the way here, I guess you were seeking comfort after your mother passed away, and when he heard of your vulnerable state, he made his move."

"Actually, I'm the one who called him and asked him to come to the inn for our opening day."

"I suppose I can see why you would. I'm sure you considered him a friend and felt it wise to have a man around when you girls opened your doors to who knows who."

Jeanne took a sip of her coffee and looked over Jo's shoulder to the street while she collected her thoughts and drummed up her courage before returning her attention to Jo. "Since we're alone, I'd like to share something with you."

Jo set her cup down. "Of course, dear. You know by now I am a good listener."

"Someone threatened me a few days before we opened the inn."

Jo's eyes widened. "Why on earth would someone do such a thing?"

"Whoever it is thought I had a hand in the collapse of the bank I worked for."

"But you didn't. I watched the hearings on television with Phoebe. Marcus is the culprit." Jo shook her head. "It's one thing to do what he did, but to threaten you takes things to a whole different level."

"The thing is, Marcus swears it wasn't him."

"I'm surprised you would believe him after how he's treated you."

"I didn't at first."

Neal pulled a chair over to their table and sat. "May I join you?"

"Yes." Relief washed through her when Neal took over the conversation. "I was telling Jo about the threats I have received. And she thinks Marcus might somehow play a part in this."

Jo raised an eyebrow. "Oh, you're familiar with what we were just discussing?"

Jeanne nodded. "Yes."

"I can see why you might think so. But I don't think he is at fault."

Jo cocked her head to the side. "What makes you so sure?"

"Although we have led the guests to believe I am a boarder, I've been working to flush out the perpetrator. I'm retired Providence PD, and Jeanne hired the firm I worked for to find out who is responsible."

Jo glanced at Jeanne. "Wise move. But still. Neal how can you be so sure with someone as underhanded as Marcus?"

"The company I worked for before purchasing the store is a private investigation firm, and Ray, the man who heads it up, had a call traced."

Jo gave Jeanne a quizzical look. "Ray? You mean the man I met when you were in Washington?" Jo frowned as if confronted with a complicated plot, not someone trying to hide behind one. "Why saddle yourself with the expense of a private investigator when caller ID tells us what we need to know these days?"

"The ID didn't offer up any clues. The caller blocked his identity," Jeanne said.

"Then how could the call be traced?"

"All calls ping off a tower." Neal leaned his elbows on the table. "Once you identify where the tower is located, you can narrow down where the call originated from."

Jo looked at Jeanne. "So, the person used a cell phone?"

Neal frowned. "Who said it was a cell phone?"

"You did."

"No, I said we traced the call to a tower."

"I thought only cell phones use towers," Jo sat back in her chair, looking perplexed but not guilty.

Neal shook his head. "The records indicate the call came from Willowbrook on Staten Island, which, if I'm not mistaken, is where you live, Jo. But you already know where the calls originated, don't you?"

⁓◌◌⁓

"Why couldn't Jeanne have waited before talking to Jo?" Hannah waited for Phoebe to pour her a cup of tea. "At least until I speak to Aaron."

"I know having those clippings looks suspicious, but we shouldn't lose sight how the calls came from Jo's hometown, not Aaron's."

Hannah covered her face with her hands. "How can this be happening? First Jo, now Aaron." Hannah dropped her hands. "This is worse than a nightmare."

The phone rang.

Hannah grabbed Phoebe's hand. "Don't answer it. It's probably Aaron. And I'm not ready to hear what he has to say. I'd rather wait to see how things go with Jo."

The answering machine picked up, and Aaron's voice floated in the air. "Hannah, I see you found the folder. Please call me so I can explain."

Hannah looked at Phoebe, tears spilling down her cheeks. "That's what Marcus said to Jeanne."

⁓◌◌⁓

"I know Hannah's here." Aaron stepped into the foyer when Phoebe answered the door. "I have to talk to her."

Phoebe led the way to the kitchen.

"I'll be in the sitting room." she told Hannah from the kitchen doorway.

"No, please stay. I'm not sure I can stay here alone with him."

Phoebe stood behind her seated sister.

Aaron took the chair across from them. "I know how this looks, but I can explain."

"Really? I'd like to hear how you can explain trying to kill Phoebe and setting fire to my clinic?"

Aaron couldn't believe his ears. Had Hannah just accused him of attempted murder and arson? "Kill Phoebe? Set fire to your clinic? What are you talking about?"

"Someone cut Phoebe's brake line and torched my clinic because they think Jeanne had something to do with the collapse of FNB."

Aaron shook his head in disbelief. "First, I know nothing about either of those two things. And secondly, how can you possibly think I would have a hand in something like that?" He gave a nervous chuckle. "Let me tell you why I had those clippings."

"Please do. I'd like to know why the big interest in FNB."

"As hard as it may be for you to believe, my collecting those articles had nothing to do with your sister. I didn't even know Jeanne worked for FNB until recently."

Hannah stood. "And how did you find that out?"

"Like half the country, I watched the hearings. I heard Marcus testify and refer to a former female colleague, which made me recall Jeanne telling me she had met Marcus at a downtown bank where they worked. And when they scanned those assembled, I saw Jeanne sitting nearby."

"I repeat. Why the big interest in FNB?"

"I—"

Hannah planted her palms on the table. "Don't waste your breath." She walked to the doorway. "Come on, Phoebe, I've heard enough."

"Hannah, wait!" Aaron jumped from his chair.

Hannah stopped short, turned, and glared at Aaron. "I think you should leave."

"Please, Hannah, hear me out."

She crossed her arms over her chest. "All right. I'm listening, but this had better be good."

"What happened at FNB has been eating me alive for months."

"Why?"

"I wanted someone to be held accountable."

"For what?"

He ran a hand through his hair. "FNB is the reason I sold everything."

Hannah huffed. "Oh, so you lied when you said you wanted to leave your past behind and be closer to me?"

Aaron went to her. "What I told you was true. But it isn't the only reason."

Hannah's bottom lip trembled and tears the size of pumpkin seeds rolled down her cheeks. "You never cared about me. You only used me to get what you wanted."

"Stop. Of course, I care about you. I love you. And this is exactly why I didn't tell you the whole story." He hung his head. "The truth is I needed the money." He raised his head and exhaled. "Gillian inherited a large sum from her father shortly before she died. She was in the process of setting up a foundation to help abused children. After she passed away, I foolishly parked her money at FNB, and lost the lion's share of it when it failed. The only way to get some back was to sell our house and my business, then add the proceeds to the little covered by insurance and fund the foundation in her name as I should have after she died."

Hannah pulled a couple of napkins from the holder on the table and wiped her eyes. "Why did you put it in a Manhattan-based bank when you didn't live anywhere near there?"

Phoebe patted Hannah's arm. "That's my queue to leave. If you need me, Hannah, I'll be in the dining room."

Aaron continued. "They had recently opened a branch nearby and since Gillian, and I trusted a man who worked at the main office and held a C level position, it seemed like a safe thing to do."

"Who did you know there?"

"We first met Ken Marshall at a wine-tasting event at my father-in-law's Southampton winery five years ago."

Hannah's eyes went wide.

"My late father-in-law thought the sun rose and set on him. So, after she died, I called and he said he could help me, until I could think clearly. I never considered the FDIC limits because I had no reason to think the bank was in trouble. After all, it had been in business for more than a hundred years." He reached for her hand. "You must believe me. It was like a punch to the gut when I heard they closed their doors. When the enormity of it all set in, there wasn't much I could do except follow the investigation. It became somewhat of an obsession." He dropped his hand, groaned, then raked his fingers through his hair. "I felt like such an idiot."

"Why didn't you tell me?"

"I was too ashamed."

She looked at him and sniffled. "Are you sure you've told me everything?"

"Absolutely. But what's this about someone wanting to kill Phoebe and torching your clinic?"

"Before we go there, do you know anyone from Staten Island?"

"Um, Jo Reasoner lives there, doesn't she?"

"How do you know where she lives?"

"She must have mentioned it." Aaron ran his hand through his hair again. "Jeez, Hannah, how could you even *think* I could have something to do with harming you and your sisters? And why would someone do the things you mentioned?"

"Because whoever it is, thinks Jeanne had a hand in the bank's failure."

"Jeanne was a financial analyst. How could someone at her level bring down a bank?"

"She tried to tell the person who had been threatening her, but until the hearings, whomever the culprit is wouldn't listen."

"I'm confused. Why did you ask if I know anyone from Staten Island?"

"A private detective Jeanne hired had the calls traced there."

Aaron frowned. "Are you saying you suspect Jo had a hand in this? *Jo*? Really?"

Hannah shook her head vehemently. "I don't. But Neal does."

"The boarder?"

CHAPTER
FORTY-ONE

Jeanne waited for Jo to vehemently defend herself when Neal had confronted her with the location of the cell tower. But when all Jo did was look from Jeanne to Neal as if watching a tennis match, Jeanne felt sick knowing Ray had finally identified the culprit.

"Jo. Why?" Jeanne asked, her eyes wide as if she had stuck her finger in an electrical socket.

The older woman's ordinarily warm engaging face turned cold. And the endearing quality of her voice they had come to love took on an icy tone. "I wanted you to know the damage you caused. What it feels like to lose everything and everyone you care about."

"But I didn't do anything."

"My son-in-law led my husband and me to believe otherwise."

"Your son-in-law?" Neal said.

"Ken Marshall."

Jeanne's head jerked back as if Jo had slapped her. "Ken Marshall is your son-in-law?"

Jo nodded. "After he lost his job, he and my daughter came to Frank and me wanting to borrow money. We told him we didn't have any to lend them even if we wanted to. And when we pushed him about why the bank where he worked failed, he became belligerent and blamed you. He said you were blinded by ambition because you came from old money and had to prove yourself or risk losing your inheritance. And when you didn't get a promotion, you thought you deserved, you threatened to go to the authorities with a bunch of half-baked ideas. He said the bank wouldn't have gone under if not for you."

Jeanne put a hand on her chest. "And you and your husband believed him?"

"He was very convincing."

"Was it his idea to threaten Jeanne?" Neal sat back in his chair and scowled at the woman.

"No. Ken's a moron. He didn't have a clue. After Frank died, I found a voice synthesizer and a notebook where he had recorded his actions and written down your name, phone number, and address. Don't you see? I had to finish what he never got the chance to since I held you responsible for his death."

"So, you sent the notes and pictures and made the calls?"

"Yes."

"And planted the rat poison?" Jeanne said.

Jo took on a smug look. "Almost as easy as the calls." She snickered. "I had Phoebe eating out of my hand almost from the moment we met. If you remember, I had complete access to the kitchen. The most difficult part of the endeavor was driving here with the dead vermin stinking up my back seat."

"What were you hoping to accomplish?" Neal asked.

She looked past Jeanne and locked eyes with Neal. "I wanted them to suffer as I did. For them to lose the roof over their head, much like my daughter and her family." She looked at Neal. "If it weren't for you, I would have gotten my revenge much sooner."

"Me?"

"I planned to add a dose of arsenic to the meatloaf I made for all of you. But you ruined it when you walked into the kitchen as I prepared to add it."

"You tried to kill Phoebe, damaged our furnace, and set fire to Hannah's clinic. Did you also sabotage my nephew's car?"

Jo shrugged. "My husband always said with any war, there is bound to be collateral damage."

Jeanne stood and began to pace. "I can't believe this."

A faint smile crossed Jo's lips before she let out a manic laugh. "You girls were so naive. So trusting. You made it easy. Oh, how I wracked my brain about how best to take advantage of your trusting nature. Then it hit me. After leaving the inn, I registered at the Seaside Manor down the street several times so I could be nearby without you knowing providing easy access to the grounds when you were all asleep."

Jeanne fought back the tears stinging her eyes. First, she had misjudged Marcus, and now Jo. What had happened to her sense of judgement?"

Neal stood. "I've heard enough. I'm calling the police."

"And say what?" Jo sneered. "You have no proof. It's your word against mine."

"Think again." Neal reached into his pocket and pulled out a palm size voice recorder. "I have it all on tape."

Jo's face went pale, and her voice returned to the familiar tone Jeanne knew so well. "There is no need to get them involved. I'll pay for the fire damage."

"Arson is only one charge you will face. The other is attempted murder."

"Wait." Jeanne put a hand on Neal's arm.

Jo smiled.

"Wipe that grin off your face," Jeanne snarled. "I have one more question. Is Aaron Downing involved in any of this?"

"Aaron? Hannah's Aaron? No, why?"

"Are you sure?"

"Of course."

Jeanne looked at Neal. "Call."

With her head held high, Jo stood. "Can you at least let me use the bathroom before the police arrive?" Her voice sounded as if she were actually contrite.

"Go ahead. But don't think about trying to escape. There's only one way out and it's the door."

"Oh, please. Don't insult my intelligence." Jo gathered up her purse, walked into the bathroom, and closed the door.

———

"She's been in there a while," Jeanne whispered to Neal, "Are you sure there's no window?"

"Of course." Neal knocked on the door. "Jo?"

No answer.

"Jo," Neal shouted. "Come out here, *now.*"

Still no answer.

Sirens blared in the background.

Neal looked at Jeanne. "Step aside." He took a few steps back and, with a sudden rush, kicked open the door.

CHAPTER
FORTY-TWO

"I need to talk to you and Phoebe," Jeanne said when she and Neal returned to the house and found Hannah and Aaron in the kitchen.

"She's in the dining room." Hannah frowned.

"I'll get her," Neal said.

Hannah peered around Jeanne. "Where's Jo?"

Jeanne looked at Hannah. "Did he explain?"

Hannah nodded.

"Are you satisfied?"

"Yes."

Jeanne took a seat and looked at Aaron. "You can stay if you like."

A minute later, Neal and Phoebe joined the others.

"It was her, wasn't it?" Phoebe asked. "That's why she's not here."

Neal took the chair cattycorner to Jeanne's. He put his left hand on top of hers and gave it a gentle squeeze.

"Yes, Pheeb," Jeanne said. "As hard as it is for me to believe, it's true."

Hannah gasped, her face turning chalky. "I don't believe it. I *won't* believe it."

"She confessed," Neal said gently.

Phoebe's hand went to her breast. "Of all the people it might have been, I never would have guessed it could be her. Did she say why?"

"She wanted me to feel the pain she thought I caused her and her family. Her daughter is married to Ken Marshall."

"Oh my God." Phoebe pressed her fingers to her lips.

"Jo was very sick." Jeanne said.

Phoebe raised a brow. "Was?"

"She had this planned down to the last detail, including taking her life if she was discovered. Based on the sudden death and foam on her lips, the EMTs said it looked like cyanide. She left a note. We gave it to the police, but it essentially said she would rather die than give us the satisfaction of seeing her stand trial."

Hannah shook her head. "This is too much to take in."

"She wasn't the woman she led you to believe she was," Neal said. "I've seen a lot during my career, and I'm telling you, she was good."

"Did she at least apologize?" Phoebe asked.

"No. She seemed to enjoy laying it all out." Jeanne wiped her damp cheeks with the back of her hands. "Everything she said and did while here was all a charade."

Hannah looked at Aaron. "So, you really weren't involved."

"I told you I wasn't."

"Do you mind telling Jeanne why you had the articles?" Hannah asked.

Aaron nodded. "I guess I owe you as much." He reiterated what he had already told Hannah.

"How did you know Ken?"

Aaron explained what he'd already told Hannah and Phoebe

Jeanne shook her head. "I'm sorry, Aaron."

"I still can't believe Jo would want to hurt us." Phoebe's eyes were filled with sadness.

"She wanted to destroy whatever was important to me. She admitted planting the poison along with the rat. She cut your brake line because she wanted me to know what it feels like to lose someone you love because she blamed me for causing her husband's death. Knowing his daughter might be homeless apparently was more than her husband could take."

"Why the fire?" Hannah asked.

"She wanted to eliminate any source of income we had."

Jeanne looked at Neal. "I still don't understand why she would want to hurt Rob."

"Phoebe's eyes went wide. "What do you mean, hurt Rob?"

"I received a call right after the holidays making me wonder if Rob had safely made it back to school. Although she didn't say what she did, since he mentioned a streaky windshield, I can only assume she sabotaged his wipers, hoping to cause an accident."

"Why didn't you tell me?" Phoebe asked.

"By then, we knew he had arrived safely. But I still asked Neal to phone the school to have his dorm surveilled and ensure he *stayed* safe. I didn't want to give you something else to worry about."

Tears ran down Phoebe's face. "How could a mother want to take a child's life?"

Jeanne took Phoebe's hand. "Unfortunately, since she is gone, there are some things we will never know."

CHAPTER
FORTY-THREE

Marcus eyed the eight packing boxes in his bedroom, then glanced inside the tank where his pet snake lay curled at the bottom. "On to San Diego tomorrow. Dad was right when he said I had a platinum tongue." He smiled. "What could have been a complete disaster turned into an opportunity that will make me untold amounts of money." He laughed out loud. "How ironic someone who could have easily gone to prison will address others on what not to do. Little do they know I would do it all again to get my hands on the kind of money I was able to squirrel away. And thank goodness I don't have to deal with my attorney's endless phone calls. My only regret is losing Jeanne. But I still have time to fix that, too." He pulled his phone from his pocket and thumbed out a text.

Leaving for San Diego tomorrow.

Come with me. We'll start over.

You know you want to.

M

~⚬⚬⚬~

Jeanne sat on a bench along Bay Street in Watch Hill's downtown area, enjoying the morning sun. She hadn't answered the text Marcus had sent but hadn't deleted it either. She picked up her phone and glanced at it. "Fat chance, bozo." She closed her eyes and thought of Neal. It was beyond evident he wanted to take their relationship to a new level. But what if she opened her heart only to be hurt again? She opened her eyes, gazed at the bright blue sky and recalled a recent conversation with Neal. "I need time," she remembered saying. But was it time she needed? Or did she have to learn to trust again before looking to the future? Maybe she should take his advice and write a book about all she had been through. Who knows it might be cathartic and would certainly be less expensive than seeing a shrink. She shook off her thoughts and headed for home. As she neared the recently opened carousel, laughter, and organ music filled the air. Vivid memories of her and her sisters in line to be among the first riders years ago filled her mind. Such happy times. Times when her biggest concern had been which gaily painted horse to choose.

She shrugged. At least she could draw comfort knowing Ken Marshall and the bank president would stand trial in a few months. On the other hand, Marcus had skated away from prosecution for insider trading by agreeing to take the plea deal his high-powered attorney had wrangled. *What a year. A man I trusted turned out to be, at best, a liar, and the woman who reminded us of Mom had masterminded the madness continuing to haunt me.*

At least the past few months hadn't been all doom and gloom. After all, hadn't her younger sister discovered the happiness she deserved with Aaron? And the thought of Phoebe living her dream cooking up a storm warmed her heart. As for herself, maybe if she opened her heart to Neal, he might be the one who could lead her out of the darkness and into the light.

CHAPTER
FORTY-FOUR

Three months later

The once vibrant fall-colored leaves had given way to naked trees and the unmistakable chill of winter filled the air.

"Will you and Neal be back tonight?" Phoebe asked Jeanne the morning she and Neal were scheduled to visit Boston to celebrate Jeanne's birthday.

"You know you're dying to ask if I plan to spend the night with him, so why not spit it out?"

"Well?"

Jeanne smiled. "All I know is we're having dinner at the Union Seafood House. For once, I've decided to take your advice and be spontaneous."

⚭⊂∽⧭⧀∾⌣

"So, I guess you didn't spend the night," Phoebe said when Jeanne walked into the kitchen the following morning.

"I never said it was definite."

"I know, but I was hoping you might change your mind."

Jeanne put a hand on her hip. "Why are you anxious to rush things?"

"I'm not. I just want you to be happy."

"If you must know, last night was wonderful."

Phoebe pulled out a chair and sat. "Tell me all about it."

"When we arrived at the restaurant, Neal pulled up to the valet. I thought it strange, because he told me in the past, he considered valets a waste of money. But I chalked it up to him wanting to do something special for my birthday. Then I saw him speaking to the attendant in hushed tones, but I let it go. After we finished our meal, it all made sense when a waiter came to the table to prepare Bananas Foster for us, and before he started, three more waiters sang happy birthday. When the dessert was ready to be served, I saw the man who had prepared it reach under the rolling cart and put a small box tied with a pink bow in front of me. This was inside." She held out her wrist, revealing a delicate gold chain.

Phoebe gasped. "Oh, Jeanne, it's elegant."

Jeanne nodded and smiled broadly. "I love it. And crazy as it sounds, I suppose I have Jo to thank."

"Jo?"

"I never would have met him if not for her. I suppose Mom was right when she said if you look close enough, you'll find a silver lining inside every dark cloud."

CHAPTER
FORTY-FIVE

Two months later

Jeanne answered the door to what could only be described as a younger version of Jo.

"You must be Jeanne," the woman said. "I recognize you from the press interviews you have done." She extended her hand. "I'm Eileen, Jo's daughter. I'd like to speak to you and your sisters if you don't mind. May I come in?"

Jeanne wasn't sure what to do. What on earth could she want after all this time? Had she come to talk as she said, or had she come to seek revenge for her mother's death?

As if able to read Jeanne's mind, Eileen continued, "Please, I've come all this way. I bear no ill will toward you."

"If I let you in, I must insist you leave your purse in the hallway, and please open your jacket, so I can see you aren't hiding anything." After what happened in the past, she wasn't taking any chances.

The woman agreed.

Jeanne motioned her inside, showed her where to leave her purse, checked her for a concealed weapon, and pointed to the sitting room where Phoebe and Hannah were watching television.

"Phoebe, Hannah, this is Jo's daughter, Eileen."

Phoebe and Hannah frowned at her.

Jeanne gestured toward a wing chair. "Please have a seat."

"Can we get you something to drink?" Phoebe asked, ever the hostess. "Tea? Water?"

"Water would be nice. I've been on the road for nearly four hours and didn't want to stop for a refill."

Phoebe returned with a glass and handed it to Eileen then joined her sisters on the couch.

"Thank you." Eileen faced the sisters. "I knew this would be awkward, but I felt I should try to explain why my mother behaved as she did." Eileen took a deep breath and let it out slowly. "Although her actions were sinister, I want you to know my mother was not evil." Eileen looked at Jeanne. "I am truly sorry for what she put you and your sisters through. Although I can't change what happened, I hope once you hear what I have to say, things might make a little more sense." She took a sip of water before proceeding.

"My mother was diagnosed with schizophrenia when I was a child. For the most part, her illness remained under control when she took her meds. And when she forgot, my father would always guide her back. I believe after he passed away is when her downward spiral began."

Hannah clasped her hands in her lap. "It wasn't until she confessed that Ken Marshall was her son-in-law and Jeanne recalled a conversation Marcus Reynolds had with your husband that we realized everything she had told us about her grandson wasn't true."

"My *ex*-husband." Eileen closed her eyes as if gathering the strength to proceed. "Unfortunately, my parents and I had been estranged for years. She never met her grandson until we were forced to go to them asking for a loan to fund our son's caretakers. My dad had a bad heart, and although he retired with a nice pension, they apparently lived month to month. I carry the guilt of my dad's death with me for asking for money I later learned they couldn't afford. I think having to turn us down was too much for him to bear and it further taxed his heart."

An awkward silence filled the air.

"I had hoped once they met our son, it might open the door to a reconciliation. But no. She didn't even call to let me know my father had passed away. I only learned of it by reading it in the newspaper. I contacted her, but she only shrieked about how she held us responsible for his death. Before she slammed down the phone, she threatened revenge. But I thought she meant against us. Then when our son passed, I hoped she might find it in her heart to come to the funeral. I left a message with the details, but she never returned my call. To make matters worse, the day of his funeral, I returned home to a message from her accusing me of not being a good mother."

"I'm so sorry for your loss," Jeanne said.

"I should have realized something wasn't right when she called a few weeks later, saying she wanted to get to know him. But I assumed she wanted me to paint a picture of all the years she had missed. My grief and guilt wouldn't allow me to think otherwise."

Jeanne couldn't imagine losing a child. "Did you see her after the call?"

"No."

"When the police told me what she had done, the puzzle pieces started to fall into place. The more I learned, I realized she had been living in an alternate world for quite some time. It all came together when I received the autopsy results which concluded there was no evidence of meds in her system."

"When Jeanne confronted her, she said your father was the one who started the campaign against my sister," Hannah said.

Eileen drank more water. "I believe that much is true. In her diary, she indicated Dad had called in some favors from his former colleagues to get your contact information, Jeanne. Because of what he had heard from Ken about the part you supposedly played in the bank's downfall, he must have believed you were the reason my life was in ruins."

"The caller used a voice synthesizer." Jeanne leaned her forearms on her knees.

"I'm not surprised. My father would have had no problem getting his hands on one."

"From what she wrote, she felt obligated to finish what he had started. But I don't think things turned dark until she learned about our son's death."

Phoebe looked at Jeanne. "Maybe she wanted me to lose my child like Eileen lost hers which is why she tried to hurt Rob."

Eileen buried her face in her hands and sobbed. "I can't believe the things she did. If I had tried to talk to her, insisted on visiting her, maybe I would have found out about the meds..."

The sisters rose and circled her. "Don't blame yourself." Phoebe rubbed Eileen's back. "You had no way of knowing she was capable of such horrific things."

Eileen raised her head.

Hannah stepped back from the circle. "What escapes me is why she returned here after she knew Jeanne had nothing to do with the failure?"

"Living with a police captain gave her insights into crime-solving the average person doesn't have. In the dark recesses of her mind, maybe she figured if she suddenly stopped coming, it would shine a light on her. Or maybe she worried she might have left evidence behind." Eileen visibly shuddered. "According to the last entry in her diary, during her final trip, she intended to dispose of any evidence and forever silence her victims."

"Did it say what her plan was?" Jeanne was almost afraid to ask.

Eileen nodded. "I assume you have a gas stove?"

"Yes," Phoebe held shaking fingers to her lips.

"I can only assume based on what she wrote, she intended to turn on the jets and leave an open flame nearby to cause an explosion."

Phoebe gasped. "She knew I always kept a scented candle in the kitchen."

Jeanne stared at her in utter disbelief. Thank goodness Neal had insisted on confronting Jo. If not for him, the outcome would have been far different.

Eileen looked at each of them. "I've taken too much of your time already. I should get going. I hope you will accept my apology for not only my mother's actions but also for Ken's. None of this would have happened if he hadn't filled my parent's heads with his baseless accusations."

Jeanne waved a hand toward the foyer. "Thank you for coming. I'm sure this hasn't been easy for you."

"Yes, we truly appreciate it," Hannah added.

"If it's any consolation, although we will never forget the last few months, we had no choice but to forgive your mother. To do otherwise would have destroyed us." Phoebe handed Eileen her purse. "I hope you will also find it in your heart to do the same."

Jeanne and Phoebe rocked on the porch while Fenway lay beside Phoebe's feet as they waited for Hannah to return from Aaron's.

Within minutes Fenway raised his head at the sound of an approaching car.

The car had barely come to a stop when Hannah jumped out, wearing a wide grin, and ran toward her sisters holding out her left hand. "Aaron asked me to marry him, and I said yes."

"Why am I neither surprised at the former nor shocked at the latter?" Jeanne giggled and wrapped Hannah in her arms.

Hannah stepped back and visibly swooned. "He proposed on the beach. Talk about romantic."

Fenway barked.

"Oh, Fens." Hannah crouched before him. "I'm afraid you're going to have to share me. But it's all good. Because now you'll have two people to play with."

Aaron walked up the stairs mimicking Hannah's smile.

Phoebe held out her arms to Aaron. "Welcome to the family. I'm sure you two will be very happy together." She stepped back. "And having a pair of masculine hands around will be good."

"We won't be far away. We intend to live at Aaron's." She looked up and gazed at him. "At least until the little ones come along."

Jeanne walked into Bigelow's as if walking on air.

Neal stepped out from behind the counter and gave her a kiss she felt clear to her toes. "Why are you so happy?"

"Well, for one thing, Ray finally worked up the nerve to ask Phoebe out, and to my delight, she accepted. I hope it works out. They would make such a cute couple, and Phoebe deserves to be happy. And secondly." She pulled a letter out of a nine-by-twelve-sized manila envelope. "Take a look at this. I was so excited when I read it. I practically ran all the way here to tell you."

Neal took the letter and read it aloud.

"Dear Ms. Stanton, I am happy to inform you Piccadilly Publishing would like to offer you a contract for 'The Day the Music Stopped.' Enclosed is our standard agreement for your review."

Neal dropped the letter on the counter, picked her up, and swung her around. "I'm so proud of you." He put her down. "I knew you could do it."

"I can't believe a publisher wants to publish my book!"

He gave her his best Magnum smile and waggled his eyebrows.

Jeanne put her arms around his neck and her lips to his ear. "Did I ever tell you it drives me crazy when you do that?"

Neal gave her the dimpled smile that always made her melt. "Good to know, pretty lady. Good to know."

ABOUT THE AUTHOR

Lorraine Solheim resides outside of Tampa, Florida, but will always have a soft spot for New England, where she lived for seventeen years. In addition to writing, she loves cooking and traveling and enjoys watching wildlife roam outside her back window. She is also a grateful breast cancer survivor.

Lorraine can be contacted via her website,
https://lorrainesolheim.com/

You can also follow her on Facebook at
https://www.facebook.com/lorrainesolheimauthor

Or Twitter at https://twitter.com/LorraineSolheim

Made in the USA
Las Vegas, NV
30 September 2023